Tales of Scales

by Michael Miele

FENRIS
™

This is a work of fiction. Any names or characters, businesses or places, events or incidents, are fictitious and the products of the author's imagination. Any resemblance to actual persons, living or dead, or actual events is purely coincidental.

TALES OF SCALES

Published by Fenris Publishing
Flagstaff, Arizona
https://www.fenrispublishing.com

ISBN: 978-1-62475-207-0
Printed in the United States, United Kingdom, or Australia
First trade paperback edition: February 2025

Cover art by Sam Gusuu
Edited by Domus Vocis and Sandy Golden

For all who believe that stories are magic

CONTENT WARNINGS:

- *Unpredictability*: mentions of physical abuse
- *Distress Signal*: discussions of disability
- *Letters From Nathaniel Hedgeworthy Addressed with Great Longing and Adoration to Symon the Dragon*: violence
- *Brunhilda*: ghosts
- *The Wyrm in the Mountain of Apples*: implied violence, death
- *At Sunset, She Flew*: suicidal ideation, suicide attempt
- *My Greatest Treasure*: Threats of violence
- *The Guardian of the Grove*: children in danger, child death
- *The Unionization of Kobolds*: death, violence, mentions of worker abuse
- *A Gentle Rustling of Leaves*: death

Introduction

A castle in the distance
The only light for miles
A welcome sight for you
Cold and road weary

Two quick knocks,
Followed by a third for good measure
The door opens and you see
A dragon towering over you

Red and white scales
With brown horns
That curve back like a ram's
Kind green eyes gaze down upon you
From behind a pair of rimmed glasses
Set halfway down his snout

He asks no questions
As he invites you inside
To share in the warmth

When you are settled with mug
And swaddled with blanket
He sits next to you
Opens a book
And by the light of his tail-flame
Tells you a story...

Unpredictability

Kinse strained under the weight of her pack as she climbed up the steep mountainside. Exhausting as this part of her job was, she was always excited to meet a new client. Though her inexperience with the dragons of Summervale Shore meant that she had packed an excessive number of supplies to try and be prepared. She paused for a second and let the pack fall off her back with a *FLOOMP* onto the ground. She raised her hand up to her face to shield her eyes from the sun as she looked around for the mouth of the cave.

Dragon's lairs were usually well-hidden, but the kobold had gotten used to finding the little tells. A small shimmer of magic next to an unassuming bush, the prevalence of dangerous rock spikes at the bottom of a hill, or even something as subtle as a construction sign steering passersby in the opposite direction. Dragons were secretive, and they liked to keep their lairs hidden from the world. This was a particularly tricky hurdle to cross with her business until a past client of hers had taught her some magic.

All these traits were common knowledge about dragons and were particularly familiar to Kinse. So, it was a shock to see that the entrance to her new client's cave was not only wide open but had a large gaudy mailbox in front of it in the shape of a fish. As Kinse walked closer to the mailbox, she could make out writing on the side of it.

It had the name "Wylia" spelled out in draconic runes and a shortened address of "12 Mountain Top, Summervale Shore". Attached were a string of brightly colored lights that led from the top of the mailbox over to the mouth of the cave. Kinse hefted her pack back onto her shoulders and walked into the entrance, a puzzled expression on her face. She had never seen a client be so brazen about their lair before. It was so surprising that she didn't even notice there wasn't a door separating the entrance from the main chamber, and—engrossed in thought—she walked right in without even thinking about it.

Kinse froze in place immediately when she realized where she was. She carefully removed her pack and set it down onto the ground as gently as she could. She'd learned firsthand that her clientele was quick to anger when it came to not showing the proper respect for a dragon. She absentmindedly brushed her hand through the fur on the top of her tail, making sure to avoid the patch of open scale that was burnt off. She hoped that this Wylia would at least be agreeable. After her last client's reaction when she'd forgotten to bow, she could use an easy job.

When she was satisfied that Wylia wouldn't come barging in with a gout of flame sending her out of the cave, Kinse began to explore the main room.

It was a quaint space with a tall, rounded ceiling, the likes of which being uncommon in mountain caves. There was a small section in the back left corner that was dug out into a small pit filled with flowing lava. Around the area were sharp utensils and some large plates with fish bones scattered on them. In the other corner there was a small stockpile of fish being kept on a line in slowly moving water, giving them a small amount of movement and served a dual purpose of decoration and food storage. There was a pile of treasure, as most dragons have, though Kinse saw it was not the standard dragon's hoard. While most dragons filled their caves with gold and jewels, it appeared that Wylia coveted the likes of records, kites, and clothing. The biggest feature in the room was a huge hole in the floor that filled into a water basin. The water was a beautiful blue and Kinse could see her brown scales and yellow eyes reflected on the surface of the pool. As she stared into the reflection, a large shape began to swim towards the surface at surprising speed.

The shape broke out of the surface and showered the room with a mighty splash, drenching Kinse from head to tail. Kinse gasped as she felt the cold-water seep into her scales and fur. Before her was a water dragon, blue and green scales swirling into each other in spiraling patterns up and down their long body. Their shape was closer to that of a sea serpent, but they still had the iconic visage of a dragon in their face. Instead of horns, they had large dark blue fins that protruded from the top of their head. The rest of their form was made up of a long tail and six legs with talons on each foot.

Kinse was about to speak but was interrupted.

"Sorry about that! I didn't think you were still in the 'Splash Zone' when I came up to breach. There's a set of towels along the wall over there. Might be a little big on you, but they'll dry you off regardless."

Teeth chattering from the cold water, Kinse was bound and determined to introduce herself first.

"G-G-Good e-e-evening M-M-Miss WW-W-Wylia..."

"Oh now, you stop that! No need to be so formal with me. You're obviously cold and wet, so go dry yourself off. Sit by the lava chute and warm yourself up too while you're at it."

"Y-Y-Yes, M-Ma'a-am."

Kinse covered herself up with a blanket that was three times her size and sat down next to the lava chute to let the ambient heat warm up her scales. Wylia had made herself comfortable and laid her long body out on the floor of the cave so she could talk to Kinse easier. She kept her tail submerged, and Kinse could see the waves it made as she moved it idly back and forth in the water.

When she felt as though she was warm enough, Kinse stood up and launched into her usual business pitch.

"Good day to you, Miss Wylia of Summervale Shore. Thank you for considering Kickbutt Kobold Parties L.L.C. for all your draconic party planning needs. I assure you that I have years of party planning to draw from to make your event as majestic as you are. I have some samples here in my pack that I encourage you to peruse at your leisure so that I can get a feel for what will give you the best experience."

And with that, Kinse lowered herself into a deep bow and waited for a response from Wylia.

"As flattered as I am, please don't bow for me. I'm nothing too special after all. But I am interested in what you have to show me."

Kinse raised herself up out of her bow slowly. She wasn't expecting Wylia to be so informal with her. The dragons she worked with never offered her that chance to let her guard down. She stood in silence long enough for Wylia to gently clear her throat to get her attention. She snapped her head up as Wylia spoke.

"So? Show me!"

Kinse scrambled over to her bag excitedly and began pulling things out. With a grin on her face, she pulled out rolls of streamers, party hats, face paint, and other various party paraphernalia. "Have you considered what occasion you want to celebrate, Miss Wylia? That would help me to pick the decorations and invitations to use."

"Oh! I hadn't even thought of that. I was just in the mood for a party!"

Kinse had to stop searching through her bag to process what she had just heard. Why would Wylia have called for her services if she didn't even know what kind of party she wanted? Usually, her clients had at least a small idea of what the party was going to entail.

"Is your hatchday close, Miss Wylia? Perhaps you'd be interested in celebrating the day you were born?"

Wylia snorted at that comment and said, "That sounds so self-serving! To think I'd have the ego to have an entire party dedicated to the day I hatched from an egg."

Kinse threw the balloons and festive party horns over her shoulder. "What about your relatives? Maybe you want to celebrate a special occasion with them?"

"I assure you that my family would rather forget that I was related to them, so I don't think that will work either."

Kinse tossed aside the ceremonial cask of wine labeled 'break in case of in-laws' as she kept digging through her pack. At the bottom she found a huge beach ball and a small kit to put together a volley-ball net. "How about a beach party then? You live in Summervale Shore after all, and getting the chance to enjoy the fresh air and glistening water must sound appealing?"

"No offense Kinse, but I spend all day in the water. I don't really feel like having a whole party centered around what I do every day."

Kinse dug into her pack one last time but found that she had finally reached the bottom. To her surprise, Kinse noticed tears beginning to well in her eyes as she realized she was close to losing her first courteous customer in years. She clinged to her business instincts to keep her composure, but could feel her resolve slipping. She closed her eyes to hold back a sob, before feeling a slimy hand rest on her shoulder.

"Hey now, little one. What's wrong?"

"I've failed you, Miss Wylia. I don't have anything that would be suitable for you. And if I'm being frank, you are much too unpredictable to even know where to begin to plan your party!"

Wylia threw her head back and Kinse braced for the worst, but all that came out of Wylia was a hearty laugh.

"Yeah, I get that a lot. Tell you what, I think I have an idea for a party after all. But it's going to be a little unorthodox. Is that okay?"

"Of course, Miss Wylia. I'm here to give you the perfect party after all."

"Splendid! Then I want you to tell me what kind of party *you* would want, and we'll set it up for you."

Kinse looked at the dragon dumbfounded. She hadn't thought about her ideal party for years and years. And the last time she remembered celebrating something for herself was back when she was still losing baby fangs. It took her a long while of thinking about it before she settled on an answer.

"I'd actually love to have a slumber party. I missed out on doing things like that with the other kobolds when I was younger. Was too busy planning other folks' parties by then."

Wylia's eyes lit up and she ran over to her hoard, pulling out a set of pajamas that had been buried at the bottom. She then took the towels in the corner and folded them using her many legs into the approximate shape of beds for them to lay on. They propped themselves up next to the lava chute to get nice and cozy. Kinse broke the cask of wine, and they roasted some fresh fish that paired surprisingly well. Wylia spoke up after dinner while picking her teeth with one of her many talons.

"Well, Kinse, I just have one more question for you and I think it's the most important one of the night."

"Alright, let me hear it."

"Truth or Dare?"

Kinse smiled the widest she had in a long time before confidently answering, "Dare!"

Distress Signal

The elderly dragon slammed his claws on the counter in a huff. He slowly looked up and into the eyes of the dragon tending the counter. Or to be more accurate, he looked into the left eye of the dragon as the right eye was made of moving metal gears and shiny glass.

"You'd think a dragon half made of metal would know how to work a cog and screw properly!" the elderly dragon spat. "Just goes to show that you can't rely on anyone anymore! Why, I've been coming to this shop for years and now I come back and find my favorite watch-smith is gone. The nerve of Dr. Greft to go off-world like that, without telling me. And now I'm stuck with a worthless hunk of metal and scales who wouldn't know a ratchet from a barrel cover! Well, aren't you going to say anything?"

Rimor held his tongue for fear of saying something that might make the elderly dragon more upset. He gazed back mildly at him.

"Curtis, I told you earlier that we no longer carry the parts needed to fix your watch. I've already offered you a new watch at a heavily discounted price, since you've been such a good customer of ours."

"Bah! That's the trouble with you youngins. Always looking to replace something before you try and fix it. No sense for sentimentality!"

Rimor sighed and held out his left hand for Curtis's watch.

"I'll take a look at it, but I can't guarantee that I can fix it for you. And it's going to cost a fair bit to make the parts custom for this type of watch."

"Forget it then! I'll take my business somewhere the help isn't a talking toaster and actually knows how to do their job!"

And with that Curtis stormed out of the shop and slammed the glass door behind him.

Rimor raised his hands to his head and rubbed at his temples. He enjoyed his job, but there were always those customers that gave him a healthy headache by the end of the day. He looked out the window to watch Curtis leave, and noticed it was beginning to turn dark outside. Blinking twice in rapid succession showed Rimor his internal clock, telling him it was now half past eight. Time to close up shop for the night.

He locked the display case, made sure to wind the clocks that needed to be wound, and threw his cloak over himself to step outside. He locked the door and then headed off in the direction of Dr. Greft's home.

As he walked, he could see some of the other residents of the town staring at him. He had gotten used to it over the last year, but it still made him uncomfortable. He didn't know if the cloak was more for him or the other dragons at this point. He fumbled with his keys until he found the correct one and unlocked the house, stepping inside.

He felt around in the dark to flip the light switch on the wall, clanking against it clumsily until a triumphant *click* could be heard. The room lit up with fluorescent overhead lights. The workshop was right inside the entrance to the house, followed by the sleeping quarters, and then the main hall, leading to the rest of the house. Dr. Greft had set things up this way to maximize his ability to work on projects without needing to go through the whole house. It allowed him the time and energy to power through his more complex work quicker. And while Rimor thought the setup was unhealthy, especially for a dragon as old as Dr. Greft, he was glad to have it after the accident.

Rimor took off his cloak and hung it over a nearby chair that had spare parts on it. He set out the watches that people had brought in for the day on the workbench and turned on the small lamp on the table. Sitting down, he grabbed his screwdrivers and tweezers and concentrated on his right eye to cause a magnifying lens to pop out of his head.

Working on watches relaxed him. Even before the accident Rimor enjoyed the work that was involved in repairing the town's watches. There was a certain feeling of joy that he couldn't get enough of when a piece slotted into place and the watch would start ticking again.

After fixing the last watch, he willed the magnifying glass back into his head, turned off the light, and stood up. He yawned and stretched, extending his wings and rotating his shoulders, opening his maw quite wide before he heard a grinding sound. Those pesky servos got caught again. Rimor was used to this now. Nothing a little oil wouldn't be able to fix.

In an attempt to walk through the bedroom doorway, he heard a *clunk* and found that he was stuck. Looking behind him, he found his wings hadn't retracted. He reached back and manually engaged the mechanism to get them to close properly and they shut with a tinny *ping*. This was also common for Rimor. He couldn't figure out why Dr. Greft had installed his new wings anyway. His added mass made it so that he couldn't use his wings for flight so why have them? In the adjacent bathroom, Rimor opened the medicine cabinet and grabbed his usual nighttime supplies before returning to the bedroom and closing the door with the tip of his tail.

He sat on the edge of the bed and used a spray bottle filled with some oil to loosen up his jaw. He moved it a few times experimentally to make sure that it wouldn't catch again and then closed it. He set the bottle down and breathed in deeply. Within his lungs, a multitude of systems were firing to make sure that the air was being filtered correctly and passed through his biomechanical body. He stared down at his hands and moved them both in unison. The left was a combination of wires, metal, and servos to simulate his organic right one. Rimor found the hardest thing to come to terms with after his accident wasn't all the new machinery strapped to him, but rather what had happened to his scales. His coat used to be a lustrous and deep green, and after months of surgeries and adapting to his new augmentations, it had dulled to a light gray. His left eye, unaltered, still blazed with the same bright orange that he was born with. The right one was a convincing replica, and Dr. Greft had made sure to install some lights into the base of the glass so that it looked more life-like.

Rimor rubbed the back of his head absentmindedly and cut himself on his horns. He often forgot how sharp the metal tips were. He chuckled a little to himself and thought he should just be happy to be alive. Life sure was strange though.

He put away his supplies and bandaged his hand before coming back to make the bed. The bedroom belonged to Dr. Greft and Rimor was told he could use it while the doctor was gone, but for the first three weeks, he couldn't sleep in it. He opted to just use the charging station in the corner of the room instead. Since most of Rimor's bodily functions were regulated for him, all he really had to do to keep going day to day was plug in and make sure he got about six hours of consistent charge. Old habits die hard, though, and after a few weeks, Rimor missed the familiar comfort of blankets and pillows. He found an amicable workaround by dragging his charging cord to the edge of the bed and plugging it into a port at the end of his tail. That let him move around the bed mostly unhindered.

As he laid his head down onto the cool pillow, he thought about Dr. Greft again. It had been about a year since he had gone off-world. Everyone had told him that he'd blow up in the atmosphere, but that only seemed to fuel his passion. He was adamant that he had to go to space.

That was just like him, Rimor thought, rubbing his cold metal arm.

He tossed and turned in the covers, but no matter what position he ended up in, the bed still felt uncomfortable. He threw off the covers and snatched up the small transceiver that was close by. He fiddled with the dials and antennae until he could hear some faint static come through. He always felt silly doing this but there was always a small possibility. Dr. Greft's ship had a transceiver and Rimor liked to imagine that maybe one day he could find the same signal. That he could talk to Dr. Greft again, across all those millions of miles. He twisted and turned the knobs incessantly. An adjustment here, a small quarter turn on this frequency. He eventually fell asleep slumped over the device, drooling out of the side of his mouth.

Rimor was woken up by his internal alarm clock and could still hear the faint hum of the transceiver. He got up and started his usual routine of brushing his teeth, polishing his cybernetic metal, and checking to make sure that all his wires were in the right spots. Once he was clean and ready to head to the shop, Rimor picked up the transceiver and plugged it into an outlet in the workstation. After flinging the cloak around his shoulders, he strode out the door.

Curtis came back again early in the morning to demand that Rimor fix his watch. He was nicer and less angry today but refused to leave without Rimor fixing the watch. Rimor relented and promised he'd see what he could do, forcing a smile as Curtis left, hearing the elderly dragon call him a 'waffle iron' under his breath. The other customers filtered in throughout the day and picked up their watches without incident. Halfway through his shift Rimor closed his eyes, and when he opened them, was alarmed to see his internal clock reading half past nine – an hour after the shop should have been closed. He scrambled to close up shop, not bothering to set the clocks before leaving. He could do so tomorrow, he told himself.

He hung up his cloak on the chair as he walked in and took out Curtis's watch. He turned it over in his hands with curiosity and decided to try and fix it now rather than wait until later.

Pulling the tools closer to him, Rimor sat down at the workbench to open up the watch and see what he was dealing with. As he poked and prodded at the mechanical guts of his patient, he grew increasingly curious as to how it ever ran at all. It took him hours of troubleshooting and rearranging spare parts to get anywhere with it. And then something miraculous happened. The watch began ticking.

Rimor could hardly believe it. He scooted his chair back, a triumphant grin on his face. He had been utterly focused on his task for so long, that he hadn't realized how tense he was. As he felt himself unclench, he slowly got up from the workbench and stretched out his cramped wings. It felt amazing at first, but as they reached their full span, he heard the horrible wrenching sound of grinding gears.

He felt a cable get caught on one of the wings and squirmed in place, not realizing that he was sweeping them over the workbench table. By the time he had clicked his wings into retracting, it was too late. The watch traveled in a perfect arc before knocking the transceiver off the shelf. The room was silent as Rimor held back his automated breathing to hear if the ticking was still going.

The longer he waited, the more upset he became. After a minute of holding his breath, he re-engaged his systems and took in just enough air to let out a roar.

"RAAAAAAAGGGGGHHHHH!!!!!!"

He grabbed the watch and threw it as hard as he could across the room. The watch sailed through the air before hitting the transceiver off the shelf and onto the floor. Rimor got up so fast from his seat that his tail tipped his chair over. He jumped over the workbench and went to gingerly scoop up the transceiver. There was a low buzzing coming from it. Rimor carried the transceiver to the worktable and set it down gently. He could hear something very faint coming from the device, but it was too quiet for him to pinpoint exactly what. He reached for the nearest set of pliers and went to bend the antennae into shape again. Halfway through bending it back up, he heard a familiar voice.

"Please help if you can...", the voice trailed off, but Rimor knew it well. He yelled into the outgoing mic on the transceiver to let Dr. Greft know that he was listening, but he received no answer. There was a long pause in the audio, until Dr. Greft's voice came through the speaker again.

"This is Dr. Harvey Greft, traveling through the V-9 sector. If anyone can hear me, I'm in dire need of assistance. My ship has lost the ability to warp and I am afraid I may not be able to make it back to my home. I've placed the ship into autopilot and will keep my physical body in a state of cryogenic sleep to prolong my lifespan. The coordinates encoded in this message will give you the location of my ship. And Rimor, if you're listening, I'm so very sorry. To all available ships, I humbly ask you, please help if you can..."

The message began to repeat and Rimor slumped down to the floor in disbelief. He felt a confusing mixture of happiness and panic as he tried to process what he was hearing. Dr. Greft was still alive, that much was at least certain. But for how long? And when was the message sent out? The doctor's electronic voice echoed through the eerie silence. Rimor got off the floor and stared down at the device, and realized that he couldn't hold back his tears. He rubbed his left eye and sniffled a little. He never thought he would get the chance to repay the doctor for saving his life.

He could never get a ship, though. Dr. Greft had assembled his over many months before he was even ready for a test flight, let alone a full launch. It would take Rimor years to replicate his research and then a lifetime to get the materials and assemble them. But Dr. Greft had managed to build a ship, despite the complications. There had to be a set of notes that would at least get him started in the right direction.

Rimor rummaged through the massive pile of papers Dr. Greft had left behind until he found one that was particularly marked up. He grabbed the piece of paper and yanked it out of the stack, only to see the rest of the pile come tumbling forward and onto the floor of the workstation.

Cursing under his breath, Rimor went to collect the papers back up into another pile as his claws fell on a particularly hefty manila envelope. He turned the envelope over in his hands and saw big letters printed in an early form of draconic. It read 'Spacecraft Mk. II'. He eagerly tore into the envelope and started to thumb through the pages. They were blueprints!

Blueprints he couldn't exactly read. He was badly out of practice in his study of Old Draconic, for which Rimor cursed himself. There was something odd about the last page in the packet as well. It didn't have any writing on it that he could discern, but the patterns looked familiar in a way that was hard to pin down. As Rimor stared at the patterns, he heard a chime in his head. Suddenly, his mechanical eye began scanning over the patterns, going procedurally through each line at an incredible speed. Soon, symbols could be seen floating in the periphery of his vision, until they completely clouded his internal display. Before it overloaded his interface, the symbols began to fade, and a singular pop-up message could be read in the center of his vision.

It read: "Installation of Translation Program initiated. Estimated time of completion: 7 hrs. 45 mins. Please connect to charging station to begin."

Rimor was stunned. He had the tools to construct his own ship all this time and he didn't even know it. He plugged his tail into his charging station and crawled into bed. Soon the only light in the room was Rimor's eye as it cast a soft orange light onto the ceiling.

Rimor dreamed very little since the accident. He would have liked to see himself soaring through the sky as his old organic self, but when he did dream, they were never so pleasant. Regardless, he could always recall his dreams when he woke up in the morning thanks to his automatic memory storage system, so it was very odd to him to realize he didn't remember anything but a vague detail or two from the dream he had seen this time. The only parts he could remember were feeling very warm, but not uncomfortable, and feeling suspended in the air, but not flying.

Rimor shook his head and blinked a few times to get his systems up and running. He checked his internal display and found that the installation had been completed overnight. He was ecstatic to begin decoding the blueprints but first he had to take care of things at the shop.

He rushed over to the shop and flung the door open. Curtis was, of course, standing outside before opening. Rimor didn't even bother addressing the elderly dragon, grabbing tools and flinging them into a spare toolbox he had brought from home. He went through and set the clocks one last time, checking to make sure everything was in its place. He found a spare sheet of paper and forced himself to write slowly and legibly. Curtis, to his credit, waited patiently at the counter as Rimor flitted around the shop in his mad dash. When Rimor moved to leave the shop, however, Curtis spoke up.

"Now that you're done running a marathon, can you tell me where my watch is? I thought you were going to have it for me today?" Curtis tapped his foot impatiently on the ground.

Rimor reached into his bag and pulled out a bundle of cloth about the size of Curtis's watch. "I didn't forget, Curtis. I've got it right here for you. Something came up at the last minute and I've got to close the shop today. Come out here and I'll give it to you."

Curtis huffed and slowly shuffled out of the shop. He waited with his arms crossed as Rimor locked the shop and hung the hand-written sign on the front of the door. The sign read, "Closed for the foreseeable future due to personal emergency".

Rimor handed Curtis the bundle of cloth before he had a chance to read the sign and took off at a dead sprint down the street. Curtis scratched his head and peeled back the layers of fabric until he uncovered the shattered watch. Springs hanging loosely out of the case, cracked bevel, and gears crammed haphazardly inside.

"Hey! This is worse than it was before. Get back here, you temperamental lava lamp!" Rimor couldn't hear him, he was already halfway home.

Over the next month, Rimor's life took on a predictable rhythm. He would wake up, immediately bring out the necessary blueprints and then start working on building his spaceship. He had opted to use the workshop as a staging area so that he could be close to his project. This would prove to be too convenient for him as he spent his every waking hour building the ship. He worked until his servos seized up and he couldn't move his left hand. Then, growling, he would pry the tool out of his left and continue working with his right. It took longer and he could feel the dull ache seep into his other hand by the end, but he'd rather work through the pain than waste even a single second.

The metals needed were a precious commodity, but luckily, Dr. Greft had managed to hide some away in a corner of the house from his last project. Rimor carefully measured and then cut the metal into strips and sheets using Dr. Greft's angle grinder. He then bolted them together using a rivet gun until they were formed into the general shape of the ship's outer hull.

While this was physically taxing, it paled in comparison to his mental strain. Rimor spent the evenings when he was too exhausted to work on the body of the ship reading and re-reading the schematics until he understood some part of it fully. This led to him taking apart and re-attaching pieces of the ship multiple times to his dismay.

The days and weeks blurred together, and he ate less and less, letting his cybernetic systems do most of the work in keeping his body functioning. More time spent working on the ship meant less time maintaining himself: he spent a whole day with his mouth agape open because an errant yawn had locked his jaw up early in the morning. He didn't feel like he had the time to waste on taking care of himself. Dr. Greft was counting on him, though, so the longer he spent time on anything else, the more worried he became. This spiral led to Rimor having to plug into his charging dock early more and more, and eventually working on the ship while plugged in to push his limits.

He was finally rewarded when on the last day of the month, he finished the ship.

The next day was clear and warm enough to heat your scales. A perfect launch day! Rimor wheeled the ship out from the house and pulled the tarp off it with a grand flourish. The ship was a small, curious contraption, big enough for a dragon of Rimor's stature but much smaller than the commercial ships more widely used for sending people off-world.

Dr. Greft's spare metals had been enough to build most of the ship, though to complete it, Rimor had had to scavenge car parts from an abandoned lot outside of town, and pawn off some of his own watches to purchase the final few bars of steel for the chassis. The outside hull was a mixture of different colored metals twisted and shaped into the semblance of a spaceship. The cockpit was made from some sturdy panes of glass from the failed greenhouse down the street. The engine was the most complex portion of the ship and looked out of place in comparison to the rest of the craft. Twin thrusters and shining chrome that cast a blinding light when the sun shone on them. They had taken the brunt of the metal that Dr.

Greft had left behind since it was extremely important that they function closely to the original schematics. The spaceship had two large wings, one on either side of the hull that broadly jutted out from the center of the craft. Rimor had brought the transceiver into the ship with him and mounted it within the ship's internal console.

Looking over his creation, Rimor felt a swell of pride. It was certainly more complicated than a watch, but Dr. Greft had trusted that he could handle it and he delivered.

Rimor loaded his supplies into the cockpit, checking to make sure he wasn't forgetting anything he'd need, and then exited to begin the launch process. When he emerged from the cockpit, he saw a small group of dragons from town crowded around him. They all had very concerned looks on their faces. No one would look Rimor in the eye, except for one wrinkled old dragon.

"What exactly do you think you're doing? You don't honestly believe that hunk of metal is going to fly, do you?"

"Yes, I do, I've done a number of simulations and in all of them I survive the initial flight through the atmosphere." Of course, Rimor thought, that wasn't exactly true. Most simulations had been successful, but certainly not all. Besides, it wasn't leaving the atmosphere that was the challenge as much as re-entering it.

"That's not the point I'm trying to make. You've been running yourself ragged. Are you so sure that your ship is up to snuff, you'd bet your life on it? No one's seen you in weeks. And then you come wheeling this contraption out and talking about space travel. We're worried about you!"

Rimor didn't know what to say to that. He tried to muster a reply and found that he was choked up. "I can't leave Dr. Greft out there. I got a transmission from him and if there's even a sliver of a chance I could help, I need to take it. He saved my life, the least I can do is *try* to save his."

Curtis frowned but seemed to relent. "I suppose I ought to be wishing you luck then. Bring the both of you back safely, alright?"

"I'll do my best, Curtis. Oh, and make sure everyone backs up. There's a blast radius for takeoff and I'd rather not hurt anybody."

Rimor took one last look at the town before closing the hatch and sat down in the pilot's seat. The spaceship looked crude on the outside, but on the inside, there was a massive array of advanced machines running simultaneously. Rimor made sure to get comfortable before plugging his head into the ship's main console. This ship was designed to work with Rimor's biomechanical components, and as he felt the familiar flow of diagnostics cross his internal vision, he knew he was connected. The next step was to hook into the adaptive touch sensors. Rimor carefully folded his wings to his sides and slid them inside two hanging mechanical slings. As they slotted into place, he could feel the touch sensors link up to the ship. He moved his wings independently to test the connection and found that he could move the wings of the ship in turn.

It was odd being able to truly flex his wings again.

Rimor reached under him to plug into the last connection. He had managed to splice his charging station into the main electronics of the ship and so he plugged his tail into the port and felt a small rush of energy flow through his body as the connection was made. Satisfied with his checks, Rimor blinked a few times to bring up the launch countdown on the main monitor display and started to count in his head.

The ship's engines roared to life as the muscles and servos in Rimor's body tensed. Slowly the ship started to move forward, then...

"BLASTOFF!!!" Rimor roared as loud as he could.

The ship roared to life, and he was propelled away from the town. Within seconds he was thousands of feet up in the air, tilting his wings to stabilize the ship. The resulting force shook the whole cockpit and Rimor could feel the force of the engine fully on him. It pressed his metal implants further into his body and he could feel the tension building across his skin. He had to escape the atmosphere, and fast, so he flapped his wings as hard as he could downward to give the engine as much of a vertical boost as possible. The wings of the ship responded in kind and the metal pushed down with enough force to create a shock wave that cracked across the sky.

WHOOOOOOOMMM!!!

The engine's fire turned a bright white as the secondary fuel kicked into gear and the ship blasted through the clouds and out into space. Before he knew it, Rimor's home planet was a speck in the reflection of the cockpit's glass. The engine quietly shifted to its third fuel source and burned a calm orange and red across the backdrop of space.

Rimor took a few moments to catch his breath and get his bearings again before pulling up the coordinates for Dr. Greft's ship. If the calculations were any indication, it was going to be a long trip. He plugged in the coordinates and watched as the computer plotted the course.

When exiting the atmosphere, the body of the ship had shaken heavily, and there was a rattling in Rimor's ears. Now that he had managed to break through it, he could keep the wings of the ship in a stable position and 'glide' through space. For the first time since the accident, he was able to feel the joy of flight again, even if only through the ship. He wiped a tear from his left eye as he looked out over the vast horizon of space. He forgot how much he missed this. This feeling of weightlessness and calm. It felt normal.

Rimor yawned, the servos in his jaw quietly creaking as he rubbed at his eyes. With his energy drained from the launch, he figured now was a good time to test the sleeping cycle he'd programmed. Rimor took his hands off the steering control for the ship and rested them on the arms of the pilot's chair. Then he brought up a program in his internal system that he had programmed to sync with the ship and ran it. The program spontaneously engaged the ship's autopilot and slowed Rimor's functions to a crawl so he could fall asleep. For the first time in years, as his breaths and heart rate slowed, he dreamt he was flying with his old wings.

When Rimor woke up, eight hours had passed, and he was stiff from sitting in the pilot seat all that time. He got up to stretch out his legs and applied a bit of graphite to his mechanical joints to lubricate them. He flexed his wings absentmindedly and found the ship dip a little from the motion. Realizing what just happened, he reached up with his hands to disengage the wing connection so that he could walk around the cockpit. He stretched them out as an alert popped into his vision.

"Didn't think I'd need to eat already," he muttered to himself.

Rimor opened the cooling unit and took out a packet of food. He was surprised that his hunger sensor was going off this early, but when he checked his internal clock, he found that it was late in the afternoon. That couldn't be right, could it?

Rimor looked out of the cockpit's glass to check the time of day and found that all he could see was the endless abyss of space. Oh right, no sun to tell the time by. That was going to take some getting used to.

He ripped open the bag of food, took out a dried piece of meat, and stuck it into his mouth. He wasn't the biggest fan of jerky, but it didn't spoil fast, and he needed the protein.

Rimor felt an alert trigger in his internal systems as a pop-up message flashed in his vision:

Warning: oncoming debris detected, collision inbound on starboard side.

Acting swiftly, he dropped the bag of jerky on the floor and rushed over to the pilot's chair. Rimor quickly plugged himself into the ship and then pushed the thrust of both engines to speed him out of harm's way. After three seconds of extra fuel burn, the alert stopped.

He eased back off the thrust until the ship was at a cruising speed again. He leaned forward to look out the window for a glimpse of what nearly hit him. The object that almost hit his ship was a large chunk of rock that slowly gave off a trail of luminescent white, green, and blue. It was a beautiful comet. He never expected them to be so pretty close up. The last dragon to speak about seeing a comet in his town was someone's great-grandfather, and they had done a very poor job of capturing the contrasting beauty of the pitted rocky surface with the delicate and freely flowing trail of dust that followed closely behind.

Rimor watched the comet for a long time, until the trail of colorful debris could no longer be distinguished from the ocean of stars around it.

Of all the problems Rimor was prepared for before he set off on this trip, the most obvious one eluded him. He was woefully unprepared for the boredom that he would face. Some days, there would be magnificent sights to see, like a new planet that he could look at or some cosmic event such as the comet, but most days nothing happened. He started to come up with small games—counting planets, making up constellations - to pass the time and keep himself sane. He could only read the schematics so many times before they started to get repetitive.

Rimor got up and walked to the rear of the cockpit, staring out the back of the ship absentmindedly. He looked at the slowly burning fire that trailed behind the engines like small geysers. Touching his snout his snout, he wondered how long ago it was that dragons could still breathe fire. From what he knew, it was many centuries since a dragon could spew flame properly. He put his face up to the glass and pressed his snout against it in such a way that if he looked down, the engines were obscured. He imagined that the engine's fire was his own mighty flames and cracked a small smile at the thought.

Months came and went and Rimor became more restless with his confined space. He started to question what all the machines that Dr. Greft had instructed him to build were even for. This machine makes a beeping sound, but what else? Did it have another function?

Rimor looked at the machines in disgust. He was constantly surrounded by them and much as he didn't want to admit it, he missed the dragons back home. Even Curtis, the stubborn old fool that he was, crossed his mind every now and again. Space was cold and uncaring enough without the constant presence of machines blinking and beeping in your immediate vicinity.

Rimor had tried on occasion to use the transceiver to contact planets he passed by but came across no active radio waves. The best he could do was patch the ship into the transceiver and listen to the pre-recorded message left by Dr. Greft. He would often put it on when engaging his sleep cycle: it relaxed him more than having to sit in the not quite silent room and hear the occasional beep disturb his rest.

The switch to having to regulate his own sleep schedule was jarring at first as well. The longer he spent in space, the harder it was to be able to tell the current time.

Rimor still remembered one 'night' when he was flying past a swirling purple and blue planet. While desperately resisting his sleep routine, he felt a slight brush against the left wing of the ship. It was a large grayish blue creature that moved as if it was floating on an imaginary sea. The body was a curious mixture of a whale and a seahorse. There were a multitude of brightly colored lights that made it look as though it was carrying a small universe in the curl of its tail. Rimor stared out the cockpit window, slack-jawed in awe and rubbed his eyes a few times to make sure they weren't playing tricks on him.

The creature seemed to move its mouth in an attempt to speak with Rimor. He tried to make signals with his hands and claws to communicate with it. The creature tilted its head to the side in confusion and slid around the ship in one graceful motion before heading back to the swirling purple and blue planet below. Rimor wanted to chase after it, but as soon as the creature was out of sight, his internal systems sent him into his sleep cycle. When he woke up the next morning, he was too far to turn back and establish contact.

A few days later as he was gliding through a section of space that was especially uninteresting, Rimor received an alert from the ship's onboard computer system that he was coming up on an asteroid field. He could try and go around it, but that would take too much time. He instead decided to fly through it as carefully as possible.

The warnings from the computer got louder and more incessant until Rimor manually turned them off. The asteroid field came into focus on the cusp of the cockpit's glass, and he gripped the steering control tight with his claws in anticipation. He pulled back on the engine's thrust so that he could move around the field slowly, but the movements of the asteroids were too unpredictable.

Before Rimor knew it, an asteroid scraped across the right wing and sent the ship tumbling in the other direction. He wanted to grab his wing but there was no time, for another asteroid was headed straight for the front of the cockpit.

Rimor acted quickly and kicked the engines into high gear so he could duck underneath it. It missed the cockpit, but he could feel the asteroid scrape the metal on the top of the ship as it went by. The next asteroid was closing in and Rimor panicked.

He frantically pulled up any programs on his internal systems that might be able to help him and found one that was labeled EMERGENCY JUMP DRIVE. He ran the program and funneled all of the ship's remaining energy to help it run.

There was a bright white flash in Rimor's vision and then he didn't feel his body anymore - he felt as though he had become the ship itself. He could feel the intense burning of the fuel from the engines as he rocketed himself out of the asteroid field and back into the safe reaches of space.

He blacked out soon after.

When Rimor regained consciousness, he was greeted with an overwhelming noise from the ship's computer. He picked himself up off the floor and went over to see how much damage was done. From the warnings he could tell that he was almost out of fuel.

Thankfully the cockpit's glass only suffered minor scratches, so he wasn't in danger of losing oxygen, but the ship's hull had taken quite the beating. The right wing would not respond to his inputs at all either. The engines seemed fine but trying to have them run faster than impulse propulsion was too great a risk for fuel consumption. The fuel he had left would get him to the last known location of Dr. Greft, but just barely. He would not be able to return home.

Rimor cleaned up the ship and went to put on the message from Dr. Greft but found the transceiver able only to produce a sputtering, buzzing sound. The speaker had been blown out when he'd used the emergency jump drive. He brought his wings close to his body and wrapped his tail around his legs as he tried to ride out his sadness. The metal wings were cold against his skin, but the weight of them was comforting.

After two more days of drifting, Rimor heard a new sound come from the computer. One he hadn't heard of before. Fearing the worst, he got up from his pile of discarded jerky bags to see what tripped the alarm. The ship's navigational computer pinged an alert into his internal systems once he got close enough.

"Your destination is coming up in about 3000 miles. Make sure to slow down," the mechanical voice echoed into Rimor's head.

He couldn't believe it. Somehow the ship had drifted back onto course, and he was only a few hours away. The only thing left to do was wait for the doctor's ship to come into view. So, Rimor sat and waited.

He checked the computer to make sure it wasn't malfunctioning again. Everything looked normal, so he sat down in the pilot seat again.

"You're being paranoid. He'll be there. He has to be there."

Though, as time went on, Rimor started to doubt himself. He was snapped out of his introspection by the sound of the computer telling him that he had arrived at his destination.

Rimor jumped out of his chair and looked through the cockpit's glass for Dr. Greft's ship. But no matter where he looked, he couldn't find any trace of a spaceship. No fuel trail, no debris, not even a light. Well, there was a light, but it didn't look like any signal that a spaceship would have.

Rimor decided that it was his best lead and used the left wing to awkwardly point the ship towards the faintly glowing orange and red light. He was worried about having to wait for a few more hours since it was so far away but found that the ship seemed to be picking up speed. When he went to check the fuel gauges, Rimor saw that they were completely empty.

"Oh no..."

The ship had gotten caught in the gravity of the star, and Rimor realized was being pulled toward it. He hit the steering column, hoping to get it to come back online, but it was no use. He tried to access the internals of the ship but didn't have enough energy left to override the automatic systems. Wherever he was going, he couldn't get away.

As he got closer to the source of the light, the internal temperature of the cockpit started to get warmer. His internal systems were working overtime to keep him cool enough that he wouldn't keel over immediately, and in time, Rimor could make out exactly what it was.

The ship's computer confirmed his fear as it read out in its mechanical voice: "WARNING: Red Giant ahead. Please steer clear or you will be vaporized."

It was too hot to do anything. He began hyperventilating, frantically looking around the cockpit for anything that might save him. The last thing he saw before blacking out was the broken transceiver sitting on the passenger's seat.

Rimor didn't know how long he had been out, but surprised himself when he realized he had regained consciousness and was, as far as he could tell, not dead. When he opened his eyes, he found that he was close enough to the Red Giant that nothing else could be seen ahead. The cockpit had cooled down as well. It was still quite warm, but not nearly as severe. He walked to the front of the ship and looked out into the center of the Red Giant.

It was spectacular up close. From where he hovered, Rimor could see all the swirling currents of hydrogen that gave the star its immense energy. He could see the dark red cracks along the surface of the star and how the bright orange center shone through the holes in the surface. Every few seconds there would be a slight discharge in the form of some energy being expelled in an arch out of the star. Strangely enough, the sparks of energy never managed to touch the ship.

It was then that Rimor heard a voice.

"Hello small one, what brings you so far away from home?"

Rimor turned around quickly and scanned the cockpit for anyone else. Had he gone mad?

"There is nothing to fear, small one. I mean no harm to you. Even now I am keeping my rays from burning you."

The voice seemed to come from somewhere, but also nowhere. Rimor looked around in confusion until, out of the corner of his eye, he saw something moving along the surface of the star. As he watched, the dark red surface bunched up and began to pool together into a large clump in the center. The clump then extended out in multiple different directions and began to form itself into a shape. A shape that Rimor was quite familiar with. If he wasn't hallucinating, he could swear it looked like a...

"Dragon..." he breathed.

And indeed, the surface of the Red Giant had transformed itself into the visage of a planet-sized dragon. The body had the same dark red color to it and beneath the scarlet scales were the same pulsing orange and yellow currents of energy present in the rest of the star. The eyes blazed with an intense orange glow, but the shape showed the years of the star in them. If you looked closely enough, you could see the small wrinkles below its eyes.

When Rimor heard it speak again, it did not open its mouth. Its voice was warm and soothing.

"I'm afraid I'm not really a dragon. I've merely taken this form to help you feel more comfortable. As for how I am talking to you, I'm speaking using the energy frequency of your brain."

"So, then telepathy?" he asked.

"Basically", the star responded.

"Since when could stars communicate with dragons?"

"Oh, for a long, long time. Back before your home planet even existed. Billions and billions of years ago, at least."

"Why are you protecting me?"

"Because I'm tired of burning everything around me. It gets boring after a few millennia. Besides, I will explode soon anyway."

"Wait, are you going to die?"

"Very soon, yes."

"How soon is soon?"

"In about five minutes."

Rimor felt the bottom drop out of his stomach.

"Unfortunately, there is nothing you can do to stop it. Your Dr. Greft, as you call him, had given me an infusion of hydrogen to keep me from burning through all my energy. But I am running out of hydrogen to spend and without it I will collapse into a White Dwarf. The explosion will kill us both, but do not fear, it will be over in an instant."

"Then why tell me all this? Why not just let me burn?"

"Because I have seen your sadness, Rimor. I know the sting of loneliness as well. At least in this way, we can be together at the end."

Rimor's anger burned away and the tears he was choking back came rushing forth. It was odd, but he felt better knowing that he wouldn't die alone either.

Rimor walked over to the pilot's seat and sat down in it. He carefully connected his left wing into the remaining sling, connected his tail into the ship's energy source, and connected his head into the ship's computer. He sat like this in disbelief for a few minutes before breaking the silence.

"How do you know my name? How did you know I was looking for Dr. Greft?"

"I can see inside your mind, into your memories."

"Since you know my past, could you tell me about yours?"

"Greft asked me the same thing and regretted it. It is intense to experience."

"I think it would be good for the both of us if we finally had someone to talk to."

The Red Giant rumbled in approval.

"As you wish."

Rimor felt flashes of the eternities the Red Giant had experienced. Planets spun into existence and winked out just as quickly. Similarly, the Red Giant saw Rimor's childhood and how different he was before the accident and Dr. Greft. It felt the pure joy of flight on newly stretched wings, of rain sloshing off bright green scales, and the wonder he had the first time he fixed a machine. It became harder to keep the connection from severing and Rimor's systems engaged his sleep cycle to preserve his remaining energy.

"Sweet dreams, Rimor."

And with that the Red Giant breathed its last, the form of the dragon crumbling into the void of space. Everything shook violently and pieces of the Red Giant began to flake off and scatter. The boundless energy began to build and then, after a short pause, the Red Giant exploded.

Strangely, the energy seemed to funnel itself directly towards Rimor's ship. The sensors in the ship kicked in and a small machine with concentric rings that only ever used to go *beep* came online. The energy hit the ship and pushed it backwards, but after a few seconds of pushing, the ship stayed in place. The energy was being funneled directly back into the ship itself.

So much energy, in fact, that failed systems suddenly came back online. The fuel tanks were replenished, and the right wing started to move again.

Rimor dreamt of struggling to put together Curtis's watch. As he woke up, though, he felt the same feeling as when he'd accidentally fixed it. A piece clicking into place. He could feel the overwhelming amount of energy coursing through his systems and felt more alert and energized than he had ever been before.

Rimor stared out the glass of the cockpit and saw the remains scattered here and there in an arc around the new shape in the middle. The White Dwarf gave off a faint white glow that barely lit the cockpit of the ship. Rimor mourned the Red Giant, but it had given him the most valuable piece to complete his rescue mission. Time.

And it was time to find him.

He turned off the navigational computer and set the engines for maximum thrust.

Letters From Nathaniel Hedgeworthy Addressed with Great Longing and Adoration to Symon the Dragon

3rd of Sumner, Year 1567

Marked upon the parchment by Nathaniel Hedgeworthy of Clan Wyldwood

I am writing this evening to commemorate my induction into the Pact of Adventure. I know not what perils and thrills lay before me, but to say I am excited would be putting it lightly. Finally, I will have my chance away from this forest of infinite dullards and get to see the world for what it is. Once I come back with stories of my adventures, the other foxes of Clan Wyldwood will see what they are missing by spending all their time tending to trees. I may even get to slay some foul creatures along the way, but regardless of what comes, I am immeasurably ready for the morning sun to rise.

26th of Autumn, Year 1567

Marked upon the parchment by Nathaniel Hedgeworthy of Clan Wyldwood

Some may say I asked for this hardship when I signed on, but I'd vehemently disagree. While I knew in the back of my mind that it would be 'rough living' out on the trails and in the country, I did not think it would be as insufferable as this.

I'm used to living off the land, but working for the Pact of Adventure has brought new challenges I did not anticipate. All of the quests worth my time require more people than just myself, and knowing this, I am not one to eschew help when it is given. However, not one soul I have proposed an alliance with has wanted to work with me. They will not risk their lives or reputation working with someone who hasn't already made a name for themselves. I am left to wonder how in the world I am to get anywhere if no one will help me as I am now? Many days, have I pondered this problem and I've not come up with a way to remedy it.

Thank goodness for my skills in tracking. Loathe I am to admit it, Wyldwood's teachings have kept me alive these previous weeks. I have been able to take small contracts that involve locating persons of importance, or those who wish to dodge their debts. They pay enough coin to get me from place to place and not much more. It's fine for now, but if I must find another lost pet to earn my supper, I may just go back home.

Sleep is another matter of contention, as I have received little rest since I started. Adventuring alone means I don't need to split my take between others, yes, but it also means I must protect my own hide. I've already had one close call where I've exchanged my coin purse for my life and that has made it difficult for me to sleep ever since. The only reason I'm coherent enough to write is because of the generosity of my previous contractee, who allowed me to sleep on the featherbed in his guest room before I leave this morning. Today, I set back out, and hope that it will be a better day.

34th of Frost, Year 1567

Marked upon the parchment by Nathaniel Hedgeworthy of Clan Wyldwood

Belize and Coriander have become my faithful travel companions. While I did not imagine a basset hound and a possum would be accompanying me, they too are seeking adventure.

Coriander has been incredibly invaluable as her nocturnal nature means that she has an easier time staying awake for the night watch. Twice already, she's helped us get the drop on vagrants who wished to kill us for our coin while we slept. It's been long enough now that Coriander no longer gives me the cold shoulder when I go to talk to her, but I suspect she steals my things when I'm not looking. Can't truly trust a thief after all.

Belize leads us the best he can and usually makes the decisions for what quests we'll take on. He's got his own sense of justice that seems to carry him through the worst days. I suppose that comes with being a paladin. That and the proselytizing about his god. For what it's worth, my skills in tracking have proved very useful. Especially in these freezing days where finding our target means getting back to our tent faster and being able to keep warm.

Perhaps my luck is turning a corner after all.

61st of Frost, Year 1567

Marked upon the parchment by Nathaniel Hedgeworthy of Clan Wyldwood

The winter has been hard on us. Little to do from the Pact of Adventure and most of our time is devoted to keeping ourselves from dying of the frost. Thankfully, we've managed to catch the attention of King Saulos and he has a quest that he promises will make us all very rich.

I must admit I've been plagued with strange thoughts and feelings, prompted by my own actions. Last week, Belize and I were lost amidst a snowstorm, and in order to keep from freezing to death, we huddled together. Despite my annoyance with Belize's preachiness, I found myself enamored by his white and tan fur, lovely to look at and so soft against my own. How the white and tan mixed with my orange in lazy soft waves. The tent was bundled so tightly that I could not escape his scent, and with the wind and snow battering us from all sides, I dared not open it even a crack. It's difficult to say what exactly spurred my boldness. I felt comfortable, warm, and safe in his arms. With his scent so close, I desperately wanted to get closer, so I chanced a small gesture of affection. I leaned forward to kiss him, and he did not shy away.

I had not thought that men would catch my fancy when I started this whole endeavor. But that's what this was about after all—discovering the parts of myself that I wouldn't have known back in that forest. He's not made mention of it since, but he does seem more relaxed around me. I'm unsure if Coriander knows of our tryst and suspect she wouldn't care even if she did. Yet I worry it might throw our group's dynamic into disarray. Especially now, we can't afford to be off our game.

We've been tasked with finding and hunting down a dragon. King Saulos has heard that the beast hoards impressive jewels and finery in its cave. At the first thawing, we are to begin our quest to track it. We've been selected for my keen knowledge of the area, Belize's impressive ability to follow scents, and Coriander's superior stealth. I've heard tales of how fearsome dragons can be. I fear they are right.

15th of Solstice, Year 1568
Marked upon the parchment by Nathaniel Hedgeworthy of Clan Wyldwood

Today my life has changed forevermore
We saw a passing glance of the dragon for the first time
He was radiant
I was so transfixed by the curves of his many horns
Spiraling as he took off into the sky
So powerful and yet so graceful
And here I find myself caught between awe and duty
What a horrible way to make a living

40th of Solstice, Year 1568

Marked upon the parchment by Nathaniel Hedgeworthy of Clan Wyldwood

I find myself needing to write. Everything has become so confusing that I'm not sure I can go through with our mission anymore. I still feel something for Belize, and we've shared each other's tent through the night enough times that I shouldn't even be thinking about that dragon. But ever since we first saw him, I've been obsessed. We were told to watch out for his razor-sharp teeth or his tail which could crush us in an instant. Every word led back to the danger he posed to us. No one spoke of his beauty.

A poet I am not, but I've felt inspired.

12th of Sumner, Year 1568

Marked upon the parchment by Nathaniel Hedgeworthy of Clan Wyldwood

It's been weeks and there's been no sign of the dragon whatsoever. Belize hasn't been able to catch his scent either. It should come as no surprise. This dragon has managed to avoid capture for years, of course he was going to be careful to cover his tracks.

Coriander and I have settled into a mutual camaraderie that I was not expecting. When I'm in a foul mood, she can always find the right thing to say to cheer me up. Not only that, but she personally stole back my coin after I was swindled by a merchant we traded with on the way to Draycott. I suspect I'll remember her grin as she presented me with my money.

For my part, I've helped her by showing her how to make an extract from local plants that would conceal part of her scent. Since then, I've noticed our communal coin purse bulging wider than before. I only hope the extra coin isn't from the likes of folks who need it.

I wish I hadn't let my prejudice get in the way of making a good impression sooner. Just because she was a thief by trade, didn't mean she wasn't a good person at heart. And this of course, turns my thoughts back to the dragon. Is he actually as dangerous as they say?

I think Belize is getting tired of tracking him. He snapped at me while we talked of strategies to find the dragon. I love him still, but these outbursts scare me. Within our tent, there is only the soft sound of breathing, but I feel the weight of those emotions.

50th of Sumner, Year 1568
Marked upon the parchment by Nathaniel Hedgeworthy of Clan Wyldwood Addressed with Great Longing and Adoration to The Dragon

When I think of your decadent red scales
it sends shivers through me
Your red is the passion of my battle cry
and the love I feel at sunset at once

And what a glorious sunset we could make together
Bright red scales settling over
the soft orange horizon of my fur

Can I kiss you, Oh Magnificent Dragon?
Your snout is so far off the ground,
one questions how I could even begin

I'd have to climb a tree that touched the sky
just to have a chance
And even then, you'd have to want me

But the thought of it stays regardless
I can't shake the wonder of your mouth entwining with mine
The forest and fire at peace, in loving embrace

68th of Autumn, Year 1568
Marked upon the parchment by Nathaniel Hedgeworthy of Clan Wyldwood Addressed with Great Adoration and Longing to The Dragon

We've gotten closer to him lately. Small things left behind as he flees from us. A scale or discarded talon goes a long way with a nose as good as Belize's. He almost threw us off his scent completely with a dip into a nearby lake. The scene of him rising out of the water was more breathtaking than I can describe. The water dripped from his wings and splashed back into the lake below. I was enraptured by his visage.

How high can you fly with those wings of yours?
Can you reach heaven above?
Or is there something better in the sky up there?
Would you show me if I asked?

Your strength scares me
With one flap of your wings
You can topple trees
And yet you never do

I want to believe it is purposeful
That you know how dangerous you can be
And that you want to be gentle
But I know that's just a fancy

How would those wings feel
if they caressed instead?
They look tough like leather
But leather can be warm too

15th of Frost, Year 1568
      Marked upon the parchment by Nathaniel Hedgeworthy of Clan Wyldwood

I'm worried you may be too smart for your own good, dear dragon. I hope I can forgive you with enough time. I'd rather not freeze to death before I get to meet you, but even now my paws tremble with cold. Writing this is taxing enough as is, I just wish...

25th of Solstice, Year 1569

Marked upon the parchment by Nathaniel Hedgeworthy of Clan Wyldwood

The chill in the air is gone, and we've managed to find our way back to civilization. I was able to purchase more parchment for when we set out again. We had to burn what little kindling we had during Frost, and a good deal of the last few months of letters were lost. I've mourned them already but admit I'm glad we were able to survive in some small part due to them. For posterity's sake, I've done my best to summarize what's happened.

We lost the dragon during the Frost last year and are just now picking up his trail again. Frost was long without seeing him, but Coriander and Belize tried to push through regardless. Morale was suffering after being on this hunt for so long. I don't think it's even about the money for Belize anymore.

Last Autumn, we ran into a trap that the dragon set for us. Coriander and I came away with superficial cuts and bruises, but Belize had a large gash along his left leg. Thankfully, the herbs to treat his wound were in season. I made a poultice and patched him up as best I could. It cost us a lot of time while he recovered, and the trail went cold just as the last leaves fell from the trees.

I think Belize was less concerned about his injury and more upset that the dragon had outsmarted him. He's been closed off lately, and I can't even reach him. He's buried himself in his holy text and seems to lash out more frequently. For the sake of his own life, I hope we find the dragon again soon, or else I'll need to explain how Coriander killed Belize out of sheer frustration.

27th of Sumner, Year 1569

Marked upon the parchment by Nathaniel Hedgeworthy of Clan Wyldwood

We're closer than we've ever been to catching the dragon. That excites and terrifies me equally. I know Belize means to kill him and I imagine Coriander will no doubt help. It's a horrible dilemma when you need to pick between your family and doing what your heart tells you. I feel like if I don't act now, then the next time we meet will be across a battlefield.

I've sabotaged the trail. It won't buy him a lot of time, but I can hope that it's enough for him to get away. This is cowardice, I know. But better he lives, and I feel this awful gnawing inside of me, than having to see him die.

8th of Autumn, Year 1569
Marked upon the parchment by Nathaniel Hedgeworthy of Clan Wyldwood

It has all been in vain. No matter the method, Belize is able to find his scent again. I've done all I can think of to keep him off the trail. Hiding scales, moving brush, covering tracks, but nothing has worked. I even used some of the scent concealer to divert our path.

What I didn't count on was Coriander getting involved. She hasn't said as much, but I suspect she knows I've been meddling. Being a thief, I'm sure she's picked up on my suspicious activity. She knows about the concealer, having used it herself. I don't know if she has discovered the reason yet, but it doesn't particularly matter. We've gotten close enough to make a move now and I must keep up the appearance that I'm amenable to fighting him.

Will we kill each other? I don't have the heart to hurt him, even now. I fear our first meeting will be our last.

9th of Autumn, Year 1569
Marked upon the parchment by Nathaniel to The Dragon

I feel as though the world has shattered
Our surprise attack was met by a surprise of your own
You were ready for us

Belize fought valiantly
Shining in his armor
His howls drowned out by your roar

Coriander tried to hide
But with a mere slide of your tail, she fell
How could you?

And with a snarl and a scream, I have my answer
How could I?

My friends broken and yet I was the only one to hurt you
Why did it have to be me?

I heard the thud of the arrow into your chest
as my heart stopped beating
There was sadness in your voice
They said you were a monster
But I cannot deny your pain

You flew into the air so quickly
That the blood had barely a moment
To splash upon the ground before you were gone

I ran to our tent and grabbed as many supplies
as my paws could hold
Stuffing them quickly into a makeshift bag
I will forage the rest on my way

My skills in tracking honed to a fine point through panic and grief
I will not let you die
I swore it to myself a hundred times as I wrote this

I take this down as the last of my feeling
Tonight, my heart will answer your burning flames
And come what may, I will finally know

10th of Autumn, Year 1569
        Marked upon the parchment by Nathaniel Hedgeworthy to
Symon the Dragon, with Great Confusion, and Possibly Love?

I did not hear you leave when the morning dawn rose
And my heart leapt to my throat
Thinking my companions had found you

But when I met them later in the day,
they greeted me as if I had been lost
They'd thought me dead

And now I can't help but think
That what I feel for you is different now
It has a different flavor in my mouth,
a different tingle in my fur
Now that I have met you, it is all so strange
You were everything and nothing that I imagined

So, until we meet once more Symon
Let the next arrow shot at us both,
be from Cupid himself

Nathaniel laughed to himself as he set the weathered parchment back down on the table. "I was a pretentious little kit, wasn't I?"

A small fire was crackling in a fireplace close by. The faint light was enough to read by but not enough to draw attention. At least that's what he thought. A large figure loomed in the entrance to the room and called out to him.

"Nate? Are you over here?"

Nathaniel closed the bound book of letters and poetry and replied, "Over here, hun."

A red dragon just barely smaller than the doorway padded into the room quietly. His head was wreathed in a crown of golden horns and even in the low light, it was possible to see the brilliance of his blood-red scales. He moved as if hesitant to interrupt what Nathaniel was doing. He rubbed his neck awkwardly and said, "I noticed you left the bed and got worried about you."

Nathaniel smiled and got up from the table. He walked over to Symon's chest and placed his head on it. Symon's massive heart thrummed in his ears. A steady beat quickened as he placed a paw reassuringly next to the scar only a few inches away.

"It's nothing, Symon. My dreams woke me up again and I felt like taking a trip through old memories."

"Nothing too painful, I hope?"

"Not anymore, no. It's nothing you need worry about."

A broad scaled hand came under Nathaniel's chin and rubbed it lovingly. Symon took extra precautions to keep his long white claws from getting near the small fox's face. His hand was a great deal larger than Nathaniel's body, but they'd had a lot of practice by now, learning how to navigate around their different sizes. Nathaniel leaned into the gesture blissfully. He opened his eyes halfway and held Symon's thumb with both his hands.

"Let's go back to bed. I'm sorry for worrying you."

"As long as you're okay, that's what matters."

With a flick of his wrist, Symon pulled the fire from the fireplace and held it within the palm of his hand. They left for their bedroom, the small light guiding their way there. In a familiar tangle of fur and scales, beneath a pair of wings that felt as comfortable as any blanket, they found rest from their past.

The forest and fire, finally at peace.

Brunhilda

Ch-ch-ch-ch-ch-ch-ch-ch-kachunk-kachunk

Sherman couldn't believe that Clive had talked him into this. While other kids were out trick-or-treating or going to Halloween parties, they were stowing away on an old timey passenger train. He didn't think the trains ran late, but the Night Express 5382 was an exception. That was a mouthful for most, so folks started calling the train 'Brunhilda', after the old conductor that used to work the cars in centuries past. There were more ghost stories about Brunhilda than there were cabs in the line. And as members of their school's paranormal investigation club, they had an obligation to check into them.

Or more accurately, *Clive* thought they had an obligation. Sherman was fine with letting the stories go uninvestigated. It wasn't like anyone else in their group was raising their paws to volunteer either. Even Raúl, who Sherman thought would be all over the particular story, didn't offer a helping hoof. Before they got on the train, Sherman tried to convince Clive that they could just take some pictures outside of the train station and tell everyone they got thrown off, but he wasn't having it.

They packed light for their mission. Sherman brought a small instant camera and Clive had a tape recorder he borrowed from his dad along with a fanny pack to hold some snacks. The idea was to get onto the train without the conductor noticing and ride it until morning. They had somehow managed to make it onto a passenger car near the caboose without arousing suspicion, and quickly hid themselves underneath the seats. It was a tight squeeze to fit underneath, especially with the size of Sherman's feathery wings, but they managed it better than he expected.

To their surprise and relief, the train took off shortly after they boarded. Picking up steam as it rattled along the tracks in its stilted, irregular rhythm.

Ch-ch-ch-ch-ch-ch-ch-ch-kachunk-kachunk

What felt like hours later, Sherman poked his beak out from under the seat and looked around the empty car. He couldn't see if anyone was waiting for him, and the only sound seemed to be the movement of the train. Hoping that it was safe, he stretched out his wings and pulled himself out from under the seat. He stood up slowly and fluffed out his feathers, preening himself a bit before finding a piece of old gum stuck to his wings. He spit it out immediately and used his beak to lay his feathers flat once more. Now that he was able to stretch out his legs and wings properly, Sherman could focus once again on being completely unnerved.

Even without the possibility of ghosts, the train car was creepy. The only light came from the full moon shining through the windows, painting the floor with ghostly shadows. There was a feeling creeping at the back of Sherman's neck that being in the passenger car when there were no other passengers was wrong. It was the same feeling he got when he would have to pick something up at the school after all the kids and teachers had left. That without others around him, he was intruding on the car's rest somehow. He let the feeling wash over him and shivered.

There was a part of his brain that insisted he shouldn't be so scared all the time. Being a falcon meant he was a bird of prey after all. Then another voice reminded him that his bones were light and hollow and very, very breakable. So, if there was a ghost hiding in the shadows of the train car, he was almost certainly going to die. Especially if the ghost decided to throw him out of the train. Sherman kept coming up with worse and worse scenarios until he noticed he was nervously chewing on his hind claws. The habit was one he was trying to break, but he was glad it had stopped him from spiraling further. He put his hand at his side and decided that he should check on Clive. He'd been suspiciously quiet through all the recent commotion.

Ch-ch-ch-ch-ch-ch-ch-ch-kachunk-kachunk

Sherman peeked under the seat across from him and saw that Clive's eyes were closed. The sound of the train had drowned it out earlier, but when he leaned in, Sherman could hear the soft sound of Clive's even breathing. He was curled up in a ball of pale yellow and dark amber scales cuddling his own tail. Sherman reached over to his snout and used his feathers to tickle under his chin.

"C'mon, ya big lizard. Time to hunt for your ghosts," Sherman whispered to Clive while moving his hand back and forth.

Clive squirmed a little and let go of his tail instinctively. He opened his eyes and pretended to yawn, smacking his lips together as he did so.

"Oh, hey Sherman. I had the strangest dream. I was an expensive vase in a millionaire's mansion, and I was getting dusted by this really fluffy feather duster."

He pulled himself out from under the seat and stood up. Clive was a skink, which meant a short neck and shorter legs. It wasn't an exaggeration to say that Clive was mostly torso, with the next biggest part of him being his tail. Because of it, Sherman was the taller and lankier of the two of them.

"You're lucky you looked cute sleeping wrapped up in your tail or else I wouldn't have woken you up so gently," Sherman teased, lightly brushing Clive's snout with his wing.

"Aww, you do care!" chided Clive, blowing away a feather stuck to his nose and sticking his tongue out.

"What am I gonna do with you?"

"I'm sure you'll think of something," Clive said after pulling his tongue back into his mouth. "Have you noticed anything weird yet?"

Sherman chirped indignantly. "You mean to tell me taking mid-night rides on old trains isn't weird enough for you? No wonder you didn't want to go to that Halloween party tonight. Not a lot of high schoolers who would pass that opportunity up for a musty train car."

"Hey, come on. Don't be like that. You know I'm missing out tonight too. I heard Mrs. Butterbean is giving out full-size candy bars at her house," Clive said while digging out his tape recorder from his fanny pack.

Ch-ch-ch-ch-ch-ch-ch-ch-kachunk-kachunk

Sherman and Clive had stood for about an hour waiting for something to happen in the train car. From the reports they had gotten from other folks, the train was supposed to be a hotbed of paranormal activity, but Clive wasn't impressed. He had expected to see something, anything within the first hour of observation. Sherman did his best to persuade his friend that the ghosts might just be shy.

Silently, he hoped nothing would happen at all. Having Clive there did help to settle some of his nerves a bit, but it was still a good deal creepier than Sherman would have cared for. Clive didn't seem to be affected by the lonesome clanking of the train and the emptiness of the train car. Or if he was, he wasn't showing it to Sherman.

They both grew tired of standing and decided to sit on the seats and wait for the ghosts to show up that way. They chose seats facing each other and sat down carefully. Hiding under the seats, Sherman had imagined them worn and antiquated, but now that he sat on them, he saw they had hardly any signs of age at all. Some discoloration from exposure to the sun, but no rips or tears to be found. The whole surface was smooth to the touch of his wingtip.

"Clive, do you think it's weird how good this train looks?"

"What do you mean, Sherman?"

Sherman clicked his beak in consternation and said, "It's just that, this is supposed to be an old train, right? From the 1800s at least. Why would a train that old have no visible wear and tear on it? Even the paint on the inside isn't peeling. It should be beat up to Hell and back."

Clive put a hand to his chin and thought for a second before saying, "Maybe it was restored? That's a big thing nowadays. Making sure old stuff can be enjoyed by a new group of people. They might've just reupholstered the seats or something."

"It just doesn't sit well with me. I get the urge to ruffle my feathers just thinking about it."

"Well, then don't think about it. That's what I do."

"You can't be serious."

Clive smiled and adjusted his tail so that it laid over his lap before saying, "It's worked for me so far."

Sherman couldn't really argue with him. He'd seen Clive's nerves of steel firsthand multiple times. It wasn't the first time they'd sneaked into somewhere they weren't supposed to be, chasing after a story. He was just surprised that the explanation for his calm demeanor in the face of mortal terror was so simple. Sherman had expected him to say he meditated or had seen something so terrifying that everything else was small potatoes in comparison.

Ch-ch-ch-ch-ch-ch-ch-ch-kachunk-kachunk

Clive was pulling out a bag from his fanny pack, with an exuberant cartoon cricket on the side and a logo in bold impact font that spelled out 'Cricket Chips'.

"How can you be hungry right now?"

Clive shrugged as he popped one of the chips into his mouth. "We've been up half the night. I'm surprised you're not. Besides, it doesn't seem like anything is gonna happen anyway. I was really hoping this time we'd get the scoop of the century."

"We've never gotten any concrete evidence before. Let's just make something up and call it a column."

"Yeah, yeah. I was just hoping this time would be different."

Sherman felt a strange mixture of relief and sadness. He hated to see his friend disappointed but was glad the ghosts had decided to keep away from them. He got up from his seat and went over to place his wing on Clive's shoulder.

"You want to take some pictures of me looking scared? That always seems to be a hit with the people who read our stuff."

Clive perked his snout up and nodded. He popped another chip into his mouth before setting the bag down on his seat. He motioned to Sherman to give him the instant camera. Together, they found some spots in the train car that had sufficiently spooky lighting and Sherman posed for the camera. As they finished their small photoshoot, Clive handed the camera back over to Sherman.

"That should just about do it. Now what?"

"Well, we'll have to wait until the train stops to get off. Come to think of it, I'm surprised it hasn't stopped yet."

Sherman couldn't think about that right at the moment. There was something terribly wrong and he couldn't put a wingtip on it. Something had changed in the train car as they were taking the pictures, but what?

Then it hit him.

"Clive? Do you hear that?"

"Hear what?"

"Exactly."

The train car had become eerily quiet. So quiet that they couldn't hear the train moving anymore. Sherman slowly turned his head to the side to look out the window. Sure enough, they were still moving. He could see the landscape sliding along just as easily as before. He wasn't sure if that was a relief or not. And out of the corner of his vision, Sherman could see a faint orange light coming from the other end of the train car. Clive had noticed it too.

"Uh, Sherman? What's that?"

Sherman turned around slowly and looked over where his friend was pointing. The orange light was faint at first, but it grew in intensity quickly. Whatever it was pushed through the closed train car door and manifested inside the train car. Now that the light was brighter, they could make out an outlined shape of a frog. He was wearing a knight's suit of armor and carried his helmet under his arm. The only truly perceivable portion of his body was his outline - the rest was a pale translucent orange. He walked slowly around the train car, turning around at random intervals. He didn't pay attention to the stunned kids at the other end of the train car who couldn't believe what they were seeing.

Sherman went to whisper something to Clive, beak chattering against his will, but Clive had already clicked on his tape recorder.

He took his eyes off the apparition for a second to look at Clive and saw the lizard's face had the biggest smile plastered over it.

"Sherman! That's an honest to goodness ghost! Do you know what this means?"

"That we're in horrible danger?"

"No! That we've got a chance at that unbelievable scoop after all. Quick, get your camera back out. I'm going to try and make contact with it."

"Are you crazy, Clive? You're not seriously going to talk to that thing, are you?"

But Clive was already walking toward the spirit, enthusiasm in his bouncy step. Sherman had never seen him this excited. He tried to follow after him but had to walk at a much slower pace to keep himself from sprinting in the opposite direction.

When he did catch up, Clive looked as confused as the spirit. He tried waving his hands in front of him. Yelling out to him. Even offering him the tape recorder. But he didn't react to any of what Clive tried. Sherman even took some pictures of him, shakily, with the instant camera. And still no reaction from the spirit. Clive turned the tape recorder to himself and said, "I don't get it. Why isn't he reacting? What do you think, Sherman?"

He extended the tape recorder over to Sherman's beak and waited for the falcon to answer. Sherman cleared his throat a little too loudly and responded with, "He can't tell we're even here. He's already looked around the train car a couple times. If we were what he was looking for, he would have said something by now. And besides..." Sherman put a wingtip on the tape recorder and slowly pushed it back over to Clive. He whispered, "We shouldn't be trying to get his attention in the first place. What if he decides to hurt us? Or worse, follow us off the train and haunt us back at school?"

"You think he would do that?" Clive asked excitedly.

"It's not supposed to be a good thing, Clive!"

The frog knight had stopped moving while the two were whispering to each other and now both had noticed that he was looking out the window. The spirit shook his head side-to-side, shrugged his shoulders, and croaked deeply in a language neither of the boys understood. The croaking sent a shiver down Sherman's spine as he willed his feathers from puffing up around him. Clive double checked his tape recorder to make sure it was recording, no doubt hoping that the otherworldly sound would get caught for reference later. The spirit moved his helmet out from under his shoulder, put it on his head, and began marching away, straight at the train car's wall. Before he could collide with the wall, however, his form dissipated into motes of orange light that scattered out until he could no longer be seen.

Sherman breathed a sigh of relief and began to chew at his hind talons to try and calm himself down. Clive clicked off the tape recorder and jumped the highest Sherman had ever seen into the air. When he landed with a thud, he was beaming.

"We've hit the jackpot! Photographic evidence AND a sound sample! The guys back at the paranormal investigation club are going to lose their minds over this evidence!"

Sherman wanted to share in Clive's celebration, but he couldn't help but notice that the orange light was entering the train car once again. And it wasn't just one point of light that entered. All around them were balls of orange light that shimmered and shifted into spirits, until the entire train car was lit up in their warm orange glow. As they moved around, the two could see a pattern forming. They were dancing. The spirits had the outlines of noble folk, looking as if they had just stepped out of a castle. They wore masks, as if attending a masquerade ball. The strangest part about their costumes though was the lack of a face under the masks. The dancers glided to and fro, and as they spun and twirled, Sherman and Clive could see that there was no head, snout, or ears to hold the masks aloft. Sherman ran to the nearest seat and ducked behind it, hoping to avoid detection. As he ran, one of the dancers passed through his body, diffusing into orange sparks, before coalescing back into shape. While he didn't notice this, Clive did.

"Did you see that?"

"Do you mean the headless parade of dancing ghosts?" Sherman warbled from behind his shelter. "Yeah, I did see that! It's very hard to miss."

"No, I mean when you passed through them. They came back together again. Look." He wiggled his tail and a couple of the dancers scattered into light, then reformed behind him. He waved his arms and legs around the middle of the circle of dancers, scattering them all. It took them longer to reform, but soon enough, they were right back to dancing.

"They're completely harmless."

Sherman poked his beak out from the side of the seat and said, "I'm glad you think so. I'll be staying over here, thank you very much!"

Clive shook his head and said, "You're overreacting! If they were malicious spirits, they would have tried something by now. Trust me, I've done a lot of research into this."

Sherman wanted to believe Clive; he really did. Maybe he was overreacting to the whole mess, but how else was one supposed to react to seeing a ghost for the first time? Let alone an entire dancing troupe of them? He tried to stand up but stopped himself when he saw that the dancers had stopped moving. They were all staring up at something above them, but whatever it was, the two boys couldn't see it. There were frightened whispers between the ghosts in that language that they couldn't make out.

And then they all screamed.

An enormous ball of orange light crashed through the ceiling of the train car and scattered the dancers beneath it. As the light coursed through the train car, Clive hit the floor and Sherman ducked back under the seat. It was chaos as the dancers were snuffed out by the bigger light engulfing them. In terror, Sherman let out an ear-piercing shriek that resounded off the train car walls and out into the night.

"AHHHHHHHHHHHH!!!"

Surprisingly, the light vanished from view. The train car was empty, save for the two boys again. Sherman's eyes were wild with fear. He darted out from the seat shouting, "That's enough! Get me off this train now!"

Clive was still stunned when he figured out what Sherman was trying to do. He got up and ran toward his friend just as Sherman had thrown open the emergency exit.

Ch-ch-ch-ch-ch-ch-ch-ch-kachunk-kachunk

The wind whistled in their ears and tugged at Sherman's out-stretched wings, pulling him up, up, up away from the train car. Clive wrapped his tail around a nearby seat and leaned out, trying to grab Sherman before he was carried away. He managed to get a hold of his legs and pulled with all he had until he was able to drag Sherman's wings through the door and back inside the train car. Sherman fell back onto Clive and they both landed in a heap behind the door. Clive unwrapped his tail and smacked it into the door, slamming it shut.

When they had both gotten their breath again, Clive asked, "What were you thinking? Are you trying to *become* a ghost?"

Sherman had curled up into a small ball and was softly crying. Clive immediately regretted his outburst as he put his hand on his friend's wing. He went to give him a hug and Sherman unfolded his wings enough to let Clive in.

When he next spoke, he said, "I just want to go home. This is all too much for me."

Clive held him as he collected himself. He wanted to tell him that everything would be okay. That they weren't in any danger and the first safe chance they had, they'd hop off the train and find a way to get back home. Yet as the orange light returned, he felt saying those things would be moot.

"Don't open your eyes. I think there's another spirit in the train car."

Sherman did as he was told and kept his eyes shut. Clive turned around and faced the new spirit that was manifesting. The glow in the cabin was immense as it arrived. The whole of the train car was bathed in orange light as a reptilian snout poked through the door. Snuffling left, then right, its nose looking for something it could not see. The rest of the head pushed through shortly after and Clive had to stifle a gasp. Whatever it was, its neck was enormous, easily long enough to reach its head all the way down the train car and look down at him and Sherman. The eyes were as big as the seats, and slit, both sharp as daggers, and pointed directly at him.

"Sherman, I think this one can see us."

"What do we do?"

"Let's try to show we mean no harm. Very slowly put your hands up."

Sherman shakily moved his wings out to the side of Clive as he too put his hands up.

"See? We're friendly."

The creature seemed to understand the gesture as its eyes relaxed and its head posture lowered. Sherman opened his eyes slowly and saw the creature was moving its head down toward Clive. He waved his arms in protest before the creature carefully opened its mouth a fraction of an inch and pinched the fabric of Clive's shirt. Clive was too fascinated by the gesture to notice that the creature was lifting him upwards. Sherman panicked and reached out to grab Clive. The next thing they felt was the sensation of being flung into the air.

For the first time that night, Clive screamed.

They were above the train, being carried in the creature's mouth as it flew past all the cars towards the locomotive. Out in the wide expanse of the night sky, Clive could look behind himself and see the creature's whole body. Two massive wings beat in a constant rhythm on its back and its four legs were tipped with razor sharp claws. A long serpentine tail trailed behind it, tracing bright orange motes of light in between the white of the stars overhead. Clive whipped his head back around to the train below when he felt the sensation of falling again.

The creature dove down and Clive braced himself for an impact that never came as they phased through the top of the engine car and down into the heart of the train. Once in the car, Clive and Sherman were let go and they tumbled to a stop just short of the engine. The creature shrank as it phased its massive body through the engine door, leaving the two boys to reorient themselves.

"Brunhilda!" a snarling voice screamed from the conductor's seat. "What is all that racket?"

A frazzled looking cougar came stomping into the room wearing a disheveled pair of striped pajamas. She took one look at the boys sprawled on the floor of her cabin and hissed.

"Stowaways, huh? Well, I know exactly what to do with you."

The cougar moved toward them both, eyes glinting like mad in the moonlight. She reached out with her claws as the sound of the train roared below them.

Ch-ch-ch-ch-ch-ch-ch-ch-kachunk-kachunk

Sitting on a blanket listening to the conductor explain how the train worked was quite a surreal experience. Clive had picked the spot closest to the engine so that he could warm his scales. Sherman had opted to sit a safe distance away for the moment. Tilly, the cougar that had found them, shed light on what the boys had experienced over a cup of warm cider.

"I find folk are more willing to accept what I tell them with a hot drink in their belly."

Clive sipped the cider and nodded, though he still wasn't sure he could follow what she had said. Thankfully, Sherman spoke up and asked for him.

"So, wait. You're telling me that Brunhilda is a dragon? Like a real, honest to goodness dragon?"

"Yes, more specifically, the soul of a dragon. But at that point we're just splitting hairs."

"And she powers the whole train from the engine?"

"Yep."

"How?"

"I don't rightly know myself. But it's a wonder innit?"

Clive held up his hand, school instincts taking over, and when Tilly's focus shifted to him, he asked, "But how did she end up in the engine? Aren't dragons, y'know, huge?"

Tilly laughed and then said, "Well, you're not wrong. Fact of the matter is, she got there because my great-great-great-great-great aunt took pity on her. She transferred her soul into the engine as the train was being built because it was a construct that would be big enough to hold the entirety of her."

"Why would they even need to do that?"

Tilly frowned a little and said, "Too many machines. Air was too heavy. The poor girl couldn't take off and fly right anymore. When my aunt found her, she couldn't lift off the ground. Couldn't move.

That's no way for a dragon to live. Brunhilda had so much life left in her, but she was bound to her body. So, my aunt gave her a way to see the world and continue living."

"That's amazing! Isn't that amazing, Sherman?"

Sherman took a sip of his cider and then said, "But that doesn't explain the spirits. What about all those dancing ghosts and the frog knight?"

Tilly looked at Sherman as though he had laid an egg. "There's no spirits on this train, boy. I think you might have had a little too much cider." She reached over to grab the mug back from Sherman, but he smacked her hand away with his wing.

"What Sherman means to say is, we saw the same orange light that Brunhilda is made of pass through the train car earlier. Do you know what that's about?"

Tilly thought for a second and then her eyes lit up. She motioned for the two of them to follow her as she walked over to the engine and pulled back the cover to the engine door. The heat from inside was tremendous, but it was comforting too. Her presence a pleasant warmth that seeped out into the cabin. Looking inside, they could see Brunhilda's spectral body coiled around the engine. She was much smaller in there, but her whole body was laid flat along the ground, and it looked as though she was sleeping.

"Sometimes Brunhilda gets restless, and she needs to run off some steam to get a good night's rest. I took her out tonight, and that's the result"

"So, she was dreaming?"

"Bingo."

Clive looked disappointed so Sherman chimed in with, "Aww, don't worry, Clive. There's at least one ghost on the train. And you got the chance to see her."

Tilly shook her head and said, "You have got to get it through your head that I say what I mean, and I mean what I say. There are no spirits on this train. Long as she's still running, Brunhilda is just as alive as you or me. And speaking of which..." A growl crept into her voice as she lowered herself down to stare at the two of them dead in their eyes. "None of this, is to leave this here train car. If the wrong person found out, they'd want to dismantle her and find out what makes her tick. I can't let that happen." She held out her palm, waiting for the boys to take the hint.

Sherman understood immediately and turned over his instant camera.

"Consider it already forgotten, ma'am." Then he nudged Clive in the ribs so he would give her the tape recorder.

Tilly smiled and said, "Much obliged, gentlemen. Make yourselves comfy. I'll make sure you get dropped off proper in the morning."

As she walked away to dispose of the evidence, Clive turned to Sherman and smiled.

"What are you so happy about?"

"After everything that's happened, I forgot it was Halloween. We managed to get a good scare in after all!

The Wyrm in The Mountain of Apples

"You can't do that! What about all the animals up there? And the trees? Don't you have any conscience?"

The large tiger in the construction uniform just shook his head dismissively at the small mouse.

"Look kid, I don't make the orders. I just follow them. If you got a problem, you shoulda spoke up months ago. All the zoning and permits are already put through and approved."

Emmanuel wasn't soothed by the matter-of-fact explanation given by the gruff man. None of the adults had talked about this at all. Had they just given up before the fight even began? It wouldn't surprise him, but the bulldozers weren't running just yet. He'd hoped it wouldn't have come to this, but it looked like he'd have to resort to Plan B. He didn't want to think of the alternative. Emmanuel stuck his tongue out at the tiger and jumped on his bike. He rode through town at breakneck speed, wind whipping at his large ears as he took each successive turn sharper and sharper. Half an hour later, he arrived at the base of the bike trail for Mt. Pomme and made his way up the crumbling and rocky trail. The whiskers on his nose twitched in nervous anticipation. He'd ridden the trail at least a hundred times before, but riding it now felt different than it used to. The trail was long and winding, coiling back on itself in parts, more like a restless snake than a well-worn path.

Emmanuel knew the way by heart, veering off the trail just after the row of rotten stumps and sending the bike downhill through the low shrubs. The timing on the next part was tricky, but he had gotten used to it. As the bike sped down the other side of the trail towards the base of the mountain, Emmanuel stood up on his pedals and let the bike coast towards the large rock at the end of the path. He squinted his eyes and braced himself, counting down in his head.

3, 2, 1, NOW!

The bike tire hit the front of the rock, sending Emmanuel flying over the top and onto the other side. He landed with a *THUD* on his tail and winced in pain. He untangled his legs from his bike and propped it against the rock. Getting up, he rubbed at his tail and looked at the small crack in the base of the mountain. He walked up to it and squeezed himself through the narrow opening, into the hidden cavern.

As soon as Emmanuel stepped through, he could hear the familiar sound of long, slow, methodical breathing echoing inside of the dark chamber. He walked closer to the source and turned on his pocket flashlight to check. And there, curled up in a ball of scales which filled the entire cavern, was the monster. A great and terrible lizard, which Emmanuel knew from looking at it that if it were to stand on its hind legs, it would tower higher than the mountain itself. Long and sinuous like a snake, but thick and strong like a dragon. The creature breathed comfortably, which was a relief. The last time Emmanuel visited, the monster's breaths were much shallower and that worried him. As amazing as the monster was, Emmanuel desperately wanted to make sure it stayed asleep. Once he had gotten over the shock and awe that came with discovering a real-life monster, the implications of what it could do if it ever woke up had dawned on him.

Emmanuel considered reporting it but knew that the adults wouldn't believe him anyway. They were obviously too busy preparing high-grade explosives and fueling construction equipment to care about some kid's storybook fantasies. He knew he had to stop the demolition, or the entire town would be in danger. He sighed as he rubbed his temples and went over the plan in his head again.

It wasn't working, though. He was too nervous. He tried instead to focus on the monster's breathing, for as fearsome as it was, its rhythm was oddly soothing to Emmanuel. He walked over closer to the creature and sat down next to one of its immense eyes. As amazing as the monster was, Emmanuel desperately wanted to make sure it stayed asleep. The first time he'd found it, he'd stumbled right into its scaly flesh and just about jumped out of his fur from the shock. Ever since then, he's known he could get close to it. Emmanuel put his small paw onto the leathery skin of the creature and began to pet it. The texture was calming to the touch and helped him to think more clearly.

If life got to be too much, he used to come to the mountain and try to clear his head. Instead, it seemed like every time he came to the mountain, his head was full of more worries than the last. Emmanuel spent most of his free time exploring Mt. Pomme. It was his hideaway, and he spent many summer nights eating wild apples from the trees and watching the town below. He knew every peak and valley of the mountain's rocks and all the plants that grew there. He sometimes climbed to the highest spot on the mountain, looked over the valley, and for a fraction of a second, would forget what it was like to be small.

Emmanuel was startled out of his reminiscing by the sound of the monster breathing shallow again. He backed away cautiously, eyes wide as he felt vibrations rumbling through the mountain. It wasn't strong enough to be an explosion, but it was long and persistent. If it kept up, the monster might wake up. It had happened before, a few weeks prior, so Emmanuel knew one way to soothe the creature, though it was risky.

He looked at the monster's body again and found that its leathery hide had some natural bumps and raises in the skin. He dashed towards the middle of the monster and gently raised himself onto its side, grabbing onto the naturally raised handholds. He put his climbing knowledge to use and looked for the next handhold as he scaled the monster. He tried to strike a balance between moving slow enough that the monster wouldn't feel him, but fast enough to make it in time. It was an excruciating process. The monster was so long that Emmanuel wasn't sure he would have the stamina to keep climbing. His arms burned from the strain and the monster's increasing movements weren't helping his nerves.

Suddenly, the monster's neck whipped up and catapulted Emmanuel towards the head. He landed, bounced, and could feel himself sliding down the body of the monster, threatening to fall off as it rose higher into the air. Desperately, he pitched himself forward and caught a new handhold before he could fall fully. He peered down to where he almost fell, seeing the creature's shifting scales, big and blunt enough to have crushed him. He climbed quicker now, scared of what could happen if he was too late.

He made it to the head and found what he was looking for. A small but clearly discernible ear hole a few feet away from its closed eye. Emmanuel got close to the ear and began to whisper a lullaby into it while gently petting the monster's scaly skin. The monster immediately stopped moving and settled itself back down. A few shaky verses of "Twinkle Twinkle Little Star" later, it was asleep again, only even deeper than before. Emmanuel let out a sigh of relief and slid down onto the floor of the cavern. He took one last look at the monster, content in its slumber, and then left the cave to go check outside.

His fears were confirmed when he saw just what had made all the noise. The mountainside was covered in construction vehicles and trucks carrying explosives. They were preparing the mountain to blow, and soon.

He rushed home on his bike to get supplies. He'd need quite the arsenal if he wanted to pull it off. He ripped open his backpack and dumped his schoolbooks out onto the floor. Then he went through the house grabbing and shoving what he needed into his bag. A pair of binoculars by the den, water and snacks from the kitchen, wire cutters and a handheld blowtorch from Mom's toolbox, and a couple chunks of wood with a box of industrial grade nails from the garage. Finally, a dark hoodie to keep out the chill and help to hide his face. He heard his mom calling after him, but he couldn't turn around and explain himself. There wasn't enough time. He could hear her use his full name as he jumped onto his bike and rode back up the mountain in the dead of night.

As the first rays of light came over the mountainside, Emmanuel stood at the top of the mountain. He watched through a pair of binoculars as a cloud of dust rolled up the base of the mountain, and soon enough a convoy of bright yellow construction vehicles rounded the corner, climbing the service road. The convoy was led by a large front loader, and its tires were the first to blow out, followed by the dump truck behind it and then a series of small forklifts carrying loads of boxes.

A smirk painted Emmanuel's face as he watched the vehicles stop one by one, rendered immobile. A large wombat emerged from a limousine at the back of the pack and started screaming at the workers. He was wearing an ill-fitting business suit and had the toupee on his head greased back. Emmanuel smiled and jumped down from the side of the mountain to finish rigging the last of his traps. He peeked around the corner of the rock closest to the workers and began to plan his attack.

In a flash he was grabbed by one of them and hoisted into the air. It was the same tiger that Emmanuel had spoken to a day ago.

"I think I found your rat, Mr. Chalk."

"Ah, splendid job, Bruce!" the wombat boomed in a voice that was much too big for his body. "You're quite the little troublemaker, aren't you, boy?"

Emmanuel looked Mr. Chalk square in the eye and said, "There's something terrible that lives in this mountain. I was only trying to keep you from waking it up."

"Oh? And just what is in the mountain?"

"A monster."

Mr. Chalk looked around at his workers and they all started laughing.

"There ain't no monsters here, boy! Just a fine piece o' real estate!"

"You've got to believe me! You're all in grave danger!"

"The only thing that's in danger is my time being wasted. Bruce, get him out of my sight."

"Sure, thing boss."

And before Emmanuel could say any more Bruce carried him down the mountainside and out of sight.

Emmanuel struggled against Bruce's tight grip, but it was no use. He looked on in abject horror as the mountain was wracked with explosions. Bits of crumbling rock and fallen trees fell off the mountainside in enormous clumps. Each successive detonation was louder and more powerful than the last, until an even louder screech pierced the air.

RRRRAAAAAAAAAARRRRGGGGGGHHHHHHH!!!!!

Everyone had stopped. Cars slammed on their brakes. People came rushing out of their houses to see what had made the terrible sound. Bruce let Emmanuel drop to the ground and stared at the mountain, slack-jaw in fear.

The monster was awake.

It had burst through the side of the mountain with ease and was now coiling around what was left of Mt. Pomme. Its scales and skin were a dark brown, the same color of the mountain interior. Its six eyes flashed open, each a piercing hazel, gazing in all directions. The mouth was easily large enough to swallow the entire demolition crew whole, along with their trucks. And its shiny white teeth were sharp enough to cut through the rock of the mountain like butter.

The monster turned its head to the source of the explosions and began to slowly move towards it. The demolition crew set off the last of their explosions to deter the beast, but the force barely moved the monster. It barreled through the last of the detonations and the monster's maw opened to its full height as it prepared to strike. A fraction of a second later, there was a deafening crash that echoed across the valley.

At that moment, everyone felt small.

At Sunset, She Flew

She was the sky and the glow of the waters below her. Purple and orange feathers flowing seamlessly to blue, and green scales gave her a unique advantage that no one else had. In twilight, she was invisible to all but the most trained eyes.

At sunset, she flew.

Flying was more than automatic to dragons. It was more than an instinct, more than an impulse. It just was. The feeling was hard for Fiore to describe to those whose lives weren't intertwined so completely with it. She didn't have the words to bridge that gap of understanding, and after a while, she stopped trying. Flight, after all, was something to experience. And when the thermals were just right, and the sun shone on her scales, there was nothing better.

Her parents had told her stories that dragons had once come from the earth below, but they all longed for the sun's embrace so fervently that they grew wings to be closer. Fiore believed this completely. There was little she would do to try and get a few more precious moments with the great warmth that gave life to everything around her. It was a tragedy then that she could not experience the sun at its brightest. Always getting the last few rays of sunshine before the night crept in across the horizon.

Fiore often laid awake at night, thinking of her hatchday. There are more types of dragons than there are kinds of fish, but feathered dragons were still incredibly rare. And with no other feathered dragons in the clutch, Fiore was left to fend for herself when it came to learning many things. Her parents, while well-meaning, did not know how to explain flight when they only knew how to use their webbed-membrane wings. Flight, after all, was something to experience.

She quickly learned the difference between falling and flying. And in what felt like no time at all, left her nest for a home of her own. It had been many years since that fateful flight. She was lucky that the storm that knocked her out of the air didn't send her unconscious body crashing against the rocks of the cliffside. When she awoke, after coughing out a slough of water, she found the raging ocean had landed her on the sandy beach of an island, painted with the shadow of a cliff. She set to work carving out a home for herself in the cliff.

She was so full of hope then. So full of promise. She dove from her home into the brine below and shot out of the water laughing, fish dangling from the corner of her snout.

Shortly after she finished carving out the first room of the cave, she went out to explore the rest of the island. She shot up into the sky mere moments before coming across a settlement of humans. They were camped out at the edge of a large forest close to her newly made cave. Though she couldn't understand their cries, she could read the expressions on their faces. Disgust, horror, anger. A few were awe-struck, but their faces blurred in the commotion. Fiore barely avoided the nets and ballistic fire. She retreated to her cave, looking over her shoulder the whole way. She didn't leave it for days.

When she did dare to venture back out, she was careful in each of her steps. She poked her head around a nearby wall of rock and found a human standing guard outside of the settlement. And though the humans that stood guard changed from day to day, Fiore knew they wouldn't leave until they'd found her and killed her. She'd been warned of humans and their violent tendencies since she was hatched. She didn't realize how committed they would be to killing her until she saw it with her own eyes. She didn't even hurt them! What excuse could they have to put her through that torture?

As the days passed, Fiore could feel herself wasting away, but wouldn't chance setting even one claw outside of her safe haven. They hadn't found her cave yet, and she wanted to keep it that way. A week later, she grew desperate for food. Just before the sun dipped over the horizon, she made the decision to leave. Her wings felt foreign to her after not using them for so long.

At sunset, she flew.

The fish in her jaws was so delicious she didn't care who saw her. Let the humans shoot her out of the sky for all she cared. Yet when her stomach had stopped growling, she realized how exposed she was. If she strained her eyes, she could see the lone lookout next to the human's settlement. Stranger still that they had not moved an inch since she last left her cave. Surely, they would have gathered up their nets and weapons by now. So then where were they? Fiore pondered it as she flew around the edge of the island. She looked down into the shimmering water beneath her and experienced something peculiar.

She couldn't quite make out the shape of her body. She found she had to concentrate hard to see the edges of her wings and the lazy swish of her tail in the air. She dove into the frigid water, the cold stabbing at her feathery wings, and stared into the murky blackness below as understanding dawned on her. They couldn't see her.

She splashed out of the water in delight. The whole of her body, from the tip of her snout down to the edge of her tail felt electric. After days of seclusion and isolation, riding the wind was more exhilarating than it had ever been. She looked to the horizon, her soul singing out with joy at the sunset. She paused, hovering in the air, as she watched the sun dip low on the surface of the water.

Night was fast approaching. Fiore knew that she would have to return to the cave before she was spotted. She turned around and flew back to the safety of her cave, just as the first fires were being lit in the distance.

At sunset, she flew.

Fiore got up, stretched herself out, preened her feathers, and promptly sat back down again. That day would be the same as before, and the day before that. She had lived a life of quiet isolation for so many years that it was routine to her. Her cave was as much a part of her physical body as her snout or her tail. She knew every crack, crevice, and wet spot in excruciating detail. Which places were the best to lay down on when the sun came up to warm her scales and what corners were the best to peek out from before leaving. It was comfortable, she had made sure of that.

She had been depressed, sure. *Was* currently depressed. Knew the nauseating feeling of a rotting fish in her empty stomach. She had thought multiple times of flinging herself from the edge of the cave and letting herself fall to the rocks below. She never went through with it. Couldn't go through with it, but the thought was there all the same. It would flit across the landscape of her mind briefly, she'd have her fantasy, and then it would be gone again. The promise of one more evening outside would always pull her back from the edge. And no matter how she felt that day, she would always try and enjoy herself when she had her few hours of sunlight. It was the only joy she had left in her small world.

Fiore had found ways to pass the time while she waited for the sunset, of course. And there were days in which she genuinely enjoyed these too. Her favorite among the many idle hobbies was carving pictures into the walls of her cave. She would sharpen her claws on a stone, pick a section of cave that was bare, and set to work. She couldn't work on it all day, lest she trim her claws down to dull nubs, but it helped Fiore distract herself. She enjoyed seeing the pictures come together over the course of a few days as well. A little bit at a time, she was making her cave more beautiful.

On particularly hard days, she would stare at the pictures she had carved before and come up with stories to keep her mind from the darkness. In a fair few of them, she would try eloping with a handsome male dragon, but it never quite felt right. Something just didn't click when she imagined them together, but she'd been away from other dragons for a long time, too. She'd almost forgotten what it was like to be around others.

She had years to come up with a plan for leaving the horrible cycle she had trapped herself in, but nothing had worked yet. Not to say she didn't try. At least once a week, back in the first few months of her new life, she had left the cave and tried to fly out in a given direction as far as she could while the sun was setting. She would always turn around before she got too far. The safety of the cave was too tempting. And even on the days when she pushed herself past her nerves and kept flying well after sunset, there was nothing but an open ocean. She would have to fly for hundreds of miles before finding land again. While her luck had prodded the stormy ocean to bring her to the island and save her from a watery death, she knew she shouldn't count on such luck to bring her to land a second time.

Fiore wondered if she was cursed. She wondered about a great many things, in fact, with so much time to spare. What had she done to deserve a horrible fate? Had some passing wizard hexed her egg before her hatching? It would explain her feathers quite well. Or perhaps, more likely, she was letting her sour mood reflect her thoughts. Like a beam of sunlight hitting a patch of scales.

She looked outside and saw the last of the sunlight as it hit the horizon. She got up, stretched, and left the cave. Maybe she'd catch a few more fish to study for her carvings.

At sunset, she flew.

Fiore hated that town, and sometimes hated the humans who lived there. Most days, she didn't even want to think about them, let alone check to see if they were watching her cave. She had considered killing them. She didn't feel confident that it would go well, though. A few humans, she could handle, but a full town's worth was likely to kill her before she could kill them.

One slow day as she was waiting for sunset, she wondered if she might be able to communicate with them, to explain that she wasn't a threat. She had tried once, hissing and growling in a manner as non-threatening as possible, and it went about as well as she'd expected it to. The next idea was learning how to speak their language, but Fiore had only ever heard snippets. And from what was being exclaimed, she figured it might do more harm than good. She left them alone, and in exchange, hoped they would do the same for her.

At sunset, she flew.

The rocks were inviting today. She caught herself just before impact on reflex, landing with a tremendous splash in the water. She did not fly for the rest of the sunset. When she returned to the cave, she laid down and watched the sunlight fade away.

At sunset, she slept.

A month after her lowest day, she woke up to a peculiar sound just outside of her cave's opening. It was wings flapping. Birds and bats had flown by her cave before and she knew what they sounded like. The sound was much louder.

Fiore's head was barely off the floor before she bounded to the front of the cave. She didn't even bother to preen her feathers as she craned her neck forward, poking her snout out ever so slightly so she could see. Her eyes were still adjusting to the early morning light, but something large and distinctly draconic in silhouette was coming towards the island.

Fiore couldn't believe it. She pulled her snout back quickly and rubbed her eyes. It must have been her imagination! What other dragon would be crazy enough to visit such a remote island? Her leg bounced in fear and excitement. What if they really were another dragon? Would they get trapped here too? Should she warn them about the humans? And most importantly, would they like her?

 She peeked back out from her cave and the other dragon was still there, standing atop the cliff. She wasn't seeing things! The other dragon was real after all. Their scales were a mixture of black and white with some patches of gray in-between. They peered out at the sea for a moment before poking their snout to the ground, pacing along the edge. Fiore had to stifle a gasp when she saw them flex their wings and take off again. The wings were a brilliant shade of red and yellow that looked like fire in motion, but more importantly, was what was left behind when they took off. A single red feather.

They were like her. A feathered dragon. There, of all places.

She felt better somehow knowing that she wasn't the only one. Even if she couldn't get the courage to leave her cave to talk to them. She could take comfort in knowing and hold that close to her on the lonely days.

A terrible thought crept into her mind at that moment. What if the feather was discovered by the humans? Would they use it to track the other dragon? Would it lead them to her cave instead? She couldn't take that kind of risk. She'd have to go out and grab it.

Fiore looked up, left, right, down, and up once more before she felt safe enough leaving the cave. It was still early enough that she'd be spotted easily if she wasn't careful. She edged her way alongside the cliff and climbed up and over the edge of the cliff, just a few feet away from the feather. She ran over to it and snatched it up in her talons. Feeling satisfied that she cleared away the evidence of the other dragon, she climbed back down and scrambled back inside of her cave. She stared down at the brightly colored red feather in her grasp and decided that when sunset came, she would try and find this other dragon. After all, she had a conversation starter! And a way to explain the danger that the humans would pose to them. She had waited many years for some company, so she could wait a few hours more.

Fiore left before sunset, wanting to make sure that the other dragon would be able to see her. Afraid that flying would create too much sound, she moved along the side of the cliff using her claws and tail. At first, she wasn't sure if she'd be able to find the dragon in time to warn them. The island had quite a bit of land to cover, especially if she was planning on traveling by foot.

Thankfully, the other dragon had made it easy for her. She followed the trail of discarded feathers, picking them up as she went, until she could hear flapping nearby. She made it to the edge of the forest just as they were landing on the top branch of a tree.

"Hey, what do you think you're doing?"

The other dragon's head picked up at the noise and looked over to where Fiore was standing. Before she could say anything more, they hopped down off the tree branch and dropped in front of her with a soft *thump.*

"I think I'm relaxing after a very long flight. The better question is what are you doing? Seems a little forward to bring me a bouquet of flowers when we've not even met."

Fiore felt a small flush of heat in her face. "It's not a bouquet, it's your feathers! And keep your voice down! There are humans on this island. Are you *trying* to get captured?" Fiore pointed to the bundle of feathers in her talon and shook them up and down for emphasis.

The other dragon snorted and said, "I'm not afraid of humans. I'm too fast for them to catch. In fact..." They stepped forward until they were a couple inches from Fiore's snout. They flexed their wings behind them and said, "How about a race? If you can catch me, I'll listen."

With that, they shot up into the air and out towards the ocean. In frustration, and despite her better judgement, Fiore stretched her wings and took off after them.

The other dragon wasn't as fast as Fiore, but they were stronger. Every time she was close to catching up, they would bank hard to the left or right and Fiore would have to adjust to keep following them. She was quickly running out of energy and needed a way to catch this other dragon by surprise. She looked behind her and saw that the sun was beginning to dip towards the horizon. There was her chance. She dropped down to the water and submerged herself until only her snout and eyes were poking up out of the surface. When the other dragon realized she was gone, they stopped to look around. They flapped their wings just hard enough to hover over the water and that gave Fiore enough time to paddle over to them. She burst from the water; talons outstretched towards the other dragon. They tried to flap their wings, but there wasn't enough time to get away, and soon they both went tumbling into the ocean in one big ball of scales and feathers.

Fiore came up for air first. She was growling when the other dragon's snout popped up. But the other dragon was in a much better mood.

"My goodness! I haven't had a chase like that in years. What a rush!"

When they both had caught their breath, the other dragon brought up one of her talons and said, "Sorry for that, it's just...I haven't seen another dragon for weeks. I should have at least given you my name before I made you chase me all over." She pointed to herself as she said, "I'm Naxelia, but my friends call me Nax."

"I'm Fiore. It's very nice to meet you, I can't remember the last time I've seen another dragon. But it's dangerous here; I wasn't kidding when I said there are humans on this island."

"And I wasn't kidding when I said I wasn't afraid of them. Let them come for me and they will learn just how well I can defend myself." Nax made a show of opening her jaw and showing off her sharp teeth. Fiore, despite her own fears, couldn't help but laugh at Nax's bravado.

"It's just that, you're the first dragon I've seen in years. And if I let anything happen to you, I don't know what I'd do."

Nax stared for a moment, as if she was very far away, before responding, "Did you say years?"

"Well, yes...", Fiore said as she swam back to shore. Nax followed close behind her. As they swam, Fiore explained how she had been tossed onto the island, ran into the humans, and realized that she was trapped. She did her best to explain how fervently she wanted to be able to fly again, to feel that sun warm her whole being. How frustrating it was that she could, but for only a sliver of the day. They pulled themselves up onto the shore as Fiore finished catching Nax up.

Nax quietly asked, "So, you've been stuck here alone, all this time?"

Before Fiore could answer, there was a great ruffling of feathers as Nax pulled her in to an awkward hug. Fiore hadn't realized how long it had been since she had been comforted until she felt Nax's arms around her. She could feel tears welling up in her eyes as she leaned her neck down into the hug and sobbed into Nax's wet wings. As she pulled away from the hug and wiped back the last of her tears, Nax spoke to her in a gentle voice.

"I can't imagine what you've been through. But if it makes you feel any better, I'll keep an eye out for the humans too. We can protect each other, okay?"

Fiore answered quietly, "Okay." She felt better knowing that Nax would have her back, but she also knew that she was losing precious time to fly. So, she leaned down to whisper to Nax, "I bet you can't catch me."

A grin spread across Nax's face as she said, "We'll see about that."

At sunset, they flew.

Nax made her heart feel lighter than it had in years. She didn't think that flying could get any better, but having a partner was a completely new experience. She could dip down or push forward and know that Nax would be close behind. Her black and white scales glistened with the spray of the ocean and her feathers burned with the passion of their dance. She wanted to savor every ray of orange-gold sunlight, every high-pitched squeal of delight, every moment free from loneliness.

As darkness crept in over the horizon, Fiore begged Nax to stay with her in her cave for the night. It was sheltered from the elements and would keep her out of sight of the humans. Most importantly, it would keep Nax close to her. She wasn't ready to be alone again. It was too nice having someone to talk to once more.

Fiore led Nax into the cave before starting a small fire in the hearth. Blowing on the fire to feed the flame, Fiore heard Nax exclaim, "Wow!" Turning to see what her guest was so impressed by her face became flushed with warmth, as she realized the fire had cast its light onto the carvings she'd made in the stone walls.

"Did you make all of these?" asked Nax.

"Yeah, I did. I know they're not much, but they help me pass the time."

"Not much?" Nax sounded incredulous. "I know at least ten other dragons that would kill for this kind of artistry!"

Fiore could feel that same flush of warmth in her face again. "I suppose you'd know better than me. I can't even imagine knowing ten dragons at this point. Though I guess I could apply what I learned from carving fish to make different scale patterns. I've only been able to practice on my own as reference."

"Have you ever tried carving feathers? I know a few dragons who would love a self-portrait."

"Of course, but it's still just my..."

Fiore stopped as her brain caught up with the implications of Nax's last sentence. She shook her head and then asked, "I'm sorry, but did you say multiple dragons? With feathers?"

"Yeah."

"How many exactly?"

"About a hundred or so."

A hundred! Fiore felt like she might burst. For years, she had been stuck on the island alone, too scared to leave, feeling so different, and there were hundreds of other dragons just like her out in the world. She could feel the weight of that realization tipping her over, but Nax had caught her before she could fall.

"Sorry, I think I must just be tired. I'm not used to flying that much in one day."

She smiled and said, "Alright, is there a spot you normally sleep in here or...?"

"Oh yes! I like to sleep over here on this patch of raised rock. Has a great view of the sunrise and keeps the heat in well."

Nax nodded as Fiore led over to her bed. Once she was sure that Nax was comfortable, Fiore padded a few feet away and laid down on the edge of the rock. She curled herself up and closed her eyes.

She found that she was having a hard time getting to sleep. So many things had happened today that threw her entire world into a tailspin. It didn't help that the wind outside of her cave was particularly noisy either. She heard the sound of ruffling feathers and opened her eyes to see Nax shivering on the bed. She padded over to Nax and gently nudged her shoulder with a talon.

"Nax, get closer to the center of the rock. It's warmer."

Nax groggily flipped over and looked at Fiore. She shyly asked, "Could we huddle for warmth instead? It's much colder here than I'm used to, it would just really help."

Fiore did her best to hide the nervous stammer in her voice as she said, "I suppose it couldn't hurt." She crawled onto the same rock as Nax and laid herself down next to her.

"Move your wing over the top of my shoulder, it's jabbing me."

Fiore slowly did as she was told and could feel Nax do the same for her.

"There, now we can both keep warm."

Nax was right. With both of their feathers layered like that, it was like sleeping under the softest grass.

She had almost drifted off to sleep when she heard Nax whisper, "Come away with me. You should share your colors."

Fiore smiled and reached out to pull her head closer to hers as she whispered back, "Let me sleep on it. Alright?"

Fiore let the warmth from Nax's body soothe her racing mind. She focused on the feeling of her wings lying over her and how safe she felt in them. She hadn't felt safe in years. It was unnerving at first, to not have the fear tugging at her mind constantly. The longer she stayed in the moment though, the more she realized she didn't want it to end. She couldn't tell when sleep took her, but she knew it was too soon.

She ran her hands over the carved pictures of her cave. A slow walk around the edges so that she could feel her artwork one more time. Nax stood at the front of the cave, wings spread wide to face the newly dawning day with confidence. Fiore walked up beside her and rubbed her snout with her own. She lingered for a moment, pulled strength from the close contact of their scales, and then Nax pulled away slowly. She nodded and took off. Fiore reached up after her and then, the reality of her decision came crashing down upon her like a wave. Her wings flicked nervously behind her as she tried to steady herself. She went to take off three times and stopped herself by gripping onto the stone for dear life. She looked up and saw that Nax was getting farther away the longer she waited.

Flying was more than automatic to dragons. It was more than an instinct, more than an impulse. It just was. So, she ran with all she had and flung herself off the cliff.

Her fall became a glide and she rose in tune to the beating of her heart. Fiore climbed higher and higher into the sky. Beating her feather soft wings so hard she left a trail of orange and purple across the horizon. She dipped into thermals, gliding out across the land and into the refreshing foam of the sea.

And for the first time in years, in the full light of the morning sun, she flew.

My Greatest Treasure

Abbeth flew in the slowly breaking light of the morning, the sun reflecting off his jet-black feathers as he swooped to land in a nearby tree. The tree branch swayed a little as he settled into a comfortable perch, before springing back, loose leaves falling to the ground below. He'd lived long enough to know the saying about early birds and worms was true and enjoyed the feeling of a full belly and a wonderful view to the horizon. Nothing could top it for Abbeth. It was the height of pleasure for a crow. The only thing that could be remotely better would be...finding a new treasure.

He used his talon to break a twig from the branch, using it to pick at his beak. As he cleaned, he thought of the places nearby where he could look for new trinkets to bring home. The forest was often hit or miss, only ever giving up a shiny beetle or bug on occasion. And Abbeth could only hold those for so long before eating them anyway. He always felt a little guilty afterward, but the shiniest bugs also seemed to taste the best, so the guilt quickly faded. He could fly over the well-worn trails that wound into and around the forest. It was often travelled by merchants and tradesmen, and the bumps in the road would knock loose small baubles and pieces of shiny metal from their carts.

He'd stolen his fair share of treasure too, but that took a great deal of energy and effort. It was easiest to steal from the wooden stalls in the town close by. He'd managed to snag a ring or three from a distracted shopkeeper when they were talking to a customer. Though he was loath to try his luck in town that day. Abbeth's last heist ended in getting the bristles of a stiff broom smacked into his beak. The force of the swing was so much that he dropped his prize and had to take off with his tail feathers between his legs. The embarrassment stung worse than the injury.

He was quickly losing his good mood. He spat out the twig from his beak and ruffled his feathers. Surely there had to be some place he could look for treasure?

And that was when Abbeth saw the light. The sun parted through the clouds and trees and shone upon the mouth of a cave overlooking the cliffside. A small glimmer of hope - treasure! He took off from the tree with a spring in his wings towards the cave. As he flew, he wondered what the sparkly bit could be. Would it be a piece of a long-lost sword? Discarded by some weary warrior as they climbed down the mountain and decided to lighten their load, or was it a deposit of gemstones? Waiting for the right bird to find it and pluck the beautiful stones straight from the veins of the earth? Could it be an artifact from a long-lost civilization? The key to finding an entire city of wealth and prosperity?

Abbeth's head swam with possibilities as he landed on the lip of the cave entrance. The cliff was a great deal higher than he expected when he first spotted it. The mouth of the cave was enormous, easily able to fit several flocks of crows along its width.

He angled his head to the sun and once again caught a glimpse of his nearby treasure. He was so excited that he almost flew over it the first time, swooping down to land and inspecting it more closely. His heart sank a little when he discovered exactly what it was, though. His beak reflected at him from a single smooth and shiny gold coin.

"How terribly mundane," Abbeth said to himself. It wasn't that he didn't appreciate finding it, but compared to the wondrous things in his imagination, it was certainly lacking.

He didn't have much gold in his personal stash. It was the one shiny that humans seemed to like more than him, to the point that they fiercely guarded it from him at every turn. Still, it was a worthwhile souvenir.

Abbeth pecked at the ground where the coin was dropped until he managed to grab an edge with his beak. He turned to spread his wings and leave, but something deeper in the cave caught his eye. He squinted, focusing on the shapes in the cave, but couldn't quite make out what was in there. He hopped along the edge of the cave, inching towards the greater mystery. There were two large shapes stacked atop each other in the darkness. The one on the bottom was a lighter color and seemed to stretch across the entire surface of the cave's floor. The topmost shape was positioned in such a way that a strange sound seemed to be coming from it when the wind passed through the mouth of the cave.

Abbeth could feel his heart beating through his feathers as he tentatively reached out a talon to touch the bottom shape. It felt cool and metallic, smooth too. It puzzled Abbeth until he moved his foot back and forth and shifted the bottom shape between his talons. The shapes made a small jingling noise as they rustled around and Abbeth could tell that they were all coins. Gold coins. An entire floor full of gold coins! And not just that, he realized as he picked his head up, scanning the rest of the room. There were other shapes buried in between the golden mounds that promised even greater rewards. His eyes widened and his beak fell open as he gawked at the sight. The single gold coin he was holding tipped forward and fell, bouncing off a nearby goblet, and made a sharp metallic note.

Ping!

The sound reverberated from the cave's walls and snapped Abbeth out of his reverie. The shape on top of the gold groaned and stretched, moving and shifting the piles of treasure along with it as it transformed from a patch of cave rocks into something distinctly alive. The cave went from eerily silent to cacophonous in an instant. Abbeth shrieked and squawked as he flitted from foothold to foothold, trying to keep up with the undulating waves of gold and monster as they moved beneath him. The treasure clinked and clanked so loudly that Abbeth was convinced the entire forest could hear the clamor.

A large serpentine head rose from the pile and twisted around the room, scanning over the nooks and crannies. Abbeth tried to squeeze into an ornate cup as best he could, tucking himself into his wings. He heard a snort of air puff out of the creature's snout, followed by mumbled curses.

"Blasted darkness! Can't see a damned thing in this cave."

Abbeth let out a breath he didn't realize he was holding. If the creature could talk, then that meant he could reason with it. He might still be able to escape with his life. He just needed to think his next words through.

The creature reached up with its massive arm and grabbed a lamp hanging overhead. It gently blew a cone of flame into the heart of the lamp until a fire roared to life inside. Abbeth peaked over the side of his cup and got his first full glimpse of the creature. It was unlike anything he had ever seen before.

Some kind of lizard, that was certain, but large enough to take up the entire width and height of the cave. The scales that covered it were a shade of gray with dark brown splotches, giving it the appearance of being a formation of rocks when it wasn't moving. The creature had four limbs that all ended in razor sharp claws with a tail that tapered to a point and snaked its way through the pile of treasure. And on its back, a pair of leathery protrusions that looked like bat's wings. Dark gray horns grew out of the back of a head that was chunkier than a serpent and sleeker than a lizard. Its pupils were slit like crescent moons and set against a backdrop of deep brown.

Abbeth felt transfixed by them and couldn't look away. He only managed to break eye contact when the creature once again spoke.

"Alright thief, come out quickly and I promise to make your death quick and painless."

There was a rumble in her voice, as if she was part of the mountains herself. It traveled from Abbeth's beak to the very tip of his feathers as he shimmied his way out of the cup to stand before the beast. She didn't seem to notice his exit, her eyes still scanning the room. He hopped up onto the biggest pile of coins that he could find, clacked his beak together, and cleared his throat.

"A-hem! I believe you may be looking for me?"

The creature's massive head swung around and pointed the full intensity of those slitted eyes straight down at Abbeth. The anger in them relaxed somewhat as her mind caught up with what she was seeing. Abbeth would have been insulted at her tone of voice, had he not been fearing for his life when she replied with a simple "You?"

"Yes, me. I wandered into your cave when I caught the distinct glint of treasure and couldn't resist taking a look for myself. And might I add that you have quite the collection!"

She growled at him and said, "A collection you were intent on stealing from. Were you not?"

"You wound me with that accusation, madam. I am a fellow connoisseur of all things shiny and valuable. If someone were to steal a piece of my own private collection, I would be inconsolable!"

Abbeth twirled around and fell in a dramatic flourish onto his back. He let his beak lay open and put a wing to his forehead as if grief-stricken. Peeking under his feathers, he could see that her expression remained largely unchanged.

"And what are you called, pernicious bird?"

Abbeth jumped up and performed a small bowing gesture, taking care to sweep his wing down over his head and across his chest gracefully.

"My name is Abbeth Grimains, my dear lady. Pleased to make your acquaintance."

She responded with, "A serious name, for such a silly crow."

Abbeth kept his head low to the ground as he said, "My parents were serious birds. But enough about me."

He raised his head and met her eyes with his own.

"It's rude for me to introduce myself and get no name in return. Would you be so kind as to give me the pleasure?"

She hesitated for a moment, and it looked to Abbeth that she might not speak. Then she smiled and said, "My name is Alluvia. Dragon of these mountains. Bane of all those who would dare to cross me."

Abbeth could tell she meant to frighten him, either through intimidation or posturing. She had made sure to get closer to his beak as she spoke. Pulling back her lips and showing him the rows of teeth that could snatch him up any second. Abbeth, however, was more interested in finding out exactly what she was.

"You say you are a 'dragon'? Splendid! I've never met a dragon before. Are they all as charming as you?"

Alluvia was flabbergasted. She didn't know how to react. Doubt crept in at the corners of her face as she frowned. She looked profoundly disappointed.

"You...aren't scared of me?"

"Not especially, no." Not quite the truth, but also not quite a lie. Abbeth hoped that his overwhelming curiosity was keeping his feathers from ruffling and giving away his fear. From the look on Alluvia's face, he guessed it must have been working.

"But surely you've heard the tales of how horrible dragons can be? How we terrorize villages and ransack kingdoms? How we eat any trespassers in our cave?"

"Are you going to eat me?"

Alluvia crossed her massive arms and let out a puff of smoke. She pouted and said, "I haven't decided yet. Usually, my meals are a lot more terrified of me."

"I assure you that I can act quite shaken if given the chance."

"No, no!" she said as she waved her claws dismissively through the air. "I won't have you patronizing me. Besides, I think I have a much better idea."

Her eyes shifted back down to Abbeth and she crouched low, shifting a pile of coins so that she could be eye level with him. "You say you're a treasure hunter? Well, then prove it. I'm giving you a month to find a treasure that is unique and valuable enough to add to my hoard. If you can find something that knocks my scales off before then, I won't eat you for trespassing."

"And what guarantee do I have that you won't just eat me after I give you what you want?"

Alluvia put her arm up and placed the back of her hand on her forehead in jest. She spoke with a dramatic tone, "Now you wound me, little crow. To insinuate that I would be so cruel. Have you considered that I might follow my own rules?"

Abbeth hopped back a few inches subconsciously and replied, "I have, but it's a fool who blindly trusts his opponent. I'm not one who jumps off a cliff, trusting in a safe landing."

She put her arm back down and said, "Such a clever bird. I'm excited to see what you'll bring to me. Now, about that cliff..."

She raised up her wings, slowly unfurling them to touch the sides of the cave. Then, with one mighty flap, pushed a wall of air towards Abbeth that sent coins, jewels, and himself tumbling beak over tailfeather out of the cave. He just barely managed to right himself in the air as he sailed over the edge of the mountain's sheer cliffside. As he flew away from the mouth of the cave, he could hear her call after him.

"Tomorrow, little bird. Don't forget!"

Abbeth woke up early, got a quick breakfast of grubs, and quickly got to work. He removed the patch of foliage he used to cover up his hiding spot and poked his beak in. He tapped it around the small hole in the tree, feeling all the treasure he had stored up. When he was satisfied that everything was in place, he grabbed the piece that he thought would best impress Alluvia and pulled it out of the hole. A shining sapphire glinted in the sun, blue and clear as the river. It was one of the few gemstones that he owned, and as such, was the most valuable treasure he could offer her. He tucked it safely inside of his beak and took to the sky.

He landed on the edge of the cave's mouth and listened intently for sounds of movement. After a few minutes of waiting, Abbeth realized that she must still be asleep and chanced a look further into the cave. When he peered around the corner, he found that she was not on top of the gold though. He put a wing up to scratch the top of his head. That was odd, he was sure she said to meet him that day.

And then his answer came flapping through the cave. Far back, he made out the shadowy outline of a tunnel, and suddenly from it came the imposing figure of a dragon flying straight towards him. He reflexively tensed his body, bristling his feathers out in a combination of fear and shock, but Alluvia knew what she was doing. She folded her wings down in just enough time to swoop low to the ground and land right in front of Abbeth, albeit with a few coins getting scattered in the process.

She smiled as she said, "Welcome, little bird. I trust you have something for me?"

Abbeth did his best to lay his feathers back down, smoothing them out with his wings as he nodded an answer. He then hopped up closer to Alluvia and dropped the shining sapphire at her feet. "I've come to offer this gemstone in exchange for my life. I think it will be more than sufficient to pay off my debt to you."

Alluvia's eyes went wide as she reached one of her clawed hands down to pick up the gemstone. She brought it close to her left eye and squinted at it. Turning it over and under. Looking over every facet and surface.

"A little on the small side, but impeccable quality. No cloudiness, good color, and a decent size to fit into jewelry." She placed the sapphire back down and lowered her head to Abbeth. "How did you come by this stone?"

Abbeth felt a thrill run through him. He loved telling the story. It was one he had rehearsed quite a bit on the days when his treasure hunts were less successful than he hoped.

"Well, my lady, it all started while I was soaring above the east section of this forest." He spread his wings out wide and tipped to the left and right to mimic the motion of gliding through the air. "I was over there to look for some fresh ticks, as the trail is heavily traveled by deer, and I was in the mood to have some for lunch. As I was scanning the trail below me, I caught sight of a large, covered wagon trundling down the road. Curiosity got the better of me and I swooped down to take a closer look.

"I landed softly on the top of the wagon, the occupants none the wiser, and hopped along the top towards the front." Abbeth took small careful hops around the piles of gold. "Once I had reached the front, I peeked out over the edge and saw two nobles riding side by side. They hadn't taken notice of me, so I stuck my head under the edge of the tarp and looked around." Abbeth spread out his wings as far as he could, "Jewels and gemstones everywhere! The entire cabin of the wagon was filled with them, I could scarcely believe my eyes. I brought my head out quickly and started to devise a plan."

He started to pace around the cave, putting a wing under his beak to show he was thinking carefully. "I'd be discovered by the nobles if I came in from the front for sure. I needed to find a different way to get under the tarp and escape without being found. I paced around the top of the canvas, experimentally poking my beak into small tears to see if it would give enough to let me squeeze through. I must have tried at least a dozen spots before I found one that ripped open." He put his wing up to his head and cupped it, leaning toward Alluvia as he said, "Then, I waited. The road we were traveling on was rough in patches and I wanted to time my entry with the biggest bump to the wagon. One well-timed pothole later and I had made my way into that trove of riches."

He flopped on the ground dramatically and began to flail in place. "What I didn't consider was the lack of light in the wagon once I'd gotten in there. I ended up making such a commotion bumping into things that the nobles pulled the wagon off the road and pulled up the tarp. Once I saw the light shine through the entrance, I nabbed the first gemstone I saw and flew out over their heads. They must have cursed me for miles afterwards. And while I didn't walk away with a king's ransom, I still managed something valuable from the caper."

And with his last line delivered, Abbeth gave a great bow to Alluvia. He waited patiently for her response to his impassioned tale.

"A very good story, but I'm afraid it isn't enough."

Abbeth felt a chill run down his back.

Alluvia reached over to a closed chest a few feet away and tipped it forward. Gemstones of unbelievable brilliance started to pour out of the opening and cascaded onto the ground in a rainbow of opulence. She ran her fingers through the pile, until she picked up the one that Abbeth had brought her. It seemed so paltry in comparison.

"Surely you must have seen at least some of the jewels I have lying around this cave yesterday. You are an exceptionally observant creature, as your story suggests. You must have known that I had a dozen others of similar quality. What made you think I'd be so impressed by yet another gemstone?"

Abbeth froze up. He had hoped the gemstone would suffice, as it was by far the nicest treasure he had in his collection. He panicked and said the first thing he could think of when he looked back up at her.

"Naturally, I chose the sapphire because it compliments your eyes."

Alluvia blinked a few times in shock. She then laughed so loud that the whole cave shook from the sound of it. "Does it now? I hadn't noticed."

She wiped tears from the corners of her eyes and settled down enough to address him seriously again.

"It was a good first attempt, but I'm going to need something else before I let you off the hook." She waved her claws through the air and said, "You're free to go. I won't eat you today."

Abbeth braced himself for being pushed out of the cave, but the gust of wind never came. Instead, he turned, looked over his shoulder once, and then flew towards home.

He should have felt terrified at the prospect of failing again. He brought the best and brightest of his collection. What chance was there that anything else he'd bring her would be good enough? And yet, his heart felt lighter knowing that he would have an excuse to see her again the next day. He fell asleep quickly, dreaming of the many ways in which he would try to impress her.

The rest of the week carried on in much the same fashion. Abbeth would choose an item from his collection and bring it to Alluvia for her appraisal. He would tell her a story about how he acquired the treasure and then, after a moment of consideration, she would refuse the gift. He should have felt frustrated, but he was having too much fun to care. Alluvia was very knowledgeable about all manner and kinds of shiny things. She even explained to Abbeth that the orange flakes on a helmet he had offered her were not exotic markings, but rather something called 'rust'. And yet, for all her vast learning on treasure, she knew naught of the world beyond her cave and the surrounding mountains and forests. Abbeth tried his best to tell her all he could. He should have been scared for his life every time he stepped into that cave, but over time it got easier. He just genuinely enjoyed talking to her.

It was on the seventh day that everything changed between them. Alluvia was grumpier than usual. Even after hunting an unlucky goat that had wandered too far down the mountain. She was half-listening to Abbeth's impassioned speech about how he had found a treasure just that morning when she started to shift around in place. Then when he showed her the beautiful and shiny beetle he had caught for her, she roared in disgust.

"Get that cursed thing away from me!"

She swung her claws at the bug, but it extended its wings and flew through the gap in her fingers. Abbeth jumped back several inches, the fear from previous visits finding purchase inside of his chest. The beetle wasted no time in leaving the cave. Its retreat was a steady buzzing that faded out into the silence of the morning. They both were silent for a few minutes, until Alluvia spoke.

"I... apologize. I should not have yelled at you."

Abbeth was in shock. As he found his voice again, an octave higher than normal, he said, "It's no trouble really. I'll just try again tomorrow."

Alluvia wiggled back and forth and reached her arms back to where her wings were. Abbeth stared in confusion until he realized what she was trying to do. She had an itch that she couldn't reach. Frustrated, she slammed her arms down to her sides, shaking the ground in the process.

"It's not your fault. I just can't stand the itching that these tiny little mites give me. They get between the creases of my wings and my back, and I can't reach them."

Abbeth hopped closer. "Do you need help?"

Alluvia scoffed at the notion and said, "No, of course not! What would you even be able to do?"

Abbeth tilted his beak curiously and responded, "I could try and pick out those mites to give you some relief. They're not my favorite snack, but I don't mind eating them."

"No, absolutely not. Out of the question."

"And why's that?"

"It's undignified! Having you root around my back like that."

Abbeth put a wing to his chin and said, "Well, maybe I could get you a long stick instead?"

Alluvia was losing the battle with her itch. She suddenly sprang up and flung herself to the back of the cave. She slammed her wings into a tall column and tried in vain to scratch her back up and down.

"I promise I'll be discreet. And I'll try to be quick about it too."

Alluvia fell forward with a *thump* and sighed through her snout. "Alright, fine. But I'm going to eat my goat while you do it, so I have something else to focus on."

Abbeth nodded and flew up to Alluvia's right-side wing. She moved it up and out from her back so that Abbeth could get at the bugs that were hiding there. She wasn't kidding when she said they were small, too. Fairly normal size for Abbeth when it came to eating bugs, but it must have been madness for Alluvia to feel them moving around. He ate the mites quickly, and when he was satisfied with that side, tapped Alluvia on the shoulder so she would raise up her left wing. They ate in silence, Abbeth too scared to say anything in fear of further irritating Alluvia. When he was done with his meal, he could feel the tension easing out of Alluvia's shoulders. Her muscles were loosening as she was finally able to relax.

"You can get off my back now."

Abbeth flapped his wings and landed in front of Alluvia. Her eyes were no longer slanted in anger, and instead she looked relaxed and relieved. She opened her mouth wide, and for a split second, Abbeth thought he was done for. Then he realized she was just yawning. She waved her claws in his direction, a signal that it was time for him to leave for the day. He couldn't believe the last thing she said to him as he left.

"Thank you, Abbeth. See you tomorrow."

When he had a chance to reflect on it later, he realized two incredibly important things. That was the first meal they had ever shared together, and it was the first time she had called him by his actual name. Not 'little bird' or 'funny crow'. Abbeth. He didn't know what to make of it. He knew what he wanted to make of it, but he wasn't quite ready to admit it to himself. Not yet. Better to get a good night's rest instead.

He knew when he woke up one morning that he was in love with Alluvia. He should have guessed it sooner, but he was too busy thinking about the treasures he would bring to her to really notice, but what should he do? It felt impossible that she would feel the same for him and yet he was determined to court her anyway. In a sense, he supposed he was doing that already. Definitely not a typical courtship, but they weren't a typical couple either.

He continued to bring her trinkets and talk to her every day. She continued in her pattern of listening and eventually dismissing the shiny he would bring to her. Ever since he gave her the gemstone on the first day, she'd always decline to take any of the treasure he brought her. Once, when he was about to leave, he caught the sun reflecting off a thin silver necklace that she wore that day. He followed the line to the gemstone at the center and saw that it was a dark blue sapphire. He couldn't be sure that was the same stone that he had given her. After all, she had dozens just like it. Yet ever since that day, he made a point to meet her eyes while she spoke. He wasn't sure if she noticed, but she was happier. And that was enough.

He was rapidly running out of time to fulfill his end of the bargain as the third week came and went, but Abbeth didn't care. Alluvia had started to let him stay later and later in her cave after their talk of treasure. He used to leave in the late morning light and now was leaving at sunset's first kiss upon the horizon. Alluvia didn't mind. She felt grateful for the company. They had even become comfortable enough with each other to let Abbeth hop onto her hand so they could communicate with each other better. Abbeth was content.

On the night before the last day of the month, disaster struck.

A storm the likes of which Abbeth had never seen was blowing through the forest. Rain pelted him from all directions as he flew home. Thunder and lightning danced across the valley and shook the trees. It was darker than Abbeth's own feathers as he tried to will himself into a shallow sleep. He heard a sickening *crack* from the tree from the tree and jolted awake as the canopy collapsed on itself. He flew out of the way just in time to avoid getting hit, but the winds tore at his wings fiercely. It was all he could do to stay airborne.

His mind raced through possibilities. With his nest destroyed, he wasn't safe in the forest anymore. He could try and fly over to the nearest town, but even then, the odds that he would have the energy to find shelter were slim. He did have one option left to him though.

Abbeth took off towards the one place of shelter he knew would be safe, Alluvia's cave. He just about collapsed when he reached the entrance. His voice was a croaking whisper, but he managed to say, "Alluvia, help..."

"Abbeth? Abbeth, what's wrong?" She rubbed the sleep from her eyes and rushed over to him.

"My tree is gone. The nest, my treasure, everything."

He coughed loud enough to make Alluvia jerk back in surprise.

"I have nothing more to offer you, except myself. I love you, Alluvia. Will you take this wretched bird in for the night?"

She looked at his deep golden eyes. So full of sadness. Of hope. Of love. And she found she couldn't look away. She turned and without saying anything, leapt out of the mouth of the cave into the raging storm outside.

Abbeth watched dumbfounded, as she battled the wind and the rain and sunk her claws into the base of a large tree nearby. With a roar that shook the valley and rivaled the howling of the storm, she ripped the tree out of the ground, roots and all. She cut through the storm and landed with a *crash* at the edge of the cave. She leaned the end of the tree trunk off the side of the mountain, dirt still hanging onto the roots. She raised her front foot and gave a mighty stomp, cleaving the trunk of the tree in one swift motion. The bottom of the tree tumbled down the mountain and was lost in the darkness soon after. She then pulled the remaining half of the tree all the way inside of the cave and dropped it next to Abbeth.

She grabbed the lantern suspended from the top of the cave and blew a little fire into it, making sure to set it next to Abbeth so that he could dry out his feathers. Abbeth crawled into the canopy of the tree and tried his best to get comfy.

When Alluvia was satisfied that Abbeth was safe, she moved away to the other side of the cave and curled around herself to go to sleep. Just before exhaustion took him, Abbeth could swear he heard Alluvia whisper to herself, "I love you too, Abbeth. You silly bird."

One night, when everything felt as it should be, Abbeth felt doubt creeping into his mind. As it so often did when he was happiest. He asked a simple question.

"Am I truly enough for you?"

Alluvia hesitated for a second, before bringing her hand down and motioning for Abbeth to jump up onto her finger. He did so and she brought him close to her face as she gave him her answer.

"Anyone can have treasure, but I have something better."

"And what's that, love?"

"I've got a treasure hunter! Worth his weight in gold, I'd wager."

"I hope I'm worth a bit more than that!"

"Oh hush! Just enjoy the moment."

Abbeth hopped up on top of her head and nestled close against Alluvia's horns. The texture of the bone took some getting used to, but Abbeth found it was almost like the rough padding of his old nest.

He slept above his greatest treasure, the love of his life, whom he wouldn't give up for all the shinies in the world.

The Guardian of the Grove

The rumble could be felt in the earth from miles away as the machines thundered toward their destination. It was the fourth attempt. The last three had failed miserably. Each time, the colonists who came would go home empty-handed. That is, if they went home at all. The small grove of trees was protected. Not by any law of man, for that was dealt with when that first expedition came and found the value that could be extracted from them.

No, it was protected by a beast from legends long gone. So far removed had humanity become on this new planet, that when word came back to the colony, only a few could discern the jabbering madness that described the creature. They would not be intimidated. They had crossed galaxies and star systems to find a suitable home. Through perseverance and determination, the obstacle would fall.

So, the machines continued their march toward the grove of trees. Each one glittering and gleaming as light from the nearest two suns reflected off their surface. Their metal plating was several inches thick, yet their strength paled in comparison to that of the wood they were to harvest. Leading the group was a score of hovering scouting bikes, their pilots leaning forward sharply, speeding over the terrain below. They were followed by three lines of transport vehicles, empty trailers rattling noisily as they travelled along the coarse dirt. Bringing up the rear was a small group of remotely piloted mechs, outfitted with enormous metal claws. They couldn't afford to send out so many mechs. They needed them for working on the upkeep of the colony, but their greed had outweighed their pragmatism, so onward they marched. Kicking up huge mounds of dirt and leaves as they did so.

In the distance, silhouetted by the trees that she protected, stood the creature from myth that had found them on the first expedition. Her body was as broad as a centuries-old redwood and similarly colored. Her wings spread out on either side of her like great drooping branches. Her neck was impossibly long, and it ended in a sharp point of a snout creased in disgust. A tail as thick as a tree's trunk swayed uneasily behind her as she watched the convoy approach. Her claws dug deep into the soil below, spreading out as if they were roots looking for water. For once they had been, millennia ago.

Her life had begun as one of these trees. From a small sapling that grew from scales shed in flight over a patch of rich soil. Over the centuries, the trees would sprout and take root, growing steadily toward adulthood and the moment they would wrench their arms and legs free of the warm soil to feel the joy of flight. She would not have these children denied their lives.

It was strange to think the adaptation of invulnerable bark would bring such danger. It was meant as a defense mechanism to keep the trees safe as they grew. She could still hear the echoes of screams from a toddler who was taken by the colonists. She had to make sure it wouldn't happen again. She couldn't even tell if the trees she protected were her own, grown from her scales. It didn't matter.

The convoy was bearing down on the grove. Cresting the hill and moving fast towards her. She raised her wings high above her head and flapped once. The wind reached out and plucked the scouts from their bikes. Tossed aside and skittering across the dirt wildly. She ran towards the transport trucks with her wings tucked behind her to reduce drag. Her feet barely touched the ground before lifting off and hitting again. She cut through the air like an arrow, aimed straight at the center of them. She twisted her body and rammed her shoulder into the nearest truck, and they collided with a sickening *crunch.* The truck lost control and began to spin out, colliding with the others in their line. She didn't look back as her attention was drawn to the nearest mech. It stopped moving, planting its feet and gripping the ground with reinforced claws. She reared up onto her hind legs, flaring her wings out behind her to slow her momentum, as her talons smashed into the waiting metal claws of the mech. The screech of scraping metal and her own unearthly roar echoed out across the valley.

The fight was quick, as it always was, with the surviving colonists limping back to their base in the remaining transport vehicles. Her blood dripped off her in heavy globs as thick as tree sap. She swiped her tail and pushed the crushed wreckage of a mech out of her way. Carefully, gently, she dug her talons in the ground up to her wrists and laid down. She canted her wings back behind her so that the light of the suns could wash over her body. She would need to photosynthesize if she wanted to heal properly.

She waited and watched for their fifth attempt.

The Unionization of Kobolds

The day was beautiful and calm, sunlight peeking out over a small smattering of clouds floating gently across the horizon, and Ember felt miserable. She was a kobold, a small bipedal lizard with a long tail and a rounded reptilian snout. A flock of crows crooned excitedly to their neighbors in the trees next to her. They hadn't seen a servant of the fearsome fire dragon, Blast, pass through in years. Ember had blood-red scales and horns the color of volcanic ash, which didn't exactly help her to blend in. The only part of her which matched her environment were her dark green eyes. She wore simple leather pants and a piece of chest armor woven together from blackened rocks. On her back was a pack filled with supplies for her journey that was larger than she was. The crows discussed whether it was worthwhile to try and steal some food from her pack when a stone came whizzing past their collective heads.

Ember was hefting another stone in her claws, throwing it up and down in her palm and scowling in the direction of the crows.

"You should know I can hear you chirping, little birds. Now leave me be, or else I won't miss this next throw."

The crows took the hint and flew out of the trees in a flurry of wings and black feathers. When she was satisfied that they were gone, she dropped the stone and let out a sigh of relief. Ember wasn't sure she would have had the energy to try and fight the nosy birds anyway. She'd been lugging around her pack for days on end, barely ever having received a break.

She held a hand up to her eyes to scan the horizon, guessing at how much time she'd have before nightfall. The sun was high enough in the sky that she felt she'd be able to sit for a while. Her feet were killing her, and her back wasn't doing much better. She shrugged her backpack off and set it up against the trunk of the nearest tree. She lowered herself to the ground, moving her tail out of the way so she wouldn't sit on it. As she lay against the pack, Ember looked up into the canopy of the tree. The sun was filtering down through the leaves and hitting her scales in a pattern of speckled dots. It was a different warmth than she was used to feeling in her home, where the heat rose from the ground and enveloped her in a kind of suffocating hug. The stillness of the forest was peaceful, especially without the constant chirping of the birds to distract her. She felt her eyelids get heavier and in the next moment, she was sleeping.

Ember dreamt, as most kobolds did, of serving her dragon in some fashion or another. She was working on moving a boulder with the help of her fellow kobolds when a large shadow appeared behind them. Ember knew without looking behind her that it was Blast. He was not himself. Before she could call out to him, she found she was alone. Trying and failing to push the massive boulder by herself. Where were her fellow kobolds? She strained against the weight, but it was no use. She couldn't make it budge. Water slowly began rising around her feet. She knew instinctively that she would drown if she couldn't move the boulder out of the way. Her claws scrabbled at the surface of the rock frantically. She could feel the water closing in around her head. With a last gasp of air, she dove down into the water and woke up.

She could feel something licking her cheek as she opened her eyes. When she got them fully open, Ember realized it was someone she recognized.

"What do you want, Woof? Can't you see I'm taking a nap?"

Ember had recently met Woof, a kobold from the beast dragon Carmichael. He looked like a cross between a bipedal lizard and a big dog. The breed he got his features from was hard to pinpoint, but he had floppy ears and light brown, almost cream-colored, fur along his head, the outsides of his arms, and down the center of his back to his tail. His feet were paws with soft pink paw pads underneath and his legs were long, which at first glance made him look taller than other kobolds. The rest of his body was covered in brown and cream-colored scales. His face was similar to a dog's, with a snout, black nose, and long floppy tongue to match. His horns weren't as pronounced as Ember's were. Small brown points that were often hidden by the tufts of hair on his head. He carried a small sword and shield on his back, but Ember was certain she'd never seen him get into a fight before.

Woof stopped licking Ember and reeled his tongue back into his mouth. He looked a little guilty and it was always hard to stay mad at him when he used those puppy dog eyes.

"Sorry Ember, I thought you might need to get up. Sun's about to set and you're a fair way from an inn."

Ember looked up at the sky and found that he was right. She must have been more tired than she realized. Reluctantly, she got up and stretched out her back. She looked at Woof again and asked, "Why are you out here? I thought Carmichael's territory was farther west?"

Woof rubbed his hands together nervously and let out a small whine. Ember could tell she hit a sore spot even before he answered.

"I'm out on a quest for him. Didn't get much info other than I'd need to pass through this way. I've been traveling for a few days now."

"You too huh? Blast has had me trekking all over the continent to deliver messages and supplies. Don't know what business he has so far from the volcano, but I could sure use a break."

Or some help, she thought to herself.

She hadn't seen Blast's other kobolds. They were all busy with their own jobs and deliveries. Split up and scattered across the forests, towns, and caves of the nearby countryside. That was just the nature of the job nowadays. Better to grin and bear it than to question her dragon's judgment.

She cinched her pack over her shoulders and dusted herself off. Woof looked as though he expected her to say more, so she turned to him and asked, "Something on your mind?"

Woof brightened up and his tail started to wag slowly behind him. He held his hands together and asked, "Can I travel with you for a while? I've been really lonely being by myself for so long and it'd be nice having someone to talk to. I think we're going the same way anyway."

He reached into a small pouch on his hip and brought out a crumpled and torn map. He traced a claw along his intended route and Ember could see that his path took him through the nearest town. On the one claw, she felt odd to be around another dragon's kobold, especially while on official business for her dragon. On the other, she was lonely too.

She nodded. "Okay, you can walk with me."

Woof's tail started to wag vigorously, and he bounced on the balls of his feet. He stuck his tongue out, going in to lick Ember again, but she put up a claw to stop him.

"No more slobber, I'm still wet from when you woke me up."

Woof nodded and pulled himself back. He glanced at the large backpack that Ember was carrying and winced. He reached a hand out to feel the canvas and she pulled away.

"What are you doing?" she asked.

Woof shrugged his shoulders and said, "I thought I would help you carry something. That pack looks really heavy."

It is, she thought.

"Thanks, but I was given strict instructions not to let people get into the bag. Blast would be furious with me if he found out."

Woof looked confused, tilting his head to the side and letting one of his ears flop over.

"But I'm not a person, I'm a kobold. So, I should be able to help, right?"

Ember shook her head and said, "Same difference. C'mon, we better get going if we want to reach that inn before it gets dark."

Ember and Woof followed the trail that seemed to be the most heavily used. Woof confirmed that other kobolds had used the path before by sniffing the grass alongside the trail. His sense of smell was much better than Ember's, so she deferred to his judgment. If so many kobolds were traveling the way, then it must have been safe for them as well.

The first hour of traveling was surprisingly quiet. Ember had expected Woof to be a constant ball of energy during the whole trip, but he calmed down considerably once they started walking. Walking—Ember had quite enough of that the last few weeks. She'd be glad to never have to walk anywhere again after her journey. It was one thing for Blast to order a bird or a fellow dragon or some other flying creature to travel around the countryside, but for Ember, if her dragon wasn't willing to pay for a horse, her only option was to hoof it everywhere she went.

It wouldn't be as bad if she didn't miss the warmth from her volcanic home. She didn't know how Woof could stand the cold. She was used to the blistering heat of lava flowing underneath her feet, not cold dirt and grass.

"How can you stand this wind? I'm freezing!" Ember shivered.

Woof looked over at her and smiled a bit. His tail swayed a little as he rubbed the fur on his arm.

"The fur helps a lot. And it's not that cold of a night. Is that why you're wearing those clothes?"

Ember responded indignantly, "Yes, of course. If I were back home, this outfit would be stifling. The chest is made from rocks around the volcano, and they help to hold in my body heat. It's about all I can do to keep my scales from feeling like they're going to freeze off."

"Oh, I just figured it was something you felt like doing. I've thought about wearing clothes before too, but they feel too restrictive to me. And keeping them clean is more hassle than cleaning scales or fur, so I just don't bother."

"I wish I could. I had to spend half my gold to get this outfit tailored to fit me. They even made me pay extra for a loop for my tail to go through. Can you believe it?"

Woof laughed and responded, "I sure can! Humans seem greedier than dragons these days. And they're always fighting each other too. I can't stand the sound of their swords clashing."

Ember elbowed Woof playfully in the side and said, "We're lucky we've got teeth and claws to fight with. Poor humans have to use swords to kill. Speaking of..." She trailed off as her gaze fell on the sword and shield on Woof's back. He caught where her eyes were looking and shifted the weapon on his back a little. When he didn't answer her, she asked. "Why are you carrying a sword? I've hardly ever seen you in a scrap, let alone a real fight. Canines get a little dull?"

Woof looked as if Ember had punched him in the gut. He slouched forward a little and crossed his arms before responding in a less-than-enthused tone. "I need it for the quest I'm on."

Ember slowed down as she put some of the pieces together. "You're on a quest to kill? But isn't Carmichael all about respecting life and nature? Why would he ask you to kill?"

Woof looked profoundly sad all of a sudden. He tried to keep it together, but Ember could tell it was hard for him.

"I don't know! Carmichael will occasionally go out and take care of threats to the natural order, but those are so dangerous I've never even seen one. Like a rampaging Tree-Eater or a Bird of a Million Feathers. And now I might be going to fight one and I don't know what to do!"

He whined a little and his tail drooped between his legs. She walked over to him and placed a hand on his shoulder, and he started to cry. Before she could react, he had swept her into a hug and was crying on her shoulder. Ember tried her best to be reassuring, but all she could manage was a few weak pats on his back. He let his sobbing drone into a low whine a few times before composing himself again. He pulled away and wiped his nose with the fur on his arm and smiled.

"Thanks for that, I uh, must have needed it."

Ember wanted to say something comforting but instead said, "You could have warned me about the hug you, know."

Woof nodded and his tail started to wag again. He seemed to be bouncing back to his chipper self quite quickly. "I'll warn you next time. I can get a little...excitable."

"That's an understatement," she quipped.

He laughed and went to turn around but stopped dead in his tracks. Ember could see his nose twitching and soon enough, he smelled the base of the nearest tree and the grass by the trail. His posture was guarded, like he was expecting an attack.

"We've been here before. I can smell us over here."

Ember rolled her eyes, "Of course we've been here before. I came this way a few weeks back. It's a heavily traveled trail. What's got you so on edge?"

Woof shook his head vigorously from side to side. "No, you don't understand. That scent trail would have gone cold by now. I mean I can smell us from an hour ago. We're walking in circles."

Now Ember was on guard as well. She crouched near Woof, placing her back to his so they could cover each other. Illusion magic was no joke and the creatures that used it were extremely dangerous. Ember could kick herself for not noticing sooner, but after traveling so long, all the trees were starting to blend together. A low growl was coming from Woof as he scanned the nearby tree line. There was something in the trees he could see that she couldn't.

She whispered in as low a voice as she could to Woof, "Switch positions with me, I'm going to flush it out."

Woof slowly slid around Ember until they were standing opposite each other and waited. Ember took a second to focus herself, breathing in deeply and closing her eyes. She hated to use it at that moment, since she could only do it a few times a day. Her eyes snapped open, and she breathed out a small plume of flame toward the top of the tree where the creature was hiding. There was a flurry of movement as the tree shook violently and something came flying out.

Whatever it was, Ember's fire had broken its concentration. The illusion spell was starting to dissipate around them in shimmers of refracted light. The late evening sky turned pitch black in undulating waves. The creature flapped its wings and settled on the ground nearby in a graceful flourish. Ember could tell they were a kobold of some sort, one she'd never met before. They had all the usual signifiers; short bipedal lizard, scales, and a tail, but Ember had never known a kobold to have wings.

The wings weren't draconic in nature either. They shimmered and moved on their own in the moonlight, dappled with streaks of green, white, and brown. They looked like a big moth, with their fuzzy antennae and big round eyes. They were also smaller in stature and build than Woof or Ember as well, which made her feel better about being able to take them in a fight.

"Why are you in Myfanwy's forest?" they asked.

Woof answered first with, "We must have gotten lost. Can you show us the way back to the main trail?"

The moth kobold laughed a little. They turned their head to face Woof.

"Oh, I know. I was the one who led you over here. And I can guide you back, if you're willing to trade me some information."

Ember chimed in, "We don't really feel like sharing, Your Mothness. Maybe you could drop the mysterious act and let us get on our way."

They turned to Ember. "I'm not 'Your Mothness'. My name is Oleander, servant of the moth dragon Myfanwy. Forgive my rudeness, but I wasn't able to introduce myself with a cone of fire pointed straight into my face. You should be more careful where you point that," they yelled, pointing derisively as the tip of Ember's snout.

"I'll point it wherever I please, you overgrown caterpillar," Ember hissed.

Oleander scowled at Ember. "You'll regret that remark." Their hands glowed faintly with white wisps of light as they began casting. Ember didn't look concerned, checking her claws and taking her eyes away from Oleander.

"You should cast your spells before making threats next time."

Oleander faltered a bit before asking, "What do you m-" Before they could finish their sentence, Woof had tackled them to the ground. With their concentration broken, the spell fizzled, white light dissipating as quickly as it came together. Woof pinned Oleander to the ground, growling lightly next to one of their antennae. Ember walked over and crouched down so that she was eye level with the restrained kobold.

"Alright, we're going to try this again. Why were you sending us in circles?"

Oleander squirmed under Woof for a moment, before sighing and slumping against the ground. They turned to look at Ember and answered, "I was trying to figure out where you were headed. A lot more kobolds have been walking through here lately and I can't figure out why. It used to be a remote location that was safe for Myfanwy, but with all the kobolds coming and going, I'm not so sure anymore."

"So then why try to trick us? I would've told you where we were going. Right, Ember?" Woof asked.

Ember crossed her arms defiantly. "Not if I thought it might put my dragon at risk. I don't trust strange kobolds. They could be plotting against Blast for all I know."

"So, you can see why I misled you. Most folks, rightfully so, won't be truthful with a creature they see pop out of the forest at night."

Woof looked over to Ember. "They've got a point there. Lots of dangerous creatures live in the forest. And the ones that can talk are usually the worst to run into."

Ember shrugged and said, "That doesn't make up for losing time on the trail. We'll be lucky to get to the inn before sunrise at this point."

Oleander chimed in with, "I can show you a shortcut if you let me go. Claws crossed I won't run away." They held up their free hand to show the overlapping claws and seemed to plead with their large eyes. It worked on Woof.

"I think we should let them go, Ember. They don't seem like they meant any harm from it."

Ember slapped the side of her head. "Don't tell them my name! What if Oleander is working against one of our dragons? And they almost used another illusion spell against us, lest you forget. We've gotta be more careful, Woof!" She slapped her claws over her snout as soon as she said it.

Oleander smiled and replied, "Well now that introductions are out of the way, if you would be so kind, Woof."

Woof obliged and got up from Oleander, who dusted themself off and shook out their wings. Their antennae twitched a little as they got their bearings again. They gestured to Woof and Ember to follow them, then sauntered off. Woof followed them immediately while Ember held off. She waited until Woof was almost to the tree line before hurrying to catch up. They all pushed their way through the foliage and talked while they traveled. Well, Woof and Oleander talked. It seemed that living in forests gave them some common ground. The night air was chilly, and Ember did her best to keep up despite it. She didn't want to lose them and have to camp out in unfamiliar woods all night. She was surprised to hear Oleander ask her a question after a while.

"When's the last time you've seen your dragon, Ember?"

It took her by surprise. She hadn't expected that from Oleander, but there was more to it than that. She realized she hadn't thought about how long it had been. It had become normal for her to get her assignments from Blast in letters rather than in person.

Woof answered first with, "About four months for me. I don't know why he can't make time to see us in person anymore. What could possibly be so important that a dragon can't make time for his kobolds?" He whined a little at the end of his question, as if he was asking the universe and not just Ember and Oleander.

She coughed a little and then answered with, "Eight months. It's been eight months since I've seen Blast." Oleander's face softened a little and they said, "I haven't seen Myfanwy in six months. I don't know what's going on, but something isn't right. The other kobolds I've talked to haven't seen their dragons recently, either. I've been trying to put together a reason, but I haven't found one yet. I was hoping you'd be able to point me in a new direction."

"I've just been doing my best to follow the instructions I'm given. It's not my place as a kobold to question my dragon's decisions. I'm sure Blast and the other dragons are keeping out of contact for a good reason. Maybe they're being hunted and had to go into hiding?"

"Then why communicate with us at all? Wouldn't it be easier to disappear if you didn't leave a trail of parchment with each of your kobolds?"

It made Ember wonder why she hadn't noticed before. She looked over at Woof and his snout was also scrunched up in an uncomfortable way. She wondered if he was thinking the same thing. What were the dragons doing?

Oleander parted a bush at the edge of the clearing and Woof and Ember could see that they had somehow ended up right on the outskirts of the nearest town. Most of the shops were dark, but the inn was still lit. A beacon of rest amongst the cold and dark. They turned back to Woof and Ember and said, "Here's your stop. And don't let what I said bother you too much. Just something to think about. I admit that I'm just very worried about Myfanwy and could be reading too much into it."

Woof perked his ears and Ember could see the idea forming in his head.

"Why not come with us? I bet between your smarts, Ember's cautiousness, and my um...good ideas we could find your dragon!"

Oleander smiled a bit but shook their head. "I miss them terribly, but I can't leave yet. If you figure anything out, you know where to find me."

Woof and Ember stepped into town and Woof called back, "Aww, alright. Thanks for the shortcut..."

Oleander was gone. The bush they had stepped through was no longer there either. Woof scratched his head in confusion as Ember pulled him along to the safety, and more importantly warmth, of the inn.

The inn was called 'The Draught of Dreams'. It was quiet for an inn; only a few folks were still up at the hour, talking over warm drinks by a fireplace that was slowly burning the last cinders of the wood in it. Ember wanted badly to sit by the fireplace, but her body ached enough to remind her why she was really there. They walked over to the reception desk and were surprised to find it was staffed by a pinkish-purple kobold wearing a bright white apron. When they approached the counter, he looked up from his book and smiled at them.

"Welcome to The Draught of Dreams, travelers. What can I do for ya?" He took off his glasses and wiped them on his apron.

"We're looking for a room for the night," Ember said.

"I can certainly do that for ya. You looking for two beds or one?"

"Oh, we're not a couple. I mean, two beds please." Ember could feel the embarrassment flush through her scales. For what it was worth, Woof didn't seem fazed by it. Then again, he'd left the counter when she wasn't looking to talk to one of the other guests. The innkeeper laughed.

"Well, when you've worked in my profession for long enough you don't go assumin'. I've got a room on the first floor open for about ten gold."

Ten gold! That was more than she'd made during the month. She only had about five gold coins on her in total. She coughed and fidgeted her claws on the counter.

"That seems a bit steep. I didn't realize rooms were going for that much now."

Ember expected the innkeeper to be upset at the insinuation, but his face softened a little instead. She could tell it wasn't the first time he'd been subjected to that question.

"Unfortunately, it's new pricing straight from my dragon, Somnir. I'm not sure why she wants to charge a horn and a tail for just one night, but I can't really do anything about it." He said the last part as though he didn't really believe it.

"I understand," and she did. It was just a fact of being a kobold. It didn't take the sting out of the price tag, but she could empathize. "Woof! Stop making small talk and get your furry butt over here."

Woof hurried over and stood next to Ember at the desk. She did her best to whisper a question into one of his floppy ears. "How much gold do you have on you? The innkeeper says it's ten gold a night."

Woof didn't get the hint to be subtle and said loudly, "I've only got two golds on me right now. Was hoping to use the money from the latest quest to tide me over a bit."

Ember turned back to the innkeeper sheepishly, but he seemed to read her mind. "You don't have enough gold, I'm guessing?"

Ember was going to lie but Woof cut in for her with, "No sir, we don't."

The innkeeper put his claws to his chin and thought for a moment. Ember wondered whether he was thinking of the best way in which to throw them out, but she was surprised to hear what he said next.

"I'll make you a deal. If you help out with cooking breakfast for the other guests in the morning, I'll let it slide. Just have to write you in as having reserved a one bed instead. That'll knock the price down to five gold." He extended out his hand and waited for Ember and Woof to react.

Ember didn't wait for Woof to say anything before she reached out her own hand and vigorously shook the innkeeper's arm. "You've got a deal!"

She reached into one of the pockets on her backpack and pulled out a small bag full of gold coins. She dumped out four onto the counter and motioned for Woof to do the same. He reached into a pouch on his waist and flipped a single gold coin onto the counter, which spun and landed neatly in the pile with the others. The innkeeper scooped them toward him and deposited them into a till under the desk.

Woof's tail was wagging steadily behind him as he said, "That's very kind of you sir, thank you."

The innkeeper smiled at him. "Think nothing of it! I could tell from just looking at you two that you're both beat and needed a break. Now if Somnir visits you in your dreams, don't rat me out, okay?"

"We couldn't even if we wanted to since we don't know your name," Ember pointed out.

"Oh right! My mistake. Call me Comfy. Everyone else does. Room is down the hall, third door on your left. Sweet dreams, you two!" And with that he tossed a small brass key to Ember and went back to reading his book.

Ember slotted the key into the door's lock and heard a small click. She opened the door to the room and found that their accommodations for the night were nicer than she had expected. There were two beds sat against the farthest wall with a small wooden table between them. On the wall closest to the door was a small dresser with a mirror set on top of it. There were also bottles of oil and polish sitting on the dresser, presumably to be used for cleaning weapons and armor. In the far corner of the room was an empty washbasin with a metal bucket sitting on the floor next to it. Ember walked in first, setting her backpack down in front of the bed closest to the door. She sat on the edge of the bed before Woof walked in.

"Wow! This room is really nice! I can see why they charge so much for it now."

Woof walked over to his bed and set down his sword and shield against the wall before turning back around.

"Hey Ember, do you think..."

She couldn't hear him, because she was already fast asleep. Woof frowned and walked over to cover her with the blanket. Then with an exaggerated yawn of his own, he put himself to bed as well.

Morning came all too fast, as it usually did. Ember woke up slowly and found that she actually felt warm for a change. The bed was immensely comfortable. She couldn't remember the last time she had sleep as deep or restful. She rolled over and saw that Woof was out of the room already. The blanket on his bed was half tossed off it, like he woke up with a start. Out of the corner of her eye she caught something lying on the dresser as well. Her stomach dropped when she realized what it must be. She'd seen that color of parchment and string used hundreds of times by now.

With a groan and some considerable effort, Ember slithered out of bed and plodded over to the dresser. The cream-colored parchment was rolled tightly in a tube and tied together with a dark red string on the top. She used one of her claws to cut the string and the parchment unrolled on its own. She was used to this whole song and dance at that point. There was a time when the enchanted messages brought some kind of awe in her, but it had become mundane seeing it every day. It was a message from Blast.

Ember,

Change of plans. Delivery route has been updated. Go to the new route ASAP. Your contact will be waiting for you there.

-Blast

Ember looked carefully at the included map and found that her new route would take her back out of town in the opposite direction. She'd have to tell Woof that they'd be splitting up. She hoped he wouldn't take it the wrong way. After all, she didn't have a choice in the matter. He'd be fine traveling on his own. She moved her claw down to the small box at the end of the parchment and scratched an X into the paper. And with that, the paper rolled itself back up and *poofed* out of the room in a small puff of blue smoke. Ember wanted to hang onto the scroll so she could show Woof, but the enchantment on them made it impossible to do so. All the same anyway, she knew he would understand.

Suddenly, she realized why Woof was gone. Breakfast! She nearly forgot! She was supposed to help Comfy get breakfast together that morning. She rushed over to the door and flung it open, racing down the hall towards the kitchen. She hoped that she wasn't too late to help, but with the way her morning was going, she didn't have high hopes.

Earlier in the morning, another kobold heard footsteps rushing down the hall and picked up his head from the pile of parchment it was buried in. He was currently pouring over a sizable pile of paper, trying and failing to make sense of it all. There was some hint of an attempt at organization in the way the papers were stacked, but the sound of the other kobold storming down the hall had startled him enough to fling the parchment he was holding onto, creating a huge mess. He pulled himself gingerly out of the pile and stretched from snout to tail. He'd been at it since the early morning and hadn't realized how long he'd been sitting down until he stood up.

His scales were a bright white with a light blue dusting on his stomach. His horns, the same light blue, curved back at the edges. His whole body had a gracefulness to it, an ethereal quality that was hard to pin down. This was aided by the fact that he wore quite a lot of jewelry. Most of which were thin gold chains that hung around his horns or dangled from his waist. He didn't wear much in terms of clothes but had a few strips of dark purple cloth draped over his neck, hips, and tail. His claws completed his look, painted the same shade of light blue to match the rest of him.

He was so busy, he had forgotten to do his morning reading. So, he opened up the top drawer of the dresser and pulled out the deck of cards that was his namesake. Tarot shuffled his cards methodically and began laying them on the desk. The daily readings were more of a habit for him than anything else, especially after having lost contact with his dragon, Fortuna. Her domain was classified by humans as divination, but that wasn't entirely accurate. It was closer to say that they looked at probabilities to help separate the certain from the uncertain. Except that didn't roll off the tongue in the same way. His job, along with the other kobolds who worked under Fortuna, was to use their magic to give credence to that separation. And while he didn't need to use his magic to do a simple reading, there was a kind of magic in the ritual, so he felt that was close enough.

Tarot didn't want to commit to doing a full reading as he had other business to attend to, so a quick three card spread would have to suffice. He opted to focus on discerning his current situation, the obstacle in his path, and advice for addressing the obstacle. The first card that he had turned over was Death, facing upright. The card depicted an armored skeleton atop a white horse carrying a black flag with a white flower in the center. It had been coming up a lot in Tarot's readings lately. *Endings, change, transformation, transition.* Next was the eight of wands, but reversed. The card depicted eight sticks tilted diagonally down and to the right. *Delays, frustration, resisting change, internal alignment.* The final card was the knight of wands, upright, and showed an image of a knight holding a stick that was riding a horse facing left. *Energy, passion, inspired action, adventure, impulsiveness.*

"Seems unlikely," Tarot muttered to himself. Ever since she had gone missing, he'd been working out of the Draught of Dreams, so going anywhere else was laughable at best. Maybe the deck was trying to tell him that he needed to move for his own sake? He scooped the cards up and gingerly put them back away in the drawer.

He walked over to the washbasin eagerly. It'd been a whole day since he had a proper bath and he felt positively filthy. He couldn't find Comfy when he went to ask for the water, so he carried the bucket himself. He almost spilled it on his pile of papers as he tipped the bucket into the basin, but he managed to catch it before it could splash over the sides. As he lowered himself into the hot water, he could feel his worries melting away in the steam. The relaxation was short-lived.

Tarot heard the telltale *poof* of one of the letters teleporting into his room and his eyes went wide. He desperately scrambled out of the washbasin and flopped onto the floor. He didn't take time to dry off as he rushed toward the source of the sound so he could open the letter. The letter, for its part, had been kind enough to materialize outside of the massive pile Tarot was collecting. Tied with a blue string, it sat alone and undisturbed on top of his bed. He ran to the bed and grabbed the letter in his mouth. He spun and his claws scrabbled for traction on the floor as he slid over to the desk, knocking his tail into it and almost tipping it over in the process. He reached out and grabbed the small well of ink before it could spill and snatched up one of the loose sheets of parchment.

Convinced he had everything he needed, Tarot let the message from his dragon drop out of his mouth and fall to the desk. He had done the process many times before, so he knew he would only have a short amount of time after opening before the letter would expect a response from him. He dipped his right pointer claw into the inkwell and used his left claw to open the letter. It unfurled itself as it always did, and Tarot began to read.

Tarot,

You must leave the inn. I have important business for you to conduct elsewhere. I will be sending along supplies today. Make sure you receive them. Do not disappoint me.

-Fortuna

Tarot worked feverishly, copying down the letter onto his scrap piece of parchment as best he could. He dipped his claw back into the inkwell every few words just to keep up with his mad pace. About a month prior, he had the idea to start keeping copies of the letters sent to him to see if he could notice any patterns. The most obvious pattern he found was the formal tone of all the letters, which was highly odd. The writing style was all wrong and didn't sound like her at all. Fortuna was never a dragon that was all business all the time; in previous communications before her disappearance, she would joke with her kobolds or tell a story in the middle of talking about something else. However, the most damning piece of evidence was her signature. She always made sure to sign, in elaborate loops and twirls, her name at the end of her letters. In all the time Tarot had known her, she had never once printed her name. All of it was speculation, of course. He supposed she could have hired a kobold as a scribe and that there was a lot being lost in translation, but that just didn't seem like the Fortuna that he knew.

He finished copying the letter in time for it to start sizzling around the edges. Before it could catch fully on fire, he flicked some of the water from his arm off to douse the sparks. Then, Tarot swiped a large check mark through the box at the bottom of the letter and it vanished in a puff of blue smoke. He took a moment to calm down. His heart was racing and anxiety high from the sudden and unexpected exertion. He was so rushed that he didn't even have time to be mad about the interruption ruining his bath. He let out a sound somewhere between a growl and a hiss as he padded slowly back over to the washbasin and climbed back inside. His tail didn't make it in on the first attempt, so he reached over the side with a grunt and pulled it in with him. The water was colder, but Tarot was bound and determined to enjoy it, nonetheless.

He felt a lot better when he got out of the washbasin this time around. As he turned his back around to the dresser to put his jewelry back on, he caught a reflection of something moving in the mirror. He finished attaching a circlet to his wrist and turned back around, putting his claws on his hips. He could see the door to his room had been opened slightly, and following the path of the movement he saw in the mirror, his gaze moved to his bed. He padded over and looked down. A dark blue snout the color of the night sky poked out from under the bed frame. From how she was timing her breathing, Tarot knew she was trying to be sneaky, but Tarot also knew this kobold already. And she was anything but sneaky. He took a claw off his hip and carefully lowered himself to his knees, peering down into her face.

"What brings you to my humble room, Shade? On an assignment from Dusk?"

Shade huffed a little and opened one of her eyes at Tarot. The purple in them was dark enough to blend in with the shadows under the bed. She grunted and replied, "No, not exactly. I was trying to sneak up and scare you."

"How's that going for you?" Tarot asked sarcastically.

"Not well. Do you mind helping me up?"

Tarot grasped her hand and helped her shimmy herself out from under the bed. Tarot had to give her credit, though. He was utterly baffled as to how she managed to fit all of herself under the bed in the first place. Shade was a bit of an anomaly when it came to kobolds: most kobolds averaged about three to four feet tall, but Shade was at least six. Unfortunately for her, her dragon was Dusk, the dragon in charge of the thief's guild and master of all things stealth. Shade had tried over the years to become better at stealth for her dragon, but a kobold the size of a human stuck out in a crowd like nothing else. The rest of her was pretty standard, as far as kobolds went: dark blue scales which helped her to camouflage against the dark of night, sharp reptilian claws on her hands and feet, and bright silver horns which stuck straight up from her head and added a few extra inches to her height. She was also bulkier than other kobolds, her muscles more clearly defined under her scales. Tarot knew from experience that she was stronger than she looked, and she already looked brawny. She wore a small set of leather armor with pockets sewn in to hold lockpicks and other tools of her trade.

Shade brushed the dust from her scales and sat down on the bed, which creaked in protest. She sneezed and wiped her snout on her arm before saying, "Comfy should really dust under these more often."

Tarot quickly grabbed one of his handkerchiefs from the near-by dresser and held it out to Shade by a claw tip. She snorted and plucked it from his claws before blowing her nose into it loudly. Tarot made a face and replied, "Well, I don't think he planned on having anyone hiding underneath them. What have you been up to?"

Shade shrugged and said, "I'm bored, mostly. I tried following Dusk's latest orders but messed that up royally. And considering it involved an actual royal family, I haven't gotten a new letter since. I think he's pissed off at me, but that's fine since I'm pissed at him too."

Tarot looked around suddenly and rushed over to his open door to close it. He spun back around to Shade before whispering, "Keep it down, you never know who's listening." It was highly unlikely that Dusk was listening in from the shadows, but it was a risk Tarot didn't want to take. "Besides, I'm quite cross at Fortuna too."

Shade's face slipped into a mischievous grin, and she tilted her head up at Tarot. "This I have to hear. What could she possibly do to make your prissy little tail upset?"

Tarot stomped his foot indignantly, hoping it would make him seem more threatening. It didn't. He carried on as though it did, holding his snout high as he walked back over to the desk with the pile of parchment on it. He sat down on the chair and dramatically waved his arms over it before saying, "Behold, the reasons for my irritation."

Shade looked puzzled at Tarot's gesture. She raised a claw in the air to point at the papers and said, "You're upset because of that mess?"

"Not the mess itself, but what the mess represents. Shade, back when you were getting letters from Dusk, did you notice anything strange about the way they were written?"

Shade thought for a moment before replying, "Nope. He always writes his letters in quick sentences. Easier to pass messages around that way. And in the case of specifying targets, the less fluff the better."

"Well, Fortuna definitely does not write her letters in such a stunted manner. And none of these letters sound remotely like her." He picked up a letter from the pile and took it over to Shade. "I've been copying the letters she sends me so that I can compare them with each other but the most I've been able to figure out is common phrases and sentences." He pointed to areas on the letter which he circled and underlined with notes of theories in the margin lines.

Shade squinted her eyes at the letter and traced her claw underneath the words as she read them. "Well, you're right about one thing. This wasn't written by Fortuna. It sounds exactly like a letter I got from Dusk a couple weeks back."

Tarot had to keep himself from gasping. "Are you sure?"

Shade nodded and slapped the paper with her claws a few times for effect. "Oh yeah, this has Dusk's claw scratches all over it. He's always super serious and to the point. In a very annoying kind of way."

Tarot put his left hand to his snout and tapped his claws to his mouth as he thought. "But if that's the case, then why is Dusk writing letters for Fortuna?"

That question hung in the air for a while, before being interrupted by a knock on the door. Shade went to get up, but Tarot put his arm out to stop her. "I should answer it. It's my room after all. It'll draw more suspicion if you answer for me."

Tarot cracked the door open a few inches and saw the outline of something ominous standing in the hallway. The silhouette was a lumpy mass with various different sharp points sticking out of it at odd angles. Tarot was just about to scream when he saw a shiny brown kobold foot stick itself into the space between the door and the wall. Before he could react, the foot had pushed Tarot back with such force that he had to catch himself to keep from falling back onto the bed where Shade was sitting.

The door swung open fully and the outline stepped into the room. It was another kobold carrying a veritable mountain of weaponry in her arms. The kobold spoke in a polite, but exasperated tone of voice, as though she was tired but didn't want to show it outwardly on the job.

"Where can I set these down for a minute? I could use a breather."

Shade was the first to respond as she jumped up from the bed and swiped her tail across the surface of the nearby desk, scattering the papers to the floor. "Over here will be just fine."

Tarot glared at her from his spot on the floor and Shade crossed her arms at him. "What else did you want me to do? Have her put them on the bed?"

The kobold walked over to the table and threw the weapons down with a tremendous clatter. She fished her arms out of the metallic mess and took a deep breath. No longer weighed down by a ton of metal, it was a lot easier to see what kind of kobold she was. Judging from the weapons it was safe to assume she served the dragon Auron, gold-scaled master of the forges. She was practically miniscule in comparison to Shade, only coming up to about the top of her thigh. While her coppery brown scales didn't match the shining golden radiance of her dragon's, her eyes were almost as bright. Her horns were a duller shade of brown and curved back, then forward again, the points sticking out in front of her.

Shade turned to the kobold and asked, "Penny? What are you doing here?"

Penny turned around and faced Shade, smiling. "Oh! Hi there again. On official business for my dragon and I've got to be quick about it. Lots of deliveries scheduled for today." She rummaged around in the pile of weapons for a minute before pulling out a nasty looking mace. "I hope those knives I gave you last week were up to the usual thieves' guild standards? I hear they can double as an extra lockpick in a pinch!"

Shade laughed and then said, "More like a toothpick for how tiny they are." Penny seemingly didn't notice or care about the comment as she pulled out a small roll of parchment from a loop around her tail and started scanning it. When she'd found what she was looking for, she bounced on the balls of her heels and stowed it away again. She hefted the mace in her hands and walked over to Tarot, still dazed on the floor, and crouched down to his level.

"Are you by chance Tarot? Servant to the dragon Fortuna?"

Tarot was a bit confused that Penny knew his name but nodded in agreement.

"Wonderful! I have a gift for you."

"You do?"

"Yep! Here you go." And with that she dropped the mace she was holding. Instinctively, Tarot reached out with his arms to catch it. It was heavier than he expected, and as a result, the mace head *thunked* to the floor as his arms were wrenched downward. Penny paid him no mind, however, and had already made her way back to the table to begin gathering up her weapons. Tarot picked himself off the floor and struggled to lift the mace. Once he had managed to heft it over his shoulder, he said, "What do you expect me to do with this?"

Penny didn't turn around, but replied, "That's up to you. You usually swing the pointy bit at the thing you want to hurt. Everything after that is up to you!"

She was trying to pick all the weapons back up off of the table but couldn't quite get her arms around all of them. After watching her struggle a few times, Shade stepped in and offered a claw to help.

"Are you sure? I would appreciate that a lot!"

"Yeah, why not? I'm not doing anything else right now."

Penny made a sound somewhere between a squeal and a shout and clapped her hands together. "Wonderful! Tinpin will be happy to see you too. We're expecting a new shipment of fresh metals for the forge today and could sure use some help."

Shade's immediate wince told Tarot she regretted her decision already, but she picked up the weapons all the same. As she and Penny strolled out of his room, Tarot wondered just how he was going to explain the hole in the floor to Comfy.

That would have to wait until later, since he needed to see what Fortuna was talking about in her letter. He scooped up a handful of the letters in his arms to take downstairs with him. Having so much evidence of distrust in his dragon was unnerving. Better to ditch some of it before he was found out.

With a great deal of effort, he opened the door to his room and then pushed it closed behind him with his tail. He started walking down the hallway only to hear the sound of heavy footfalls coming toward him, followed closely by the scrabbling of claws on wood.

Tarot felt the impact a moment later and was bowled over by Ember. The letters in his arms went flying up into the air and fluttered down gently. Ember went to untangle herself from the strange kobold she hit. When she had managed to get back to her feet, she reached down a hand to help Tarot up.

"Sorry about that, but I'm in a hurry. Let me help you up."

Tarot mumbled out, "Thanks," and grabbed Ember's hand to let her help him back upright.

Ember looked around at the explosion of letters which had littered the hallway. "Let me gather some of these up for you. It's the least I can do."

Tarot panicked and began snatching up the letters as fast as he could. He laughed nervously and said, "No, no! That's quite alright. I can clean it up myself."

Ember ignored his request and kept stacking up a small pile of the letters next to her. One of them caught her attention and she paused to read it. Tarot, noticing her, grabbed onto it and pulled to try and wrest it free from Ember's grip.

"The contents of that letter are highly personal. I'd thank you to mind your business," he said frantically.

Ember looked at Tarot, shock and confusion in her eyes. She let go of the letter and he pulled it free of her claws. He tried to turn around and pool all the letters he could, but his nervousness made it hard for him to hold them all. They kept slipping out and falling back down to the floor. Ember held a stack of them in her right hand, the paper creasing from the force of her grip.

"These are letters from your dragon, aren't they? How'd you get them to stick around for so long?"

Tarot stopped and turned back to Ember. He'd already told Shade about his suspicions, what was one more kobold? He leaned in close and whispered, "I can explain, just not here. Come back to my room and I'll let you in on my current theory."

Ember picked up the last letters in her left hand and said, "Lead the way."

They walked back to Tarot's room. He motioned for Ember to put the letters down wherever and brought the chair over for her to sit on. He had opted to sit across from her on his bed.

"First of all, I'm Tarot. If I'm going to be sharing potentially dangerous secrets, I'd like to know who I'm sharing them with."

"Fair enough. I'm Ember. Now Tarot, what is going on here?"

"I've been copying down the letters I've been getting from Fortuna so I can study them. Too many things aren't adding up. The way my dragon writes letters is nowhere near this formal and to the point. I think someone else may be writing them."

Ember thought for a moment to let that sink in. "I noticed that the letter I was holding in the hallway looked like one I would receive from Blast. It was jarring. Like a letter I had missed and was just now getting a chance to read. If this is true, and I'm not saying it is, who do you think is writing the letters?"

Tarot wrung his hands together and said, "I don't know. I haven't figured out who would do such a thing. And isn't it just as likely that our dragons would hire a scribe? I need more evidence to get anything conclusive."

"Well, what a slap in the face that'd be. I've been busting my tail to do right by my dragon and you're saying he might not be giving the orders?" Tarot tried to say something, but before he could Ember interrupted him, visible heat rising from her chest. "I've spent the last three weeks hiking nonstop to deliver some mystery backpack and I'm exhausted! The week before that, I had to push myself to use my fire so much I was freezing and almost died. And don't even get me started on..."

Before she could finish that thought, there came a creaking from the hallway. Ember and Tarot turned to look, and suddenly the door swung open and in fell a pile of fluffy brown fur. He flopped to the floor with a thud.

"Woof!" Ember said, "What are you doing here?"

"I, uh... I needed some help in the kitchen, and I thought you were still asleep, so I came looking for you. I heard your voice, and I came and..."

"Oh no you don't!" shouted Tarot, "Get out of here. This is my room, and you shouldn't be here."

Woof had managed to readjust himself and was sitting cross-legged on the floor. "That's not fair. Ember is here and she's supposed to be helping me. If you're going to kick me out, she shouldn't be allowed to stay."

Tarot looked over to Ember and asked, "You know this kobold?"

"Yes, as a matter of fact I do. And he's got just as much right to know if the letters aren't from our dragons as us."

Tarot's eyes went wide, and he rushed to shut the door. "Keep your voice down. Do you want the whole inn to hear?"

"Well, if something is wrong with the dragons, wouldn't their kobolds like to find out? I know Carmichael has been acting weird lately for me and I'd rather know," Woof said.

Tarot rubbed his claws over his head in exasperation. "If only it were that simple. We're discussing a conspiracy here if you both aren't aware. And if the dragons *are* just sending strange instructions, we could get punished for our disobedience. I'd rather not find out what that entails."

"But we should be doing something. Especially if the other kobolds of Carmichael are getting the kind of assignment I've been put on." Woof realized too late that he might have said too much.

"What *is* your current assignment, Woof?" Ember asked. "You've been very careful not to say anything about it and that doesn't seem like you."

Woof picked up his tail in his hands and ran his claws through it to calm himself. "Alright, I'll tell you. I've been sent on a hunt to kill a rampaging Tree-Eater. They're uh, extremely dangerous. Big enough to uproot and eat a sequoia without trying. Normally, Carmichael would take care of these kinds of threats to his forest himself, but now he's asking the kobolds to do it. I'm supposed to meet up with a squad of two other kobolds where it's last been seen, but I'm dreading it. I can't help thinking that I'm being sent to my death. I mean, come on, three kobolds against a monster of that size and strength? It's been tearing me up inside because I don't know what would make Carmichael be so careless with us." Woof looked like he was about to cry when his stomach interrupted him. He grimaced and said, "And now I'm starving to boot."

Ember crossed her arms over her chest. "I think you're onto something here, Tarot. The more we talk to each other, the weirder everything gets. Especially knowing that all our dragons have been telling us not to talk to each other. Can we come back after we finish up the dishes? I wanna get your side of what's been happening too."

"I don't see why not. I must admit that I don't feel particularly compelled to be obedient today after all these new pieces of evidence coming to light."

Woof jumped up and started wagging his tail. "We'll bring you back some leftovers!" And then he grabbed Ember and pulled her out of the room.

When they had finished with their shift, Ember and Woof returned to Tarot's room with a plate of fruit, dried meat, a generous hunk of cheese, and a portion of bread. They snacked as they discussed what's been asked of them by their dragons recently.

"Fortuna has been asking for more guidance lately. This isn't unusual, especially if she's trying to get more perspectives before looking into something herself. But the way that she's asking for that guidance is much more concrete. She would rather we gather, for lack of a better term, intel instead of providing our interpretations. That's not how divination works. There is a magic in the grey areas. So now, I've been crunching probabilistic opportunities instead. Particularly ones that have to do with how much gold this or that will fetch at the market. It's incredibly taxing, with all the angles and possibilities she's asking me to consider when I make my analysis." Tarot nervously nibbled on a piece of the cheese he had cut off earlier.

"That's rough, Tarot," Woof said. "Have you found a way to keep yourself from having to do all those calculations yet?"

"If only I could! It takes me hours at a time, and I see none of the gold it supposedly makes her."

"Well, have you thought about just telling her what she wants to hear?" Ember asked.

"What exactly are you implying?"

"Exactly what you think. Just make it up. If she's asking you about this every day, there's a good chance she's not going to notice or check."

"I think once she stopped making gold, she would notice."

"I'm not saying you do it all the time, just every once in a while. That way you get a break, and she doesn't get to make as much."

"That's a pretty slick plan, Ember, where'd you come up with that?"

"I've had to get a lot more creative ever since Blast started sending those letters. Used to be that we'd have a whole crew to work the vents over at the volcano. Diverting lava and shoring up magma channels to the areas that needed heat the most. But I suppose that keeping your kobolds happy and the volcano stable doesn't make enough gold. Blast split up the groups of kobolds into smaller and smaller teams until we could barely do our jobs anymore. The only reason I'm even doing deliveries for him from what I can tell is that he figures my side of the volcano isn't crucial to preventing an eruption. It's been emotionally exhausting knowing that if I had the help, I could do my job, but he refuses to budge."

"I know how you feel, Ember," Woof said. "Carmichael's kobolds will often keep detailed maps of the forest so that we know if we're walking into a dangerous animal's territory. Helps to keep us safe and gives a certain peace of mind when traveling that you won't have to run for your life. But now they haven't had the time to update the maps. I counted seven different kobolds with pieces of them missing the last time I went on a patrol. The saddest part of it all is that those injuries could have been prevented."

The afternoon sun was beginning to creep into the window when they heard a loud and boisterous knock at the door. Tarot was the first to speak, doing his best to sound unfazed by the sudden noise. "Go away please. I'm busy right now."

"Taking another bath, Tarot? Don't you ever get tired of being wet?" It was Shade's voice.

He got up and opened the door just a crack to talk to her. "What do you want?"

"I have some info that might relate to your suspicions with the letters. Y'know how Penny and I went to drop off those weapons for Tinpin? We can't find him anywhere..."

"That's strange indeed. Are you quite sure that he didn't just step out for a bit?"

Shade grumbled, "Penny looked everywhere she could think he would be and a few places he wouldn't. She's convinced that he would have left a note, at least."

Woof chimed in, "Now that you mention it, I haven't seen Ramiken in at least a week. He was only supposed to go out and gather some firewood and I haven't seen him since. Cotton too, though she had a particularly nasty job from Carmichael to do. I've been so busy and scared for my own fur that I didn't realize how long they've been gone."

"I mean, they're probably just busy like we've all been right? Every kobold I've seen is spent from all the dragon's demands. Blast keeps separating his kobolds all over the countryside, so I haven't seen or heard from Ash and Silta in months," Ember said.

"But I talked to Plumb a couple days ago and she said she would be right back after her job. She's a professional, through and through. Something had to happen to her since she's not back yet."

Tarot placed a clawed hand under his chin and thought for a moment. "Perhaps there is more to this after all. I've been so preoccupied with the letters that I haven't been looking for other connections."

Shade flashed a toothy smile, "Are you going to let me in now?"

Tarot let Shade inside and introduced her to Ember and Woof. They talked deep into the night, going over how unfair it was that their dragons were all treating them this way and which kobolds were still accounted for. Through their discussion, Ember felt bold enough to look inside her backpack and found the missing metals that were meant to be delivered to Penny. That much raw material could be used to make a lot of weapons. Woof fidgeted uncomfortably at the implication that more kobolds would be sent on missions like his. Tarot looked warily at the mace he was gifted earlier in the day and Shade held a hand over her new daggers. Something had to change or a lot more kobolds were going to get hurt.

They decided that they'd need more help and came up with a plan to send out letters of their own. A call to action to all the kobolds they knew and trusted. Tarot agreed to write the letters if Shade could help get them distributed without attracting too much attention. They'd need a place to meet in secret, so Ember and Woof agreed to contact Oleander and ask them if they could use Myfanwy's forest as a meeting spot. Even dragons would think twice about dealing with the fae. With their plan in place, they all agreed to meet up again when the time was right.

Five hundred kobolds showed up. They had sent out more invitations, but the number of kobolds that had gone missing had been steadily increasing in the weeks leading up to the meeting. In each of their hands was a letter that read, "To all kobolds concerned with the safety and proper treatment of their fellows, there is to be a meeting in the Forest of Myfanwy under the supervision of the moth-winged kobold Oleander. We wish to discuss the disappearance of our masters and our treatment since."

To say it was chaos would be an understatement. The growls, hisses, barks, and screams all faded quickly when a white-scaled kobold with sky blue horns stepped into the center of the clearing. He was struggling to push a wheelbarrow full to the brim with parchment over to where Ember, Woof, Shade, and Oleander were standing. When he at last set the wheelbarrow down, the overall cacophony of the proceedings had quieted enough for him to be heard.

Tarot picked up a roll of parchment and addressed the crowd. "We've called you all here today to share a most startling discovery. I've done extensive research into the writing habits of our dragons as well as comparing the letters we've received with each other. And one thing is abundantly clear..." He paused as he considered the weight of his suggestion. "These letters are not written by our dragons." The whole crowd started yelling, hissing, or some combination of the two. Tarot tried to wave his arms to get the crowd to settle down, but it only seemed to make them more upset.

Only when Oleander stepped forward did the kobolds quiet down again. They were guests in their dragon's forest after all, and they were expected to pay proper respects. Oleander's antenna on top of their head twitched as they approached Tarot. They stopped by the edge of the wheelbarrow and picked up a random piece of parchment, quickly scanning it over. Finished, they placed the piece of paper back in the wheelbarrow and fluttered their wings absent-mindedly. They looked over at Tarot, making sure he was making eye contact, and asked, "Do you have any proof?"

Tarot was taken aback. He didn't know how to react at first, but once the shock had subsided, he gestured wildly to the papers beside him. "Yes? Don't you see the avalanche of evidence I have stacked up here?"

Oleander nodded and said, "I do, and for what it's worth, I think you're right. Myfanwy never talks like this. But unless we have a way to prove that our dragons aren't writing these letters, then we have to assume it's them."

Shade spoke up, "From the way that they're written, they all sound like they're coming from my dragon, Dusk. He always writes in this short, matter-of-fact tone. It's possible he's writing all of the letters for all of the dragons."

Oleander snapped their claws together and Shade saw a small flicker of light come up from their fingertips. "Is it possible that he's deliberately writing this way, with the knowledge that it would seem odd to those who knew him?"

Shade snorted, "Sure, it's possible. But to make that kind of leap in logic you'd have to be..." She stopped herself mid-sentence, looked down at the ground, and swore.

Oleander smiled, "Myfanwy loves riddles, so I'm always looking for, let's say, unconventional solutions."

"But then what are we supposed to get from the messages? I haven't found any pattern to go off of," Tarot chimed in.

"It wouldn't be a pattern between letters," said Shade, "that'd be too easy to track..."

"So then how are we going to contact him? It's not like we can send back a letter. These things only go one way," Tarot said while striking the parchment in his claws.

A larger brown kobold in the crowd raised her voice, "Actually, they don't."

All three of them spun towards her. Oleander was the first to ask. "What do you mean?"

"Well, last week I was frustrated with the directions I was given. In my anger, I clawed a short question into the parchment. I thought my dragon was going to be furious with me, but it felt so good at the moment! Anyway, later that night, I got a follow-up letter with better directions. I thought it was a fluke, but I've heard other kobolds have the same thing happen to them."

Shade smiled wider than Tarot had ever seen. Oleander, for their part, seemed equal parts excited and unnerved by her reaction.

"Who's still getting messages from Dusk? Raise your claws up!"

A smattering of kobolds raised their hands and Shade motioned for them to join her, Oleander, and Tarot at the center of the circle. After a few minutes of deliberation, the kobolds had decided on the question they would pose. They just had to wait to get a letter. Thankfully, it didn't take long as the tell-tale *poof* of the letter sounded in the clearing. The letter was tied with a ribbon black as night in a small but tasteful bow.

Shade cut the ribbon with a knife and unfolded the letter. It didn't matter what was on the inside, as the kobolds hoped the tone of their response would give them a reaction. Tarot waited just on the other side of her, ink and paper at the ready. Shade dipped her claw into the ink and scratched out her missive.

"Being followed. Write only in Draconic."

Sensing the scratching was done, the magic on the paper rolled it up and disappeared in a puff of blue smoke.

It was only a few minutes later when a new letter had popped into view. Oleander reached out to grab it, nodding to Tarot to get ready. They cut the string on the letter and as soon as it unfurled, Tarot set to work. Tarot swiped and cut dark lines into the parchment below him, a kobold possessed, until he came at last to the signature. Out of breath and sweating, he feebly reached an inked claw forward and scratched an affirmative so the original letter would disappear.

The letter they received read:

Good thinking. Keep them off the trail. Change route to go past Accosto Mountain. Kobold to give additional supplies. Do not get trapped.

-Dusk

Dusk's kobolds could see immediately that the letter was noticeably different from Dusk's previous letters. The way in which the words 'mountain' and 'trapped' were written included more slashes than normal. The arrangement of the words was suspicious as well, with 'mountain' positioned directly above 'trapped' on the page. Taking all of it in, the kobolds had deciphered Dusk's message.

"Trapped under mountain."

Upon Tarot announcing the deciphered message, the crowd erupted with noise. Kobolds yelled back and forth, arguing over what it could mean, if anything at all. Ember stepped forward and said, "We've been at this for hours and all for a cryptic message that might not lead anywhere. I want to get to the bottom of this too, but I don't think this is a solid enough lead. And if I'm being honest, I'm worried about how long we've all been here. Blast has never been the charitable type when it comes to punishment."

A scarlet kobold from the other side replied, "But you're here. And if you are then that means you can feel it too. The dragons aren't acting like themselves. We need to send a group to the mountain to find out, once and for all."

"But who would volunteer? It's not like we can guarantee they'll even make it back to us", a lime green kobold asked.

"I'll go," Woof said. "I have to see Carmichael for myself."

A small but energetic voice came next to join Woof's. "Send me! I haven't heard from Tinpin in weeks. I've got to find out where he is." Penny's copper scales shone in the mid-afternoon sun as she stepped forward to stand by Woof.

Tarot spoke up next, practically tripping over his tail as he ran up to join the others. "I could help you foresee any dangers we might come across. Better to know ahead of time if there's something waiting for us in that mountain."

Oleander had waited long enough and turned to join the small group. "I've been waiting for an opportunity like this for months. I'm not going to miss it for anything. Myfanwy is waiting for me there, I'm sure of it."

Shade was leaning against a tree with her arms crossed over her chest. She pushed off the trunk with her tail and went to join the others. "Can't let you go without me. I've got a bone to pick with Dusk over these letters."

Ember looked around the group of assembled kobolds. Most had bandages or were nursing wounds and those that didn't had quite a few new scars running over their scales. Everyone looked exhausted. She saw the soreness in their scales and felt it just as deeply. If she didn't go, she risked Woof getting hurt like them, or worse.

She raised her hand, "I'll go too."

"Anyone else brave enough?" Oleander's question hung in the air as no one else came forward to join them. Whatever waited for them in Accosto Mountain, six kobolds would have to be enough.

Though the other kobolds would not volunteer, they were more than willing to help the group of six prepare for their journey. The kobolds that worked fields and grew food for their dragons brought salted meat and vegetables, packed together for easy storage and travel. Water kobolds, from salt to freshwater, made sure that they had enough drinking water for the trip. They even threw in a few scrolls of water purification, just in case. The tailor and armorer kobolds made sure to give the six the best they had to offer. The other kobolds pooled the remainder of their adventuring supplies as well, managing to give the six a few yards of rope, some assorted lockpicks, and a couple planks of wood to use as torches. With their backpacks full and their spirits high, they were ready to depart. Just before they left, though, Ember could see a pinkish-purple kobold rushing up to them with something in his claws.

Comfy approached the group and held out a blanket. "You never know when you might need to rest out there. I thought this might help." The blanket looked as soft as a cloud and felt twice as plush. On the front was a stitching of his dragon, Somnir, watching over crude representations of the other six kobolds. Ember made sure to pack it away carefully.

The six volunteers set off from Myfanwy's forest early that morning. The dew on the leaves had not yet dried when they made their way out of the clearing. The remaining kobolds were busy heading back to work. If their plan was to succeed, then they had to make it look like everything was normal. The less clues they could give to their dragons the better.

As they hiked through the woods, the kobolds got to know each other. A small part of Ember was hesitant to speak with the other kobolds, for fear of upsetting Blast if nothing were wrong after all, but she was glad to be able to see Woof again. And the fact that they didn't have much else to do but talk made it harder to avoid those conversations.

"What's it like living in this forest, Oleander?" Woof had been curious about the moth kobold ever since they had met. Ember couldn't blame him. Oleander had an air of mystery to them. Whether that mystery was intentional, and therefore dangerous, was something which Ember couldn't help but speculate about as they walked.

Oleander took a second to answer Woof's question. Weighing out exactly how much they should tell Woof. They eventually settled on saying, "It's a lot more dangerous at night. Most of the creatures here are nocturnal and so aren't as active during the day. That's why I insisted we set off as soon as possible."

"I didn't think 'early' meant 'crack of dawn'. Feel like my tail hasn't even fully woken up yet and I'm still not used to this tail satchel," Shade said.

"Better to be tired now, then dead later."

"Is it really that dangerous?" Tarot asked meekly.

"Yes. Probably more so than you're imagining. Besides, we've got a lot of ground to cover. You're lucky I know a shortcut to cut down on travel time. It's also easy to get lost in the forest at night. Traveling together in daylight keeps us from losing track of each other."

"Makes it easier to see all of the lovely flowers this way too! Your dragon has such a pretty territory, Oleander," Penny said.

Shade mumbled under her breath, "Kiss-up."

Penny glared at her but didn't say anything. "It's the complete opposite of Carmichael's domain," Woof cut in. "It's more dangerous during the day there; nighttime is when everything settles down and stops trying to kill each other."

"So then, hypothetically of course, if some creature was to jump out and attack us, you'd be prepared to fend it off?"

"Well, not exactly. I don't have a lot of experience fighting the nastier beasts that roam the forest."

"That's not very reassuring. What if we need to defend ourselves from a surprise attack?"

"And what will you be doing during this hypothetical 'surprise attack'?" Ember asked.

Tarot shifted uneasily on his feet, "I'm more of a planning and strategy kind of kobold. I'm not used to being 'in the field' as it were. Fortuna usually relies on me to help her with minor prophecies and planning for the major ones."

Penny turned around and started walking backwards so she could talk to Tarot face to face. "Oooh, fate magic! I've not met someone who can do that! Did you see into the future for us, Tarot? Are we going to get attacked?"

"I can't say for certain, but it's a possibility. The deck revealed a chance for unexpected surprises, so it's possible that we could get attacked. That and the card for Death was overturned today as well."

Penny's face fell immediately. "Death! You mean we're going to die?"

Tarot waved his claws back and forth frantically and said, "No, you're thinking about it literally. There's a chance we could die, but that's always a possibility. Death signifies the process of change."

Ember shook her head. "Do you even know who the cards are talking about?"

"No, that kind of specificity is out of the scope of the deck. But it never hurts to be prepared. Which is why I think we should come up with some kind of fighting formation. Just in case."

"Why don't you work on that and get back to us when you've got something?" Oleander asked. "I'm sure with your highly tactful brain, you'll make the best use of our skills."

Tarot smiled back, missing Oleander's sarcasm.

"Well," Penny said, "if we are ambushed, I'm sure we'll be fine. We've got weapons from Auron's forge with us so we can't lose! Tinpin helped me design this latest batch and they turned out great!"

"Tinpin sounds pretty important to you, Penny. Isn't he the reason you're even coming with us?" Ember asked.

Penny nodded her head vigorously. "Yep! Tinpin taught me everything he knows about smithing! I figure if the dragons are doing something super-secret that they'd need one of Auron's best to help out! Why else would he disappear out of nowhere?"

"Maybe Auron got jealous of him? If he's as good of a blacksmith as you say," Tarot said.

"No, I don't think that's it. Tinpin is good but he can't match Auron. Auron can mold metal into shapes I didn't even know existed! And he can power the forge with his own breath without breaking a sweat! And-"

"Great lurking shadows, can you stop bragging about your dragons for one second!" Shade shouted.

Penny covered her mouth quickly and the group fell into an uneasy silence. She turned back around and kept her snout low. After a few moments of walking without anyone daring to say anything, Penny piped back up.

"Why don't you talk about your dragon, Shade?" Penny asked.

Shade flicked her tail dismissively and said, "Me and Dusk don't really get along. You could say I'm not his favorite kobold."

"Then why come on this trip?"

"Getting abandoned has helped me out, somehow. I've got to talk to him. He should've treated me better and I'm just realizing it."

She pointed with a claw back to Ember.

"She is too."

Ember growled, "What does that mean?"

"You should know, Red. I've seen how you talk about Blast. Making excuses for how hard he's worked you."

Ember's growl grew deeper, "He uses us as he sees fit. That's how it's supposed to be. Kobolds are summoned for their dragons. And the volcano is a dangerous place. He's just looking out for us."

Shade shrugged her shoulders and threw up her claws. "Not pushing you into a volcano should be the baseline, not him on a good day."

"How dare you say that about my dragon? I should roast you for that!"

She lunged at Shade but felt a furry pair of arms wrap around her waist to hold her back. Woof held on tight, letting out a small whine in his effort to keep her from clawing Shade to shreds.

"Get mad all you want; you know I'm right."

Woof held firm as Ember wriggled and hissed at him. She thought breathing a little fire might scare him and let her pounce on Shade's smug scales. She gathered the fire into her mouth, feeling it welling upwards from her chest, but just as she was about to fire, she stopped herself. She let the fire die back down and stopped struggling.

When he was satisfied that Ember wouldn't kill Shade, he let go of her arms and stepped back. She expected him to say something to her, but he just continued walking as if nothing had happened.

"It's pretty impressive that you got her restrained without any magic, Woof," Oleander said. "Good job."

He looked down at the ground with a frown. "I wouldn't have used it even if I had it."

Tarot's jewelry jingled violently as he spun around and shouted, "What! Don't you have any magic?"

"None that I know of. Never really needed it so I never tried."

"None at all?" asked Shade.

"Nope."

"Doesn't that bother you?" Penny cut in.

"Not really."

"By my calculations, Carmichael has one of the largest territories of all the dragons. He can certainly spare enough magic for you."

"Oh, I'm sure. But that's fine. I've managed this far without it."

"So, you're not good at fighting or magic. What are you good at?"

"I'm really good at picking up scents. I like singing too. Relaxes me and the other kobolds. But I don't think a song will help too much today."

"It might! What traveling songs do you know? I know a few we sing to keep spirits up in the forge," Penny said.

"Just 'The Scaly Scalawag Seeks Solace' all the way through. Bits and pieces of others."

"Hum a few bars, I could be persuaded to join in," Shade said.

Woof's first few bars were shaky, but Shade joined in regardless. By the time Penny and Tarot were singing too, Woof hit his stride. Belting out the lines with confidence he didn't realize he had. Ember and Oleander joined in at the end and they all sang the final chorus together. It was off key and not quite in sync, but it eased the tension in the group considerably. By the time they had stopped to eat some of the packed food and drink some water, everyone was feeling more cordial. And when they set off again, Woof let Shade pick the next song to sing. She chose 'The Tale of Tails' and was surprised to learn that Penny knew the dirty song by heart.

It was a rough start, but there was hope that they could get along after all.

Accosto Mountain was a well-known landmark in the area. Its jutting peaks were used as a point of navigation for those traveling by foot. Since none of the kobolds were sure where exactly to start their search, the whole mountain was fair game. Penny had delivered a small stack of weapons near the base of the mountain a few months back and suggested they start their search there for a way in. The mountain was large enough to house multiple dragon lairs, but at least as far as the kobolds knew, no dragon had claimed the mountain as their own.

So, when Woof's more sensitive nose picked up on the scent of other kobolds, ones that weren't at the assembly a few days prior, they were rightfully suspicious. For where there were kobolds, there were certainly dragons. The group followed along behind Woof as he snuffled his way along the base of the mountain, scanning their surroundings for any signs of fellow kobolds. He led them to an indentation in the mountain that looked to have been carved out fairly recently. Any traveler passing by the mountain would think it was just how the mountain formed, but Oleander knew better. They put their arm out to stop Woof from sniffing any closer.

"Hey! Why'd you stop me?" He sniffed one more time in defiance and waited for Oleander's answer.

"Because that wall is an illusion. I can see the light reflecting from the mountain above it. Not a very sturdy illusion spell either. The seam where the current mountain ends, and the illusion begins is clearly noticeable. Looks like it was cast in a hurry."

"Do you think it was Myfanwy who cast it?" Woof asked.

"I don't know. It seems unlikely. But then again, I didn't think I'd see an illusion spell this far from his forest either."

"Can you dispel it?" Tarot asked.

"Oh, of course! You should brace yourselves, though. There might be a trap hidden behind it for all we know."

Oleander began to concentrate as white light gathered around their hands and clawtips. With a gentle pulling motion, they extracted the light from the illusory mountain face. Motes of light traveled from the illusion into their hands as they cast. As the light was pulled away from the mountain, the illusion began to wear off and the other kobolds could see the hollow indentation begin to appear behind the veil of light. Oleander reached out and grabbed onto an invisible sheet in front of themself and yanked downwards hard. The motion was the last piece needed to break the spell. The kobolds readied themselves for a fight as the veil of illusory light fell away. They quickly put their weapons away when they could see what was being covered up.

It was a massive iron door. Easily twenty times their height and thirty times as wide. There were large deadbolts on the surface of the door that kept it secured from any potential intruders. The door itself didn't have any rust or other signs of age on it, meaning it must have been put here recently. More troubling than that though, was the fact that the door was big enough to allow dragons entrance into the mountain.

Oleander let the collected light magic on their fingers and claw-tips dissipate into the air as they stared up at the door. Their snout pulled down into a frown as they tried to think of a way inside.

Shade was the first to speak up as the other kobolds stared dumbfounded at the door in front of them. "Whatever they're hiding, it's got to be something good if they're using a lock this big. This kind of security doesn't come cheap either. Would've had to have paid a small fortune to set the locking mechanism inside of the mountain."

"So, then we're stuck," Tarot sighed.

"Pretty much. Unless we can find a way to disengage the lock. And even then, I'm not sure how we'll push the door open. On account of how huge it is."

Ember stepped forward and asked, "Can you pick the lock?"

Shade laughed and then replied, "No, Red. My tools are way too small to be able to get at the tumblers that are set up inside of this thing. We'd have better luck if one of us crawled into the keyhole and tried to unlock it from the inside."

"Then you can unlock it?" Woof asked expectantly.

Shade crossed her arms and said, "I was speaking metaphorical-ly. And even if I could, I'd have to hope that when the door opens, I wouldn't get squished inside by the mechanisms shifting around. I'm not risking my scales on a hunch I can't prove."

Penny piped up with a question, "What if we went around the door? There's no reason we need to unlock it right?"

"How else do you think we're going to get in if we don't unlock the door?"

Penny reached down and unfastened one of her tail bags. She stuck her tongue out of her mouth in concentration as she rummaged around inside of it before her claws settled on a small glass bottle. She pulled it out of the bag and showed it to the other kobolds. The bottle held a granular black powder and had a cork firmly placed inside of it at the top. Around the side the words, 'DANGER: Highly Explosive' were written in bold red letters.

"The kobolds that work with alchemy told me that they've been working on this for a while now. They told me very explicitly to not let Ember hold onto it, since fire is what sets it off." Penny looked over to Ember expectantly and said, "But you can use your fire and we could blow open a path into the side of the mountain!"

"Penny, that's genius!" cried Tarot. "If we're careful about where we set the powder, then we can get in on the side of the door instead. We'll just have to hope that the resultant blast doesn't cause a rock-slide that buries us all alive."

Everyone turned to look at Tarot, concerned looks on their snouts.

"What? It's a possibility after all."

Ember could feel the other kobolds waiting for her answer. "Hold on a minute! If this mountain really does belong to a dragon, then I don't think we should go blowing holes in it for no good reason."

"No good reason! What better reason is there than to see our dragons again?" Tarot asked her.

Ember stumbled over her words. "Well...we don't know if the dragons are even in the mountain."

Oleander was quick to jump in, "Then they won't care if we blow it up, right?"

Ember was running out of excuses. She didn't really care about the mountain. It was a pile of rocks in their way after all. It was the implication of blowing up the mountain that nagged at her. The size of the door and the spell used to guard it pointed to dragons being involved and she didn't want to risk crossing them. Or worse, risk hurting them.

"I just think it's too dangerous. What if Tarot is right and the rocks come falling down on us? Is it really worth the risk?"

Woof chimed in and asked, "Penny, how were you planning on having Ember light that stuff?"

"Oh! I figured I could just pop out the cork and she would light the powder that way."

"Wouldn't that make it explode in her face?"

Penny put a claw tip to her chin as she thought. "Y'know, now that you mention it..."

"See! Exactly what I was talking about. Now, let's see if there's some secret button or switch next to the door." Ember moved her hands across the rock looking for any bits that stuck out or sections of the wall where the stones were loose. As she patted the wall down, Woof made another suggestion.

"It's too bad we don't have a way to delay the explosion. That would give Ember enough time to light the powder and get out of there."

Tarot grabbed Woof's arm and shouted, "THE LETTERS!"

"What about the letters?"

Tarot turned to Woof, his eyes huge and excited as he said, "The letters are on a timer! If you don't respond back to your dragon in enough time, the paper catches on fire. I had to deal with that all the time when I was transcribing the letters addressed from Fortuna."

Penny lit up next, adding, "Oh I get it! So, if we put the powder in the letter and wait for the time to run out, then it'll blow itself up!"

Tarot beamed at Penny. "Precisely!"

Woof called over to Ember and said, "Don't worry, Ember! It turns out we didn't need you for this after all."

Ember walked over from the door and joined the other kobolds as they planned out how they would do it. The first step was to have a letter they could use to begin with. And so, everyone looked through their bags to try and find an unopened letter from one of their dragons. Ember didn't bother to look as she knew she hadn't packed any. She was too afraid she might get tempted to open them as they traveled.

While the others were searching, Ember noticed Tarot stop for a second. He whispered some incantation and moved his right claws through the air slightly. It was a small movement, but Ember could see he was casting. There was a faint light blue glow that swirled around his claws, and it looked as though he had pulled a thread taut before releasing the spell. When he finished casting, he picked himself up and looked over at Ember. At first, she was worried that he had seen her looking his way, but when he spoke, she felt immediate relief.

"Have you checked your bag yet, Ember?"

"I don't have to. I didn't pack any letters from Blast."

Tarot looked nervous for a moment, shifting his weight from foot to foot. "Can you check again? Just in case?"

Ember sighed and said, "Sure, but I'm telling you I don't have any in here..."

As she moved her claws through the bottom of the bag, she heard the telltale crinkle of paper being shuffled around. It stopped her dead. Slowly, she reached in and grabbed the paper, pulling it out as if it was a snake coiling around to strike at her.

She was holding a letter from Blast in her claws, complete with the blood red ribbon that usually accompanied the outside. She didn't have the time to be dumbfounded as Tarot raced over and swiped the letter from her claws in a flash. "Wonderful! This should work nicely indeed." He rushed back over to Penny with haste, avoiding eye contact with Ember, who stared at him in shock.

Shade had cut the ribbon already when Ember re-joined the group. They were all crowded around Penny and Tarot as they worked to make their impromptu explosive. Penny was carefully pouring the powder into the center of the paper as quickly as she could. Tarot waited until she stopped pouring to start rolling the paper back up into a tube. He was careful not to go too fast and spill any out of the sides. When he had the letter rolled back up, Oleander stepped in, antenna twitching nervously atop their head, and tied the ribbon back on to keep the powder contained. Using his nose, Woof had found a small divot in the face of the mountain on the right side. Penny grabbed the explosive and ran over to the wall, stuffing it inside of the divot just as the letter began to hiss and burn.

She had enough time to jump and shout, "Duck!" before the powder ignited.

BOOM!!!

Chunks of rock flew out from the wall and a fine dust coated the scales of each of the kobolds. Woof was the first one to raise his head, shaking his fur out as he stood up. He could see from the sizable chunk of mountain missing that their plan had succeeded. The door was a tiny bit singed on the right side, but otherwise untouched by the blast. The others got up and shook off the dust as well, Tarot taking longer to recenter himself than anyone else.

"I'm going to need a long, hot bath after all this is over. I feel absolutely filthy!"

Woof laughed and said, "It's not that bad. You've barely got any dirt on you."

"Barely! Need I remind you what could have happened?"

"And yet we didn't die. Guess your prediction was wrong then?" Shade teased him.

"It wasn't a prediction! It was a worst-case scenario!"

Penny wasn't as concerned with the dust as she was with the massive explosion that she caused. "Did you see that? I can't believe we all survived! That blast was humongous! Those alchemist kobolds really know what they're doing, I'll say!"

Oleander started walking towards the hole next to the door. They turned around and said, "Let's keep moving. I don't want to lose our opportunity to get a head start over anybody who comes to check out what made that sound."

Each of the kobolds could walk into the opening in the wall except for Shade. She had to duck down and shimmy her way inside of the mountain. When her hips got stuck, it was Tarot and Oleander who pulled her loose and made sure she was alright. The inside of the mountain entrance was as tall as the door leading in, which meant that the room they were all standing in was exceptionally large. The only light was the narrow beam of sunlight cutting through their makeshift entrance. They could only see darkness further down the cavern.

Ember clapped her claws together. "Well, we can say we tried, at least. Not any real reason to keep going when we won't be able to see anything. I bet if we turn around, the dragons might even look the other way for blowing apart a mountain."

Oleander shook their head and said, "Oh no, you're not getting out of this that easily. We brought torches just for this reason. And I know you have fire magic to light them, so get to it. The faster you cooperate, the quicker you can turn us in for treason, if you're really all that concerned."

Ember hissed at Oleander and rummaged around inside of her bag. She dug out one of the torches that was given to her and concentrated. She focused on the feeling of the warmth of her fire as it traveled up her chest and then out her mouth in a small jet of flame. Soon enough, the torch was lit.

"Grab your torches and light them on mine."

Shade whistled. "Shoot, Red, I didn't realize you could actually breathe fire. I thought you were just bluffing."

Ember glared at Shade, hoping that the faint light of the torch under her chin would make her look more imposing. "I want to save it if I can. That way I'll have it if we find some trouble, like your unchecked attitude."

Ember was expecting Shade to say something snarky back but instead she smiled.

With their torches lit and only one direction to head in, the group of kobolds walked deeper into the mountain. The rocky walls trapped in the torches' heat like a greenhouse, which Ember cherished after the trek through the cold, shady forest. The same couldn't be said for the other kobolds, though. Woof was having the hardest time, his fur matted with sweat and his tongue panting. Oleander's wings were drooping slightly in the heat, and they seemed to be walking slower than usual as well. The rest of the group just seemed uncomfortable. Ember decided not to say anything, opting to enjoy the warmth in silence.

They had been walking for a long time on the same path through the mountain. No one could tell exactly how long since there wasn't a way to check the position of the sun. If the amount of times Tarot complained about his feet being sore were any indication, it had been at least several hours. When the pathway split off into two different directions, the kobolds were faced with a choice. Complicating matters was the fact that the left path was intentionally larger than the right one. The right path started out just as large at the beginning, but gradually sloped inwards on itself. If there were dragons in the mountain, then it would follow that they would take the left path. However, the right-side path looked like the more appropriately sized passageway for the kobolds who would serve the dragon. The group decided to take a break and rest their feet as they talked it out.

"I say we take the left path. It'll get us closer to whichever dragon has claimed this mountain," Oleander argued.

"My vote is for the side that gets us out of this heat faster," Woof said between gulps of water.

"I don't think it's a good idea to go barging into where the dragons might be. What if they get upset at seeing strange kobolds snooping around their mountain? Need I remind you we're not the most inconspicuous group of kobolds?" Shade asked.

"I could fix that problem. If I cast an illusion spell on all of us, I could make us look like whatever we want. It might not be enough to convince them, but it would buy us some time," Oleander suggested. There was a hesitation in their voice that Ember picked up on. It might have been her imagination, but they sounded tired.

Tarot had used the break to polish some of his jewelry and perform a quick reading. The faces he was making as he flipped the cards over didn't give the others much confidence. Penny was the one to break the ice and ask what the cards were saying.

"Well, I'm not sure. I've turned over a few more cards to ask for more information and I think it's just making me more confused. I don't know what to make of this right now, maybe it'll become clearer later?"

As the other kobolds were thinking, Penny had an idea. She jumped up and stretched out her back, making sure to wiggle any cramps out of her tail. When she was all stretched out, she took a small breath and coughed into her hand. The sound drew everyone's attention to her, and she smiled as she pinched a small copper coin between her claw tips.

"Since we can't decide on which direction to head, I say we let luck decide for us!" She palmed the coin and flipped it over a few times so the others could see the front and back sides. The front had a picture of a kobold's head on it with some tiny draconic scribbles around the edges while the back had a kobold's tail with a slightly different inscription.

"Heads, we all go right. Tails, we all go left. Sound fair?"

"Equal probability for either path, I like it," Tarot said.

"Beats arguing about it, I guess," Shade replied.

"Now wait a minute!" Ember interjected. "What if we just split up and half of us each take a different path?"

Oleander growled, "We're not splitting up and that's final. I won't hear any objections." Their wings were held still behind them, and their gaze was harsh and unwavering.

Everyone was stunned at the sudden shift in Oleander's demeanor. Even Ember didn't feel like talking back to them. Woof was the first to speak up and break the silence.

"As long as we all stick together, I think it'll be okay."

Oleander relaxed somewhat and nodded their head at Penny in agreement.

"All right, here goes!"

She moved the coin to the top of her closed fist and flipped it up into the air. The other kobolds watched intently as the coin spun a few times and landed on Penny's outstretched palm. They all crowded around her hand to see that the coin had landed heads side up.

"Right path it is then. Come on, let's not waste any more time," Oleander said before moving towards the rightmost path in the cave. The other kobolds collected their bags and packs, heading after the moth kobold as they made their way into the narrowing cavern.

"I've got a good feeling about this direction!" Penny said enthusiastically. "Heads usually means good luck!"

"Why do you say that? Aren't both sides equally likely to happen?" Tarot asked.

"It's just an expression, Tarot. Something I heard from a group of humans who visited the forge a while back."

Tarot wasn't sure if he believed in human superstitions, but the glow in Penny's face kept him from pursuing it any further.

They made their way along the passageway until it narrowed to the point that they had to travel single file. Oleander was at the head of the group and Shade brought up the rear. When Oleander stopped abruptly, the kobolds ended up bumping into each other before they realized what was going on.

"Oleander!" Ember shouted as she rubbed her snout. "Why'd you stop?"

"I don't know. But something doesn't feel right about this passageway. Especially up ahead. I think we should check for traps."

"Are you sure you're not projecting? It doesn't look like anything's wrong to me," Shade said from the back.

"It just feels too intentional. Why make the entryway this narrow? It feels like a trick."

"And you're familiar with the 'feeling' of a trick?" Tarot asked.

Oleander scowled at Tarot. "I live with the fae and spirits. So yes, I know what a trick feels like."

"Oh, uh, sorry. I didn't mean..." He trailed off as he avoided meeting their eyes.

"No need to get your antennae in a twist over it, Oleander. I'll come up there and check myself," Shade said.

"Uh, exactly how are you going to do that?" Woof asked.

Shade grimaced and shook her head. She hadn't considered how much of a logistical nightmare it was going to be to move herself to the front of the line. It also didn't help that she was twice as tall as the other kobolds.

"Just duck down a little and I'll step over you. Make sure to tuck your tail in if you don't want me to step on it."

She waited as the other kobolds tried to make themselves as small as possible so she could step by them. It didn't give her much room, but it was barely enough to squeeze by if she was careful. She took a tentative step forward and immediately stepped on Woof's tail. Woof yelped out in pain and shot up immediately, knocking his head into Shade's chest. Shade was caught off guard and fell over into Penny who took a tail smack to the ribs before she could get her bearings again. She scraped her ankles on Penny's horns and winced but continued moving forward. She managed to make it past Ember without any trouble. Only her backpack was showing, no tail or horns to get caught on. The relief was short lived, however, as when she went to step by Tarot, she caught herself on the torch he was still holding.

"Yeeeeooooowwww!" She screamed as she catapulted herself towards Oleander, landing on them in a heap in front of the suspicious passageway. She let out a long sigh as she lay there on the ground tangled in Oleander's wings. Oleander squirmed and did their best to extract themself from Shade without touching her new burn. Thankfully, they managed to get unstuck within a few minutes and Shade could stand up again.

"See, I told you it would work out," Shade said.

Oleander flitted their wings and twitched their antennae angrily as they stepped to the side.

"Alright, get on with it. We don't have all day after all."

Shade put her hands on her hips and leaned down into Oleander's face, emphasizing her height even more.

"Well, look who's all bossy now? What got wedged in your teeth?"

Oleander merely grumbled and pointed to the suspicious hallway.

Shade snorted and walked over to the spot without saying anything more. She set her bag down and retrieved her thieves' tools from it. She wasn't very good with them, but the others didn't need to know that. She grabbed an extra stick from the bag and walked over to the nearest wall. She inched slowly along the wall, tapping the stones with her claws and giving some a hard shove with her stick. After a few moments of scanning the wall, she turned around and put on her best confident face.

"Alright, we should be clear. I didn't see anything that would set off a trap. Now let's get going..."

As she took a step towards the other kobolds, she felt her foot press down into one of the stones. The hallway behind her groaned and shifted as holes were revealed on the left side of the wall. On the right side of the wall, large stone spikes shaped into pointed cones emerged. Then the right-side wall started to move slowly inwards, towards the holes in the left side wall.

"Oh no..."

Shade dropped to her knees and scrabbled at the stone button with her claws. "Pliers! Lockpick! Throw them to me, now!" Shade screamed.

Seeing her panic set the other kobolds on edge as well. Woof started to pace around the room and whine while Penny, Ember, and Tarot were checking the walls on either side for a viable way to escape. Oleander kept calm, immediately reaching for Shade's bag. After rummaging through it for a moment, their claws snagged on the pliers and a set of lockpicks. They ripped them out of the bag and hurled them through the air to land at Shade's feet. Shade used her free hand to pick up the pliers and pry the side of the pressure plate up. It was just enough to get the lockpick wedged inside, which gave her a way to lever the plate back out of the floor. Slowly, the button started to move upwards and after a few seconds of pushing it was set back into its original position. The right-side wall stopped moving and the kobolds settled down some when they realized they were safe. For the moment, at least.

"What in the Midsummer's Moon was that?"

Shade growled as she looked over to Oleander and said, "A careless mistake. You can yell at me later when we're out of danger. Right now, we need to move."

"But we're safe now, aren't we? The walls stopped moving," Woof mentioned.

"No, we're not. I can still feel the pressure of the spring trying to force its way down though the lockpick. If we want to get out of here, we need to come up with a plan. And fast."

Ember looked down the long hallway and then back over to Shade. "I guess we could all run to the end of this hallway while you hold the plate, but that means..."

"What? No!" Penny shouted. "We're not leaving Shade here while we save our own scales! There's got to be another way!"

Tarot came over and meekly said, "I don't think there is, Penny. Shade must hold down the lockpick or else the walls will start to move again. If she lets go then we'd all get crushed by the spikes."

Shade cleared her throat and the other kobolds looked over to her. "I'm glad you're all worried about me, but did it occur to you to ask if I had a plan?"

Oleander crossed their arms across their chest and asked, "Well? What's the plan, Shade?"

She motioned her snout over to the torch and explained, "Tarot, bring that torch over here. See if you can wedge it in between the rocks in the ground. Make sure it's pointed so that the light casts a shadow over my claws."

Tarot walked over and fiddled with the placement of the torch, being careful not to get it too close to Shade. Once he was sure that it would stay in place, he stepped back and nodded to Shade. She swallowed and said, "okay, that should be good. Now to see if I can remember how to do this."

She closed her eyes and concentrated, focusing on the shadow that was cast by the flickering of the torch. When she cast her spell, the others could see her hand floating out of the shadow, still holding onto the lockpick for dear life. She stepped back, and from her arm trailed a black wisp of smoke, right where her hand should have been. She turned to them and said, "Let's go! I don't know how long I can hold a spell like this. Especially the further away we get from the torch."

The other kobolds were uneasy about walking through the trapped hallway, but there didn't seem to be any other way forward. Ember followed Shade first as she walked along the passageway and the others soon followed suit. Before long, they were traveling single file again, trying not to think about the spikes that could crush them at any moment. Shade's spell had held out, but the pained expression on her face made Ember wince. No one said anything for fear of breaking her concentration.

Woof occasionally sniffed the air as he walked and could tell that it was changing. The air was less stuffy, more circulated somehow. And up ahead, the scent of the kobolds they were following earlier was getting stronger. He desperately wanted to tell Shade and the others what was happening, but kept his muzzle shut.

The passageway was quite dark. With one less torch to light their way, the journey through the narrow space was barely visible. The darkness made the spikes along the wall seem even more intimidating, like lances moments away from charging them through. So, when a bright light appeared in front of them, they weren't sure how to react. It was possible that it was an exit from the passageway, but they couldn't be certain. Shade tried to turn her snout back and ask Oleander to see if they thought it might be an illusion but stopped halfway. She had the distinct feeling of her spell being broken and held up her hand to her face. Back in the alcove at the start of the passageway, the torch had gone out.

"Run!!!"

The walls came to life again as the right side slowly moved inwards once more. Kobolds crashed into each other in a frenzy of limbs as they tried to push down the rapidly narrowing hallway. They scraped their scales along the left side, desperate to get away from the spikes. Tarot had dropped his torch in fear and as a result, they were fumbling about in the darkness, trying to scramble their way over to the light coming from the doorway.

Woof made it out first, panting and whining as his claws skid on the unfamiliar stone that greeted him. Penny and Tarot were the next to emerge, with Tarot screaming while holding onto Penny's waist. Ember jumped out and landed onto the stone floor unsteadily yet managed to catch herself before falling over.

Shade was just about to leave the hallway herself when she noticed that they had lost track of Oleander in their panic. She looked behind her and found them walking slowly along the left wall while holding their right side. A blue-green liquid was dripping down their claws onto the floor as they shuffled along as best they could. Shade realized with a sinking heart that they must have been pushed into one of the spikes. She took another look toward the exit, the other kobolds watching expectantly for the two of them to run out. She could leave Oleander there to die. It would be the choice her dragon would want her to make. To save her own scales at the expense of another. Let them pay the price for her mistake and run away to live another day. It was cunning, ruthless, and the most advantageous to her personally. And it didn't feel right.

Shade turned around and ran down the hallway towards Oleander. She dug her claws into the floor, pushing herself to run faster and faster, her tail snaking behind her purposely as she shifted her weight back and forth. Oleander barely had the chance to be surprised as she pulled their arm up and over her shoulder, hobbling forward with them. They walked for a few moments until it became clear that the spikes would impale them before they made it out.

Shade looked down at Oleander and asked, "Can you still use your wings?"

They looked confused but answered, "Yes, but I don't know-"

Shade didn't wait for them to finish their sentence as she picked them up off the ground. They were a lot lighter than Shade had imagined they'd be, which allowed Shade to hoist them over her head with little effort. She positioned Oleander so that they were facing toward the exit and cocked her arms back in anticipation. With a mighty heave, she threw them forward. Oleander soared through the air, equal parts confused and alarmed. Their instincts kicked in before they dropped too far out of the air, catching them just in time for them to glide the rest of the distance into the bright room.

Despite the rough toss, Oleander landed the most gracefully out of all the kobolds, arriving feet first out of their gentle swooping glide from the treacherous trap-filled hallway. Once they touched down on the ground again, they grunted and grabbed their side.

The others quickly came up to them to see what happened, but Oleander ignored them. They turned around and focused on the hallway with one hand outstretched before firing off a light spell that flashed brilliantly in front of the passageway. The others caught a brief glimpse of Shade in the passage, back against the wall and spikes inches away from piercing her scales. They could see the fear in her eyes as the walls closed in on each other with a tremendous *boom*.

Penny looked away. Ember covered her mouth, suppressing a gasp. Tarot and Woof tried their best not to look at the closed passageway, but Oleander's gaze never drifted. They were still focused on the entrance, waiting for Shade to come out the other side. Barely a second had passed, but it felt much longer.

So, when Woof looked up and excitedly pointed towards the ceiling, it took the others by surprise. There, at the top where the passage met the rest of the cave, was a large swirling black shadow. A claw-tipped hand poked through first, followed by an arm, and then quickly the rest of her body. The excitement at seeing their fellow kobold safe from harm was short-lived, however, as she fell limp and started plummeting towards the cavern's floor.

Ember was already pulling the blanket that Comfy had given them out of her backpack, frantically unfolding it in her claws. She thrust fistfuls of the fabric into the other's claws and said, "Hold it taut and get underneath her!"

The others followed her lead as they scrambled to position themselves in a way that would be able to catch the rapidly descending Shade.

They managed to get into position just in time as she fell into the blanket with a loud *foomph*, popping her body up into the air a little before falling back down again to settle. Assured of her safety, Ember released her end of the blanket and let the fabric lay on the floor. Both her and Oleander rushed over to check and see how Shade was holding up.

Other than a few scrapes and bruises, she looked to be fine. No puncture wounds or a missing tail. Shade blinked her eyes blearily as she came to, fully aware that everyone was staring at her.

"See? I told ya there was nothing to worry about," she groaned.

"Shade, how on earth did you do that?" Woof asked.

"Oleander's light spell gave me just enough space in the corner of the wall to shadow walk to safety," she replied.

Ember sighed in relief and Oleander reached a shaky claw out to touch Shade gently. They needed some reassurance to know she was really safe.

"Oh, thank the Moon above! I don't know if I could handle..." Oleander cut themself off as they winced in pain.

Ember led Oleander away from Shade towards Tarot, who was already busy unpacking some of the bandages. The added exertion had taken a toll on the moth kobold. Their wound was bleeding down their side and dripping past their leg onto the floor. Shade felt a stab of guilt at seeing them in so much pain. If it wasn't for her messing up when looking for traps, none of their injuries would have happened. She wanted desperately to keep wallowing in her self-pity about her lack of thief skills, but the furry figure of Woof coming into her view interrupted her.

He had brought a small potion of healing and some bandages over to tend to her scratches, which only made her feel more guilty. However, Shade didn't say anything as he dabbed at them and helped to patch her up. It wouldn't do any good anyway. She sat up so he could get at her back and was reminded once again of her larger body. Even sitting, she was almost eye level with Woof standing on the balls of his feet. It was a feeling she had gotten used to early in her life, but it was still strange. Another reminder that she wasn't cut out to be a good thief.

Woof must have picked up on her grumbling, since he asked, "Are you alright?"

Shade let out a long sigh. "I will be. Just a little shook up is all."

Woof barked out a laugh. "Yeah, that was quite the close call." He paused for a moment before asking, "Is that the closest you've come to dying?"

Shade hesitated, trying to think of a good reason to lie, before settling on telling the truth.

"Yes."

"It's scary, isn't it?"

Shade nodded solemnly, "More than I can say."

Woof responded with, "It's a new feeling for me too. I don't like it, but what can you do?"

"What did you do after you almost died?"

Woof stopped dabbing at Shade's scratches and answered with, "I ran away with my tail between my legs. I knew I was going to lose, so I got out as fast as I could. Then I went somewhere I could get patched back up." He applied a small wrap to Shade's cuts "While I was recovering, I had a lot of time to think. And I realized I didn't want to risk my life for Carmichael. There were a lot of other kobolds who were in much worse shape. I got lucky."

He finished with the bandages and stood up, offering his paw to Shade to help her stand. She took it and pulled herself upright.

Shade frowned and said, "Well, I'm the one who almost got us killed back there. If I was more careful with the trap..."

Woof interrupted to say, "You did the best you could, Shade. Try not to beat yourself up over it." His tail started to wag a little, "And I believe that whatever happens, we can face it together. I've seen the stuff the other groups of kobolds can do, and it gives me hope we can fight back."

Shade couldn't help smiling despite herself. "Sounds a little corny, if you ask me."

Woof put his other paw on top of hers and replied, "Sometimes we need a little corny optimism."

Shade and Woof made their way back to the group, rested enough to figure out what to do next. Tarot had bandaged Oleander up across their middle and they were looking tired, but better. Penny was busy putting the ointments and bandages back into the bags while Ember walked along the edge of the room.

The space they were in was much larger than the narrow hallway. Wide enough to accommodate a wingspan, and tall enough that a fully grown dragon could traverse it without having to dip their head, this room could probably even allow them a bit of flight.

Ember was trying to inspect the wall sconces, placed equally apart, and each carrying a small but brightly burning orange flame. The sheer number of these torches made the cave look as bright as if they had stepped back outside again. Ember put her hand next to one of them and felt the heat radiating from it. There was something intensely familiar about the way the fire danced and gave off light. She knew she had seen it before. When she had gotten close enough, she dared to put her claws into the flame.

It didn't burn her.

"This is Blast's magic," she said while pointing to the torch. She had definitive proof that Blast was in the mountain at some point. What would it mean if he was still there? She desperately wanted to believe that he wasn't involved in whatever was happening, but it was getting harder and harder to deny the connection.

As if sensing her distress at this revelation, Penny spoke up.

"It might not be Blast! It could have been one of his other kobolds, right?"

Ember shook her head. "The magic is a feedback loop. Drawing heat from the earth to power the flame. A spell like that is out of the scope of what a kobold of his can do. I've tried it myself and the flame fizzles after an hour or so."

"Fascinating!" Tarot exclaimed. "Do you think if your connection to your dragon was stronger that you'd be able to maintain the spell for a longer period of time?" Shade came over and smacked Tarot on the back of his head lightly. He turned around and met her eyes glaring down at him. Slowly, he stammered out, "Ah, my apologies. I was just...curious."

Woof came over, sniffing the air periodically. "I think I picked the scent of the other kobolds back up again. It smells like they went down this cavern slightly to the right."

Oleander started walking again and called over their shoulder, "Then what are we waiting for? Let's get going."

Woof quickly caught up and took his position at the front of the group, guiding them down the twists and turns of the cave system. The corridor they walked down was as dragon-sized as the room they came out of, making the path ahead seem ever greater to the group. Thankfully, the torches provided plenty of light for them to see their path forward and the extra room allowed them to spread out.

Tarot took advantage of the space by reaching into a pouch on his tail bag and pulling out a few items: a small white cloth and a vial of clear liquid that was given to him by the alchemist kobolds. Once he had managed to get the cork out of the vial, he placed the cloth over the opening and tipped some of the liquid out. He then proceeded to twist around his body, rubbing and buffing the jewelry wherever he could reach. He did it while trying to keep up with the rest of the group which caused him to look as though he was desperately close to scratching an itchy scale but couldn't quite reach.

"Do you have to do that right now?" Ember asked.

Tarot twisted back around to face her and nodded his snout up and down. "After all of the commotion earlier, my jewels are looking much too dusty. And I didn't have the time while we were sitting down since I was tending to Oleander's injuries."

He finished the last sentence with a flick of the cloth and went right back to polishing his jewelry.

"I don't know why you're bothering to polish it in the first place," wondered Woof. "It's just gonna get dirty again in a little while."

Shade laughed. "It's less about it getting dirty again and more of a comfort thing for him. He likes looking good and the gems and baubles help him with that. I even picked out a few of the necklaces he wears around his neck."

Tarot stopped polishing as the other kobolds looked over to him. He tried to put the cloth away quickly and wrapped his tail around his midsection to cover up some of the jewelry. He was doing a bad job of hiding the fact that he was incredibly embarrassed.

"Shade, you didn't need to tell them all that..."

"What? It's true, isn't it?"

Penny giggled. "Well, I think it looks very dashing on you, Tarot! Like you've just popped up out of Fortuna's hoard and are trying to run away with the treasure!"

Penny's comment got Tarot to relax a little, his tail lowering slowly as he walked. "Do you really mean that?"

Penny looked puzzled at that. "Why wouldn't I mean it?"

"Well, not every compliment I've gotten has been particularly nice."

Penny turned around to face Tarot, walking backwards as she talked to him. "It's not a compliment if they're being mean, Tarot! And if you let some random group of people ruin what's important to you, then you'd never be able to enjoy anything!"

"You sound like you're speaking from personal experience," Oleander noted.

Penny swiveled back around on the balls of her feet so she would face forward again. "And what of it? I'm not ashamed to be who I am. Auron taught me not to be ashamed of being enthusiastic about my interests. I know at least a few dozen kobolds who could live life a little more freely. Thank the fires in the forge I get to do what I love every day."

Tarot had finished his polishing and grabbed his tail so that he could put away the cloth and vial in the satchel. He could have buffed out a couple more scuffs, but with the conversation centering on him, he had started to feel self-conscious. When he looked up, he noticed that the other kobolds had stopped before a large oval-shaped room. He couldn't quite see over everyone, so he tapped on Shade's leg to get her attention.

"What's going on, Shade? Is there something wrong with the room?"

"Not exactly, but well..."

She moved to the side so that Tarot could peek around her. It was much bigger than Tarot originally realized. Easily big enough to fit at least three dragons. Around the edges of the room were open wooden doors that led to other sections of the mountain. Stranger still, the doors were different sizes. The majority were big enough for a kobold to slip through and there were a few that were twice as tall as that. Except the biggest door was directly behind a towering suit of knight's armor in the center of the room. It stretched all the way up to the ceiling and was made of a mixture of wood, stone, and metal. Even from this far away, the group could notice its ornate decorations shining in the torchlight.

"Do you think it's a trap?" Tarot asked Shade.

"It sure looks like one," she responded.

"What do you think we should do?" Oleander asked her.

"We'll just have to be extra careful. Fan out and try to walk slowly and evenly."

The kobolds all picked a direction and started walking forward. Woof cautiously sniffed the air, trying to find where the other kobolds' scent might be coming from. His head twisted back and forth, trying to pick back up on the scent trail. "The room's too big for me to tell where we should be going. Is it too obvious for the answer to be the big open door?"

"Yes," Oleander replied.

"At least this door is open this time," Ember sighed. "I've had enough explosions in one day that's for sure."

"Aww, party pooper!" Penny said while sticking her tongue out at Ember.

They each moved towards a door on the perimeter of the room, stepping across the stone floor as though it would spring back at them at any moment. Penny inched closer and closer to the statue at the center of the room. She wanted to get a better look at it. Something about it seemed incredibly familiar, but she couldn't put her claws on what.

The other kobolds were busy moving towards their chosen doors, so they didn't notice when Penny stopped to inspect the suit of armor. It was bigger than she initially thought, at least three or four feet taller than Shade even. The suit of armor was posed standing at attention with its hands resting on the pommel of a massive two-handed sword that impaled the stone platform it was positioned on. The helmet had three spikes placed in a circle around the head that stood straight up to form a kind of crown. The visor was odd as well, with a thin slit that ran horizontally across the front of the helmet. Much too thin to give enough of a line of sight for battle.

The feature that was most interesting to Penny, though, was the metal it was made of. An alloy that shined in streaks of silver and black depending on the angle it was viewed from. She had never seen a metal with such type of composition before and was momentarily transfixed at the rippling waves of color that played across the armor's surface. It was shinier than she expected too. She thought that being in this cave for so long it would have accumulated a fair amount of dust. She leaned in closer to get a better look.

"Penny, watch out!" Tarot screamed at her.

It was too late. Penny felt the full force of the toe of a metal boot connect with her midsection. Thankfully, since she was so close there wasn't a lot of space for it to build momentum. Penny flew backwards and rolled a few times before coming to a stop on the ground. She had the wind knocked out of her, but otherwise felt fine. The other kobolds rushed towards her as the rest of the room came to life. Each of the open doors slammed shut starting with the doors closest to the entrance and working inwards. The whole room rumbled as the door in the center scraped across the ground and closed itself.

The armor in the middle stomped its outstretched foot on the stone pedestal. An eerie red glow shone behind the horizontal line in its visor. Its movements were jerky at first, as if it was remembering how to move at all, pushing its arms out and moving them back and forth. Crouching for a second before standing back up, it knees began springing back more and more each time.

"Should we do something?" Woof asked cautiously.

The kobolds heard a horrible wrenching sound as steel ground on stone and they saw the suit of living armor pull its massive sword out of its pedestal. In one fluid motion, it swung the sword over its right shoulder, metal clanking on metal with an ominous *ping*. Then, it charged.

The kobolds scattered chaotically, each picking a different direction to flee from the suit of armor. Shade jumped back, landing on the balls of her heels, knives held defensively in front of her body. Woof ran to the left of the armor, hoping that it would ignore him. Penny backflipped into a crouch and drew her metal staff from off of her back, spinning it in front of her. Ember and Tarot didn't move as they were too surprised by what Penny had just done.

"Since when could you do that?" Ember asked incredulously.

The suit of armor readied its sword and swung down at an angle, trying to hit as much of the group as possible in one swing. Oleander managed to jump and barely dodge the blow, gliding a little to put some extra distance between themself and their enemy. Tarot felt the weight of the sword sink into the ground directly to the right of him and let out a small cry when he realized how close it was.

The suit of armor didn't seem to pay attention to him though, as it worked on getting its blade free. Tarot rushed over to Ember and hid behind her the best he could. Ember rolled her eyes and turned to face the suit of armor. She blew a quick burst of flame onto her stone chest plate to warm herself up, a habit she fell back on when stressed.

She called out to everyone, "Do we have a plan for how to fight this thing yet or what?"

"Working on that!" Shade screamed. Ember could see her eyes darting over the suit of armor, looking for any kind of weak point to exploit. The suit of armor pulled on the sword, and it came up a few more inches.

"It moves fast until it swings. If we can bait out an attack, we might be able to hit back," Oleander realized.

The suit of armor pulled the sword free from the ground and swung it back up onto its right shoulder again. Before it could move, Ember called out to it. "Hey, you wannabe golem! Why don't you come take a swing at me instead? Give ya a challenge for a change!"

The armor pivoted and then started to run directly for her. It flipped the sword in the air and caught it low to the ground. It was winding up for one hell of an uppercut. Ember realized too late that she wouldn't be able to get out of the way. Panicking, she looked behind her and saw that Tarot was casting magic again. His claws moved through the air, light blue trails following them. He wrapped his claws around something invisible suspended in the air, and Ember watched as long, thin lines of light circled around his claw tips and tapered off into nothingness. The magic around his hands glowed brighter as he quickly pulled with two fingers on the strings. She turned back around in time to see a blur of fur jump in front of her. A broken sword skittered across the ground as she heard the screech of metal hitting metal while she felt Woof collide with her.

She landed in a heap sandwiched between Tarot and Woof but was still in one piece. She peeked around the curtain of Woof's tail in front of her face and could see the armor's right arm slightly out of alignment. Its sword was being balanced by its left hand as it tried to roll its shoulder back into place. Ember couldn't believe their luck! The shoulder must have popped out during the swing and thrown off the sword's trajectory. It had hit Woof with the flat of the blade instead.

While it tried to fix its shoulder, a ball of light smacked into the back of its helmet. The suit of armor didn't move, but the helmet did turn around to face whatever had hit it.

Smiling, Oleander shouted, "Now!"

Shade threw her knives at the top portion of the helmet, aiming for the glowing energy behind the slit. The first knife bounced off as it was aimed too low, but the second knife struck true and hit directly into the small slot.

"Bullseye! Can't hit us if you can't see!"

The suit of armor stopped moving. The energy behind the slit began to dim. All the kobolds waited to see if it would collapse in a heap.

Woof's voice was muffled underneath his crumpled shield, but he asked, "Did we win?"

And then the energy brightened until the entire room was bathed in the eerie red light. The knife began to droop and drip out of the helmet as the suit of armor melted it down. It used its left arm to stick the sword into the ground so it could grab the handle of the knife and throw it aside. It grabbed its right shoulder roughly and with a sickening scrape of metal, popped it back into place.

"I'm guessing that's a no," he whined.

The suit of armor swiveled its body to match up with its head and took a step towards Shade and Oleander. It went for the sword to pull it back up out of the ground, but stopped when it encountered resistance. Its head turned to the left and it saw Penny there, metal staff placed over the sword to keep it from being pulled out.

She was grinning like a maniac. "Not so fast, big boy! It's my turn to dance!"

The armor grabbed the sword with both hands and heaved, spinning it around its body. Penny kicked her staff up and grabbed it in the air. She slid backwards and wound up with a strike of her own.

While she was distracting it, Tarot, Woof, and Ember had managed to disentangle themselves. Tarot and Ember stood up while Woof opted to continue laying on the ground.

"How are we supposed to fight this thing?" Ember quavered. "We're running out of ways to take it down."

"I'm thinking, I'm thinking! It's incredibly difficult to come up with a plan when under this much pressure."

"What about what happened to its shoulder earlier? We could really use another bout of luck like that."

"Luck! That's it!" shouted Tarot, his face beaming. "Thanks, Ember!"

He rushed over to where the others were distracting the suit of armor. He tried to wave Penny down as he ran. Ember watched on, dazed in confusion.

"I'm just gonna lay here if no one needs me," Woof said, still under his shield.

Ember sat down on the ground and said, "Thanks for the save back there. I owe ya one."

"You owe me a bit more than that."

"Yeah, I suppose I do."

She reached down and gently pet the top of his head. Even though she couldn't see his face, she could see his tail start to wag slowly.

Tarot called out to Shade, Oleander, and Penny. "Lead it over to me! I've got a plan!"

"Are you sure?" Penny called back. Her voice strained as she parried a blow from the sword with her staff.

"Yes! When I give the signal, everyone rush the suit of armor."

Penny let go of her staff and rolled out of the way of the next sword swing. She got to her feet and ran over to Tarot with the suit of armor close behind. Shade and Oleander flanked the armor on either side of it, trying to keep up with its pace.

"Woof, Ember! I need you two to come over here!"

Ember stopped petting Woof and took off in the direction of the rest of the kobolds. Woof sighed and slid his shield off his body. "Well...it was nice while it lasted."

He was the last to arrive and saw Tarot pull the vial of polish out from his tail bag. He stood in front of the armor, claws trembling as it prepared one of its massive uppercuts. He took deep a breath to steady himself and then threw the vial on the ground. It shattered, liquid spilling out to coat the floor in front of him. He jumped out of the way as the suit of armor swung. The armor stepped into the small pool of polish and its momentum made it slip backwards.

It fell onto its back with a massive *thunk*.

"Quick! Everyone but Ember and Penny, grab its arms and legs so it can't get up."

The other kobolds dove onto the suit of armor and tried to keep it pinned down as it thrashed back and forth. While they couldn't keep it from moving, they did manage to keep it from being able to stand back up again.

Penny shouted over to Tarot, wildly flailing back and forth from the armor's right arm, "What are we supposed to do?!"

Tarot's words came out in small bits and pieces, "Use...coins... melt...ground!"

"What is he trying to say?" Ember hollered.

Penny understood the idea and was rushing over to the right arm. Ember followed her and Penny motioned for her to help pin the arm down to the ground. With all three of them, it was just enough to keep the arm from moving for a moment. Penny felt her magic gather in her chest and threw her head back before breathing out a small stream of copper coins that landed around the hand and wrist with a *plink, plink, plink* sound.

Ember's eyes lit up and she gathered magic of her own, breathing fire along the coins to melt them to the armor and attach it to the floor underneath. Tarot worked quickly, unscrewing the cap to his canteen so that he could pour water over the molten metal and cool it into a makeshift restraint. They moved to each of the other limbs in turn and repeated the process of melting and attaching to the floor until the whole suit of armor was trapped.

It still struggled, but it wasn't going anywhere.

Tarot brushed himself off and noticed that in the scuffle, his flowing purple sashes had been ripped in multiple places. Worse than that was the pieces of jewelry with broken chains that were scattered around the floor. He did his best to pick up the ones he could find and rejoined the group with a heavier heart.

Shade picked up the armor's sword, more so to keep it out of the armor's reach than anything. Experimentally, she swung it and found that it had a good weight. Much more comfortable than her daggers. She strapped it to her back using some of the rope they packed and met up with the rest of the group.

"That won't bind it forever. We need to figure out how to get out of here before it gets free," Oleander said.

"What are we waiting for then?" Ember asked while pulling on one of the closed doors frantically. "Start checking the doors!"

The other kobolds each ran to a door and tried to move it. Oleander pulled on the handle of their door, hovering a little each time as they tried to put their wings to use. Shade scratched and hit her door, hoping that the force might knock something loose. Tarot was too busy thinking about the best way to open his door to actually try, so he mostly stood with his chin in his claws trying not to be anxious. Ember was desperate enough to try gnawing on the handle of her door. It wasn't getting her anywhere and it tasted like old metal, but it was the best her panicked mind could come up with. Woof tried to knock on his door as politely as he could. He stepped back and waited for the door to open.

The noise was loud enough to get everyone to stare at him.

"What? It was worth a try."

Penny yelled from over by her door. She had the end of her staff wedged between the door and the doorframe. "This one has an indent! Help me pry it open!"

The other kobolds ran over to her and each grabbed onto the staff. Penny leaned in and ordered, "On the count of three, everyone pushes. Ready? One, two, three!"

They all pushed on the staff as the door groaned in protest. It moved a few inches forward. "Keep going! Push!" Penny exclaimed. They could see the space behind the door through a small crack that had formed. The light from behind it shining through the ominous red surrounding them. "One more time! Push!"

The kobolds put their all into the last push, so much so that Penny's staff bent at the place it was jammed in the door. The door swung open and hit the other side of the wall with a *clunk*, to which they all cheered.

They quickly made their way into the next room, with Tarot being the last to enter. As he stepped through, he closed the door as best he could behind him and then followed the rest down the new hallway they had found themselves in.

The corridor was big enough to accommodate Shade's height, but just barely. She had to duck her head down a little to keep her horns from brushing the top of the ceiling. The lights along the wall were different as well. While it was a relief to not have everything backlit in red, the stark white light emanating from the lanterns gave the hallway an oddly clinical feel. The light was not harsh, but it lacked the warmth of the yellowy orange from earlier. The floor was made of heavily varnished wood and polished to a shine.

Oleander was the first to notice the black stains that traveled along the floor and ended at odd intervals as they walked. It was clear from the feel of the wood that the stained strips were polished more often. Small divots worn into grooves that could be felt by the kobolds' feet.

"What's with this strange hallway?" Ember asked as she walked. "Gives me the creeps."

"Does anyone see a way out of here? I'm with Ember on this. Something doesn't feel right," Woof muttered.

His fur was standing on end from some imagined danger in the hallway. He hadn't told the others yet, but he had lost the scent of the other kobolds entirely when they walked through the doorway. More than that, he couldn't smell anything else. Without his sense of smell, he felt as though he was walking blind. Whatever was in the mountain wanted to make sure that it couldn't be tracked, and the thought of that put Woof on edge.

He wasn't the only one who was nervous—Oleander's antennae twitched erratically as they moved along the corridor. They had opted to lead the group after discovering the black stains, and since then the feeling in the air had changed. They were quite familiar with the unease that strange magic could inflict, having experienced it when living with the fae.

At first, Oleander had hoped that it was a sign they were getting closer to Myfanwy, but as they focused on it, they realized it was different. Oleander was familiar with Myfanwy's illusion spells, familiar with the feeling they imparted on their antennae, the same feeling as if they had told a lie. This was not the same feeling—it was a kind of falsehood, yes, but not one born out of illusion. Oleander didn't like it one bit.

Penny was busy trying to fix her staff's bent end but couldn't quite get the metal to give enough to make any progress in repairing it. After the fourth attempt didn't get her anywhere, she secured it to her back with a small sigh. Shade made her way over to them and said, "It's a shame about your staff, Penny. But at least it got us out of that room."

Penny looked over and replied, "I'll be able to fix it if we get to a forge, so I'm not too worried. Just have to account for the balance being shifted!"

Shade's eyes lit up a little at that. "You mentioned being able to use the weapons you make. Have any idea how to swing a sword this big?" She motioned to the armor's sword strapped to her back with her thumb-claw and grinned.

Penny laughed, "Why'd you pick that up?"

"I thought it was a good idea to take the huge sword next to the deadly evil suit of armor that tried to kill us."

"I wasn't sure if this is something that Dusk's kobolds do or if it was just one of your quirks."

"What kind of quirk?"

"Taking a trophy from your enemies, naturally."

Now it was Shade's turn to laugh. "What? Who even does that? No, I don't take trophies."

"Oh! Yeah, me neither," Penny said while sliding a small trinket slowly back into her bag. She cleared her throat and continued, "You wanna know how to swing it? Let's start with what you do know. How do you normally move when you're fighting someone?"

Shade put a few claws under her chin and thought for a minute before answering. "I normally try to lower my center of gravity by crouching down, then move my arms to keep my opponent guessing where my next strike is going to be."

"I could see that. Constant knife movement is good for dual-bladed combat but doesn't translate well to swords. You want to make sure you're moving your body when you strike. Hips and shoulders together, kinda like how the armor was swinging at us. Did you notice how it was using its whole body to make the strike?"

Shade was going to reply, only to be interrupted by Tarot. "I don't mean to cut the lesson short, but don't either of you feel that?"

"Feel what?" Shade asked, a little annoyed.

"I don't know exactly. I just have the sense that something bad is going to happen."

"You're about two deathtraps and three suspicious hallways too late on that prediction, Tarot," Shade said.

"It's all right Shade, I can go over this later when we take another rest. That way I can show you how to move your feet. Footwork is more important than you probably think."

Oleander overheard Penny. "We're not going to rest here, for sure," he said. "Tarot's right about this place. I don't think it's safe either. We need to find another path quickly."

Shade sighed and responded, "Not you too, Oleander. Can't this just be a creepy hallway? Maybe we'll get lucky, and this will open out into a big bedroom chamber."

"Is someone tired already?" Ember asked playfully. She was busy feeling along the side of the rightmost wall looking for a way out. Woof was on the left side doing the same.

"We've been walking all day and almost died twice now. Let a girl dream, Red."

Woof turned around from his wall to say something but stopped suddenly. He tilted his head up and inhaled deeply through his snout. It was faint, an incredibly small smell, but it was something. He turned in a circle and followed the path of the scent down the hallway, almost bumping into Oleander as he walked past them. As the scent grew stronger, he walked faster. There was no doubt about it, he'd picked up on a kobold's scent. Not just any kind of kobold either, the smell was wild and woodsy, like Carmichael's kobolds.

Before long, Woof was running down the hallway towards whoever was there. He could hear the others screaming behind him, but he didn't slow down. He had finally found the kobold who might be able to explain everything. The mountain, the traps, all of it!

He stopped dead in his tracks when he looked around the corner. The others caught up to him quickly soon after.

"Lava cleanse us all," she whispered. "What is this place?"

The room was enormous. Tunnels moved in every direction through parts of the mountain. Down some of the tunnels were minecarts heaped with gold and jewels that traveled along metal tracks into rooms that were too far away for Ember to make out. The other tunnels fed into each other as empty carts were wheeled from one section to another to be filled up and then pushed down one last set of passageways towards their destination. And all the carts were being moved by dozens of kobolds.

However, these kobolds were different. All of them had scales a sickly shade of grayish green. Their eyes were vacant with a white film over them. They didn't speak to each other. Their only communication was occasional shrieks and moans if one got too close. Not a single one of them moved without taking shaky, shambling steps forward. Most were intact, but there were a select few who missed parts of their body.

Ember could see one without a lower jaw, its grey, dried tongue dangling loose over its neck and swinging with each step. Another had lost its forearm, with a bone exposed through their scales, marrow festering.

She stepped away from the door and whispered to Woof, "What are they?"

He paused before saying anything, afraid to even consider what he was thinking. When he spoke again, it was so quiet she had to strain to hear him, "I think they're undead."

Ember's eyes went wide. Already the others were looking through the door and could see what was in that room. Tarot was the only one who said what they were all thinking.

"These can't be the missing kobolds, right?"

"No! Of course not! These are probably just kobolds who live around here..." Penny's voice shook.

"Woof, have we been following these things' scent the whole time?" Shade asked, her voice wavering too, as though she was afraid of the answer she might get.

Woof didn't meet Shade's eyes when he answered, "Yeah. I thought there was something wrong with their scent at the beginning too but chalked it up to how the mountain smelled. I never thought we would find this."

Oleander suddenly stumbled back, barely catching themself before they could fall to the floor. Tarot rushed to help them steady themself. "Are you alright?"

"Yeah, I-I'm fine..." muttered Oleander. They held a hand over their wound, still bleeding. "I just...really need to get away from this smell."

"I don't think we're going to be able to sneak by them," Shade said. "They'll notice us once we step foot in the room, won't they?"

"Maybe not." Penny helped Oleander walk over to the crack in the doorway and asked, "Do you think you could make us look like them with an illusion spell?"

Oleander gave a weak laugh, "I'll try."

They began to pull light into their claws and pulled them close to their chest. Oleander then whispered an incantation into their hands and pushed away from their body, spreading their claws. The light rippled out in a wave and as it moved over each of the kobolds, their scale color and eyes took on the appearance of the undead. Oleander's antennae and wings drooped even farther, but they had managed to pull off the spell.

It was convincing enough that when Tarot looked down at himself, he screamed out in shock. Woof was quick to put a paw over his mouth to keep him quiet as they all moved into a line behind the door.

Woof had also grabbed a piece of cloth from his pack and wrapped it around his nose to keep from smelling the undead kobolds. He didn't want to chance vomiting from their combined rotten smell hitting him at once. It was going to be difficult enough to keep his composure as they moved through the source of the scent trail. He tried not to think about how long it was going to take to get the smell out of his nose after everything was over.

Penny positioned herself at the front of the group. "Alright, follow my lead. And try to act like you're dead. Oleander, this won't be a problem for you, hun, but do try to keep up with us."

Oleander responded with a tired groan but didn't say anything more. Penny opened the doorway wide enough for them to walk through and the group shambled out into the light.

Ember tried not to look at the faces of the undead kobolds as they moved past them, shambling and groaning as convincingly as they could. She didn't want to know if she could recognize any of them.

Blast could never do such a thing. No dragon would ever do such a terrible thing to their own kobolds. Ember had to hold onto some hope that this horror was caused another way, but by who, then? And why kobolds of all things to raise from the dead? Weren't there scarier creatures to bring back to life? None of it made any sense.

To Oleander's credit, the illusion spell was working well. None of the undead kobolds turned to look in the group's direction. They were too focused on carting around the gold coins and jewels. So much so, that one almost bumped into Woof as he went to step over a section of metal track. Dedicated to the role, Woof hissed and spat at the undead kobold, which jerked its body sharply to the right to avoid him. Penny was leading them through the main tunnel towards one of the offshoots where the treasure was set up to be stored.

The group was almost to the offshoot when, suddenly, an oncoming undead kobold pulled a switch on its minecart, sending it onto the group's track. The group quickly ducked out of the way, all but Ember, who was knocked roughly aside and let out a loud scream in pain.

"YEOOWCH!"

Suddenly, the undead kobolds next to the tunnel stopped what they were doing and looked in the group's direction. They moved slowly towards the source of the sound. The kobolds froze in fear, surrounded by the oncoming horde-all but Oleander. Ember watched in silence as the moth kobold shuffled slowly forward, muttering to themself as if in a trance.

"Myfanwy must be close by now. Surely, they're just around the corner. Surely..." And then Oleander collapsed onto the ground in a heap.

The illusion spell started to wobble and waver. Rippling back and forth between living kobold and undead disguise. Within a few moments, the light from the spell had dissipated, leaving the group of kobolds vulnerable. The undead kobolds screeched and limped towards them faster.

"Someone wake Oleander up!" Ember shouted as she ran forward and gathered fire in her mouth.

She breathed out a small cone of flame on the ground, creating a wall of fire to keep the undead kobolds from getting any closer. There was at least a dozen of the undead, with more on the way if the sounds of shuffling feet were any indication. Ember could feel her fire breath slow until it was barely a trickle of heat. When she closed her mouth and tried again, all that came out was a puff of smoke.

"Damn it all, I'm out!" She yelled as she turned around and ran back to the group. Shade and Penny were busy fighting the kobolds that Shade had initially alerted while Tarot and Woof were trying desperately to get Oleander to get up.

"Move the sword from the pommel, don't just swing it willy-nilly!" Penny shouted.

"Can you not critique my technique while we're in the middle of a fight?" Shade said while she swung wildly at the back of an undead kobold.

"You're the one who wanted pointers!" Penny shouted back as she jammed her staff horizontally into the same undead's mouth to prevent it from biting her. It had clamped down and was trying to force its way through by biting down repeatedly. "Now pivot with your hips and follow through!"

Shade swung and cleaved the kobold at its neck. The body slumped to the ground with a thud. Penny shook the head off her staff until it fell onto the ground as well.

"Great job! What was different that time?"

"You didn't tell me I should be taking my tail into account when I go to swing!"

"I thought that was obvious?"

From a few feet away, Tarot was shaking his tail up and down to jingle his jewelry and wake up Oleander. No matter how much he jumped around, Oleander didn't notice. Still peacefully asleep and only occasionally murmuring an odd sentence or two.

Woof said, "Wait, let me try something." He leaned into Oleander's face and then gave it a big lick.

When that didn't work, he tried smaller consecutive licks. After Oleander's face was soaked in slobber, Woof took a step back and scratched his head in confusion.

"Huh. That worked on Ember before. I was hoping it would work for them too."

Ember skidded to a stop on unsteady feet in front of them both. She took a moment to catch her breath before asking, "They're still not awake?"

"No, and we're running out of ideas," Tarot said.

Ember's mouth cracked into a wicked grin. "I've got one."

She spun on her left foot and whipped her body around in a circle. She aimed her hand for Oleander's snout, and it connected with a loud *slap*.

"I've wanted to do that for a long time!" She said once she stopped spinning. While it was cathartic for Ember, Oleander did not stir from their sleep.

"They're not dead, are they?" Woof asked.

Tarot carefully held his right hand in front of their snout and waited a few seconds. He wiped his hand off on his clothes before saying, "They're still breathing, at least."

"What are we going to do with them if they won't wake up?" Ember asked.

Tarot put a claw under his chin and thought for a moment. "Do you think we could lift them into the minecart?"

"If we all work together, maybe? Oleander is pretty small, but they're also dead weight right now. Why the minecart?"

"Well, how else do you expect to move them while they're unconscious? "

Woof bent down to grab Oleander by their feet and said, "I can get their bottom if Ember can support their head. Tarot, make sure we don't hurt their wings when we set them down."

Ember looped her arms around Oleander's and picked them up with Woof's help. They shuffled awkwardly towards the nearest minecart and swung Oleander back and forth to build up some momentum. After a few swings, Woof said, "Okay, toss them on three. One, two, three!"

Ember let go just a bit faster than Woof and Oleander spun a bit before landing with a *thunk* on their side in the bottom of the minecart. Tarot winced and ran over to try and reposition them. Ember dusted off her hands before saying, "That takes care of them. Any ideas on how to get out of here yet, Woof?"

"We could try pushing the minecart and leave down this tunnel?"

Ember shook her head. "How could we push something so heavy with just our bare hands? It was heavy enough without Oleander in it!"

Woof's tail started to wag at an incredible speed as an idea popped into his head. "What if we don't have to push it?"

He took off towards the wall of fire, and before Ember could ask what he meant, just about collided with Penny as he rushed over to where she and Shade were standing. They had finished killing the undead around the minecart and were both facing the wall of fire to take out any that might try to slip through.

"Penny! Do you still have that explosive powder from earlier? I need it!"

Penny rummaged around in her bag and pulled out the bottle of gray and black powder before handing it over to Woof. "Sure, I do. What do you need it for?"

"Something incredibly stupid."

He rushed off towards the left side of the wall of fire as Penny called after him, "Wait, then give it back! Woof, don't blow yourself up!"

Shade's eyes narrowed as a shadow appeared behind the middle of the flame wall. "Look out! Something's coming through!"

The shadow jumped through the fire and landed with a horrible shriek on the other side. Flames licked hungrily up the sides of its gray-green flesh as it shuffled slowly towards them. Penny's eyes went wide when she heard it scream, recognizing its voice. Distorted as it had become, there was no mistaking it. The undead kobold stalking toward them was Tinpin.

Penny went through a whirlwind of emotions. She was initially happy that she found him, ecstatic even, but when the reality of his condition dawned on her, she could feel tears well up in her eyes. Tinpin was the whole reason she was in the horrible mountain stronghold. Would it all be for nothing if she couldn't save him? And was there even a chance to save him now? Would he even want her to try?

Shade squared her shoulders and stepped forward as if to strike. Penny acted quickly and hooked the curved end of her staff around Shade's ankle lightly. Shade looked back at her, confusion plain on her face. Her expression softened as she saw Penny's eyes. Tears dripped down her snout and rolled off the side of her face.

Penny's voice cracked as she told Shade, "Don't you dare touch him." She sniffled and continued, "I'll talk to him."

Shade relaxed her posture, but her eyes kept darting back and forth from the wall of fire back to Penny. She could see from the number of new shadows that appeared behind the wall that the other undead kobolds were going to try to step through.

Penny unhooked her staff from Shade's leg and walked over so that she was only a few feet away from Tinpin. Close up, Penny found herself even more intimidated by the sight of him. His scales still had a slight silvery-white to them in spots along his body. She drew in a shaky breath and tried to speak without letting her voice crack with grief.

"Tinpin?"

Tinpin's head swiveled in the direction of Penny's voice. He looked confused, as if that sound was familiar but he couldn't explain why. He had stopped moving forward and let the word rattle around the inside of his rotting skull. He went to speak, and it came out as a guttural groan. Then, his body jerked in a spasm, and he tried again. This time he was able to parrot Penny's word through his distorted voice.

"Teeeeennn...piiiiiinnn"

Penny lit up as she heard him say his own name. There was hope yet for him. She said, "That's right. That's your name. Do you remember me?" She pointed with her staff to herself and waited for him to answer her.

"Rrrreeeembbbburrrrrrr miiiiiiii?" He responded automatically. His snout tilted up at her inquisitively as he cocked his head to the one side.

Penny's tears dripped onto the tracks, her throat tensing up, "I'm Penny. We both worked in Auron's forge. You worked with me every day. You must remember that!"

Tinpin cracked his neck in the other direction and brought his head backwards. He pushed out his next word with great difficulty. "Pe-pe-pe-peeeeeeeeen-en-en-ennnnniiiiii..."

Penny smiled despite herself. He did recognize her after all. She just had to find a way to get him out of there. It would be hell trying to leave, but as long as everyone helped, they could still pull it off.

"Peeenny, Peeeennnnnnyyyyy, Pennnnnnnnnyyyyy!" He repeated while jumping forward, snout first with teeth bared, ready to bite down into Penny.

Before she could dodge out of the way, Shade had intercepted his strike with a running charge into him. She led with her shoulder and bowled him over so that he tumbled and fell snout over tail onto the ground.

The other undead kobolds screamed as each passed through the wall of fire and limped towards them. Penny could hear Woof, Ember, and Tarot screaming for her. None of their voices registered. She had to save Tinpin. She wouldn't let Shade kill him again. She tried to run to him, but her hand was caught by Woof.

Before Penny could wriggle free, Ember had caught her under her arms and was pulling her back to the minecart. She thrashed her tail and kicked her feet, hitting Ember in a desperate attempt to get free. She twisted her head back and forth, screaming to let her go. She could save him if they just listened! She could fix this. She would fix this. Except when Woof and Tarot picked her up too, she knew it was hopeless.

She watched helplessly as Shade placed her feet, wound up with tail raised for balance, and swung with her body to cleave Tinpin in two. Penny wailed, scratched, bit, anything she could to express her fresh grief. She felt the sensation of being tossed into the air and landed roughly into the minecart next to Oleander. When she hit, she felt her sadness overwhelm her. By the time Tarot and Ember had climbed in, she was a mess. She alternated between heavy sobbing and full-body shakes, whimpering, "Tinpin... Tinpin... Tinpin..."

Woof was busy putting the last of his plan into motion by pouring out the rest of the black powder in front of the minecart. His confidence drained as he turned and saw one of the undead kobolds, engulfed in flame, brush past the line of powder. The powder ignited and started speeding towards the minecart.

In a panic, he yelled to Shade. "Shade! Get in the minecart now!"

She turned around and saw the fuse quickly rush by her and took off in the direction of the minecart. Her legs burned and her chest heaved from running with the weight of her sword, but she couldn't let it beat her.

Shade yelled out to the others, "Make some room!"

She braced herself and jumped with everything she had. She landed in the middle, squishing everyone else with her weight a moment before the fuse reached the pile of powder.

BOOOOOOOM!!!

The undead kobolds were blown back as the powder ignited and blew the minecart forward on the track. The momentum of Shade's rough landing and the explosion was enough to carry them down the minecart's track and well out of the undead kobolds' line of sight. The air in the tunnel rushed past them as they huddled together in the minecart. The group's ears rang, heads pounded from the explosion, and the walls seemed to spin around them as they rushed along the track. They let the ride down the tunnels pass in silence.

The only sound was the whimpering cry of Penny as she tried and failed to pull herself back together.

The kobolds were jolted back to awareness by the cart coming to an abrupt stop at the end of the track. Shade was the first to peek out over the side of the minecart. There was only one path to go down, an elaborately carved tunnel with warm, flickering torches hung in regular intervals along the walls.

Along the tunnel were scattered remains of the gold and jewels that were mined from the surrounding rock. They glinted in the yellow light and provided some semblance of normalcy to the strange cave. Every kobold knew the feeling of walking around a dragon's home and finding the occasional piece of treasure out of place.

Shade ducked her head back down and looked at the others. They were exhausted.

Tarot had taken a moment to pool their healing salves, potions, and bandages into one big pile in the cart. He and Woof were busy tending to the group's various wounds accumulated in their fight with the undead, and in their struggle to pull Penny onto the minecart. Woof, Tarot, and Ember were all bleeding in one way or another. Ember in particular had a nasty bite from Penny, which Tarot dabbed with a healing salve.

Woof turned to Shade and offered her the last healing potion they had. "Take it, you deserve it after that jump."

Shade shook her head and replied, "You should take it. You look worse off than me."

Woof smiled weakly and leaned towards Shade. At first, she thought he was going in for a hug. While not much of a hugger, she opened her arms up to receive his embrace. She was surprised then, when instead of a hug, he pressed his hands gently on her side where her ribs were. She drew in a sharp breath and felt a stabbing pain that wasn't there before. When he let go, she could feel the pain persist, albeit less sharply.

"You've been breathing pretty shallowly, so I thought something might be wrong. Take the potion, Shade. It'll help heal you."

She reached her hand out to take the offered potion, uncorked it, and drank the contents slowly. It tasted of medicine and sweetness, coating her throat as she drank it.

"Are we going to talk about how we just killed other kobolds?" Tarot asked as he finished bandaging Ember.

"It's not like we had much of a choice, Tarot," Ember mentioned. "Would you rather we had been eaten?"

"No, of course not. I'm just having difficulty parsing what just happened."

"It's not that different from everything else that's happened today," Shade offered.

"I didn't want to hurt them, even if they weren't technically alive."

Shade looked over at Penny, but she wouldn't make eye contact with her. She was uncharacteristically silent. Tears still dripped from her snout and the area around her eyes was slightly swollen, but she had stopped wailing. Her body would occasionally shudder, and she'd hold her shoulders to ride out the feeling until it passed. Ember carefully tended to Penny's wounds as Woof and Shade checked on Oleander. If they were hurt, they couldn't tell. They were still fast asleep even through all the commotion.

Tarot sighed, "That's the last of our healing supplies. I tried to stretch it as best as I could."

"Thank you, Tarot," Penny said in a soft whisper.

Tarot nodded solemnly as he asked, "What do we do now?"

Ember looked around the group and saw the same thing in all of them. They were tired. She felt it too. Perhaps more acutely without her fire to help keep her warm. "I think Oleander has the right idea. We should rest for a while."

Shade's shoulders tensed a little and her tail swished nervously. "I don't know about that, Red. What if the undead find us?"

Ember shrugged. "If they followed us here, we wouldn't be able to fight back anyway. At least if we stop for a while, we might have a better chance." She reached into her bag and pulled out the blanket that Comfy had given them.

"I'm all for a nap," Woof whimpered. "It'd be nice to escape into my dreams for a bit; I'm getting real sick of this place."

Penny shifted uneasily and said, "I can't. What if...what if I dream about him? I don't think I could handle that."

Ember gently grasped Penny's hands in her own and squeezed. "If that happens, you wake me up. Alright? I know how it feels to have bad dreams and I can talk you through it."

Penny returned the squeeze, nodding silently. Ember started to unfold the blanket and spread it out over the top of everyone. While she didn't initially want to, Woof convinced her and the others to huddle together to share their body heat. Once they had all gotten comfortable and she let herself feel the heat from her fellow kobolds, she could feel her eyes get heavy. She nestled in against Woof's fur and found herself enveloped in comfortable fabric and warmth.

Sleep came quickly and deeply to Ember. She didn't want to admit it to Penny for fear of making her more uncomfortable, but she was worried about what her dreams would contain too. When she dreamt, though, she found herself rolling through fields of flowers, surrounded by the laughter of other kobolds. Everyone else in the group was there and were frolicking with her. Kobolds she didn't recognize flitted across her vision as they ran through the grass. Their snouts changed shape as she tried to look at them and the color of their scales shifted as quickly as she blinked. The place she inhabited in the dream was an undulating, undefinable thing. At times, the sky was a peaceful sunny day and then it would shift to a cloudless nighttime sky with thousands of stars lighting their reverie.

When she looked up at the night sky, Ember saw a purple whale soaring through the cosmos, filling her with calm. She felt a kobold tackle her to the ground and kiss at her neck. She laughed and returned the kisses as she felt happy and relaxed for the first time in what felt like years.

She came back to the waking world slowly, unwillingly. When she was awake enough to open her eyes, Ember rubbed at them furiously until she was sure she was up. She looked around and saw that the others were stirring as well. They couldn't tell how long they had slept for, but it felt like a full night had passed. Ember quietly hoped that wasn't the case but found she didn't care after getting up and feeling how well-rested she felt. She stretched out and wiggled her tail as the others helped her to fold up the blanket. There weren't any undead kobolds in sight. They must have lost interest once they were out of their way.

"I feel amazing!" Woof yawned with his tail wagging fast behind him. "That was a really good idea, Ember."

"Indeed!" Tarot agreed. "That was the best sleep I've had in months. Even better than the bed at Comfy's inn."

Shade stood taller in the minecart when she got up. She carried herself with a lot more confidence after the nap. She was even smirking as she said, "Not exactly the way I expected sleeping with a group of kobolds to go, but it was nice. Your tail was really comfortable, Red."

She felt a short-lived rush of heat to her face but shook it off as she finished packing up the rest of her supplies.

Penny had stopped crying, but her spirits weren't as high as the rest of the group. She barely spoke above a whisper and her voice remained flat and monotone. She was the last before Oleander to climb out of the minecart and join the rest of the group in the archway that led to the next section of the mountain.

Even after the nap, Oleander would not stir from their sleep. Shade shrugged her shoulders and just decided to pick them up to carry them. "They're not that heavy anyway, I can handle keeping them safe. Besides," she smiled as Oleander wrapped their arms around her neck drowsily, "they're kinda cute when they're asleep like this."

They set off from the safety of the minecart deeper into the mountain. To their surprise, there weren't any more traps waiting for them in the rooms they passed through. And each room they found was nicer than the last. The ground had shifted slowly as they walked along it from dirt to stone and then the same varnished wood flooring from before. They passed through spaces designed for relaxation with chairs and tables so plush that it was difficult to believe they were being hidden away underground.

The kobolds ate the last of their rations in a kitchen fully stocked with food and enough blocks of ice to keep it from spoiling for months. Tarot had to be dragged out of a room that functioned as a kind of massive library, with books stacked upon books that reached up so high that the kobolds couldn't see the top. If the dust was any indicator, they hadn't been touched since they were placed upon the shelves.

Occasionally, the group's passage became slow-going, as Penny was struck by crippling waves of grief. Woof and Ember took turns comforting and consoling her. She wasn't used to being laid low. She had been sad before, of course, but nothing touched the deep ache in her chest that gripped her heart when she thought about losing Tinpin.

She didn't talk to Shade as they moved through these rooms. She knew logically that Shade was only trying to protect her and the rest of the group, but knowing that and accepting it were two different things. Maybe when she had time to grieve, she would be able to forgive her.

The kobolds walked from a musician's room where instruments hung from every corner of the walls into the largest room in the mountain yet. The transition was so seamless that no one noticed they had entered a new room until the archway opened into the center.

The room was massive, with tunnels branching out at regular intervals around the circular wall. Yellow and orange lights hung on sconces on the walls distributed equally throughout the room. The floor was made of burnished granite, carved with intricate designs that spiraled and swooped along the ground. To their left was what appeared to be a circular jail cell, made up of metal bars which were easily fifty feet tall and three feet across. From where they were standing, the kobolds could see an immense pile of gold and jewels that was piled so high it was spilling out of the cage onto the floor surrounding it. On the right side, there was a desk piled to the brim with blank sheets of parchment and different colors of string.

They had made it to the center of the mountain.

Penny whistled through her teeth as she spun around and looked at the room from every angle. "This is amazing! The patterns on the floor must have taken ages to carve." She got down onto her knees and ran her hand over the swirls and loops, admiring the craftsmanship.

"Well look at that, Red," Shade told Ember. "A whole table set up with all the stuff you'd need to send out a bunch of letters to every kobold. Seems like we might have found our ghostwriter after all...."

"Indeed! Now if we can just wait for the person who uses those materials to show up, we'll have the final proof we've been looking for," Tarot said.

Ember tried not to think about what that might've meant. "We've seen a ton of strange and out of place stuff today. I don't think a personal stationary collection is all that important."

Shade snorted. "Oh, come on! Even I can tell that the string over there matches the colors used on the letters. Besides, we haven't seen any dragons yet, so they're probably fine."

"The fact that we haven't is the part that worries me," Ember mentioned.

"I'm going to go take a look. After copying so many of those letters down, I'm intensely curious of how they work," Tarot said.

While Tarot, Shade, and Ember talked about the desk in the corner, Woof caught a whiff of something he hadn't smelled in months. Dragon. He lifted his nose into the air and sniffed deeply to find out where the smell was coming from. He followed the scent trail over to the prison and yelped in surprise.

"Everyone, get over here now!"

The rest of the group ran over to him to see what the matter was. When they looked inside the jail, they couldn't believe what they discovered.

It was all their dragons, sitting on individual piles of treasure. Somnir had plush animals, Carmichael sat on a giant scratching post, Fortuna had a pile of extremely weathered books, Auron had a brand-new anvil, and Myfanwy laid peacefully on top of a honey-suckle bush. Blast was the only dragon whose pile was comprised entirely of gold and gems. They looked like exceptionally large jewels shining with their colorful scales. Each of them had their eyes closed and weren't moving. They were spaced out evenly in the cell and the jail stretched from the room out and back into a completely different section of the mountain. In the back corner was a dark shape of scales that furiously scribbled on pieces of parchment one after the other. As soon as they finished one letter, a new one took its place with the old one getting wrapped up with a string and teleported out of the room.

"They're all here," Tarot said breathlessly. "All of them. Every single one..."

"Why are they sleeping?" Woof whined to them. "Is this what happened to Oleander? Is it going to happen to us?"

"Dusk! Dusk, is that you? Stop writing letters for a second so I can yell at you."

The sight of Blast sitting catatonic atop that pile of gold hit Ember like a brick. Those dark red scales, those flaming eyes, those four black horns which curved upwards and framed his snout that so very seldom smiled—had this beastly dragon truly been trapped the entire time?

Tears welled in her eyes as she shook the rattled the bars, yelling at him.

"BLAST! Wake up, Blast! I'm here for you! I've come all this way! Please don't ignore me, Blast, please, please! Tell me you're okay!"

She rattled the bars of the cage and stomped her feet. Her tail lashed behind her and she alternated between hissing and growling at full volume. Tarot tried to pull her away from the bars but was interrupted by a rush of magic that swept all of the kobolds off of their feet. As the wind carried them to the center of the room, they could feel the string wrapping around their wrists and pinning their arms to their backs. A door at the far right of the room opened and two figures stepped out into the light.

"There's no need to make so much ruckus, they can't hear you anyway," said the pig in a low and husky voice.

"Quite right. And even then, they're happy right where they are. They don't need you to wake them up," chided the cat, his voice suave and cocky, almost nasal. He pulled a wand from his suit jacket and gave it a wave as kobolds dropped to the ground in front of them both.

They were both roughly the same height, about six feet tall, with the cat having a few extra inches over the pig. They wore the most elaborately tailored clothes that any of the kobolds had ever seen. It looked as though they were poured into their clothes with how well it fit and moved with them. Tarot was awestruck at the patterns and jewels that were sewn so seamlessly into the fabric. They each wore a black-and-white suit which complimented their style. The pig wore his shirt with the top button open, the chest tailored wide to allow his large torso extra room to breathe. His suit jacket was clean-cut with sharp angles and razor-straight lines.

The cat's suit was more flamboyant, with frills, an overcoat, undercoat, coattails, and even a tall jet-black top hat atop his head. The cat's fur was a light orange speckled with yellow and the pig's skin was a healthy pink. They looked down at the kobolds bound before them and the pig spoke next.

"I suppose an introduction is in order. I am Baron von Brookshire. Goldmancer and half of the duo that has acquired the dragons."

"And I am Count de Cornelius. Bureaucratic wunderkind and fashion genius," the cat introduced himself.

To everyone's surprise, Oleander was the first of the group to speak.

"That's great, but can you explain where I am?"

"Oleander! You're finally awake?" Woof asked.

"Kinda hard to sleep when you're getting tied up."

"You slept through a whole explosion!" Shade chided them. "I carried you for the past seven rooms!"

"Well, excuse me for being nocturnal! I tried to stay up all day and collapsed. Now can someone explain why we're tied up?"

"We found the dragons and then these two clowns showed up," Ember said.

Oleander lit up at the mention of the dragons. "Did anyone see Myfanwy? Are they safe?"

Brookshire cleared his throat and explained, "I can assure you that all of your dragons are safe and that no harm has come to them."

"It's bad form to kill your investments. Can't really make any profit off them if they're dead," Cornelius chimed in.

"What do you mean by 'profit'?" Tarot asked.

Brookshire clapped his hooves together and his hardened fingers clacked against each other joyously. "I'm so glad you asked. It's not often enough that we get to boast about our accomplishments after all. With an operation this secret, we can't be going around telling everyone now."

"We were approached by Blast with an initial idea of finding more ways to make him extra gold from your services. His problem was primarily in management. Too many kobolds for him to keep track of. There was plenty of work for them to do and money to be made, but not enough Blast to go around. So, he reached out to us to workshop a better solution. But his proof of concept was...lacking."

Brookshire nodded and said, "He wasn't willing to go far enough to get the most out of the new system. He would stop us from making adjustments for better productivity and return on investments. We didn't expect him to be so attached to his workers once they started to die on the job. Running a business takes sacrifice, and he was standing in the way of that. Not to mention the pittance that Cornelius and I were getting for all our hard work. So that's when we came up with an improvement that made all the difference. With control over the kobolds, we would have unfettered access to the largest and most willing workforce in the entire continent. And you, my fine scaly friends, have proven incredibly fruitful."

"Indeed, they have! And this way we get to keep all the money. We wouldn't have to split profits with any of the dragons. It required a bit of setup, what with the research for binding spells and having to gather these treasure hoards for bait, but it was all worth it in the end. Once we were sure we had a successful business model on our hands, it was easy to expand and capture additional dragons to increase our workforce, and subsequent income."

"The letters are all from you?" Ember asked incredulously.

"Oh yes," Cornelius sang, "every single one. We don't write them ourselves, that would be tedious. So, we subcontracted it out to a dragon who wrote the fastest. He has been doing an amazing job, don't you think?"

Whatever shred of respect Shade had for her dragon flared to life as she screamed, "You're forcing Dusk to do your paperwork! What kind of spineless worms are you?"

She wriggled her hands back and forth in her bindings and could feel them give way just a little. Brookshire looked over to her, a smile never leaving his face.

"A very rich worm. Which is all I want, honestly. And the way I see it, we've held up our end of the bargain quite well. Your dragons sit on a trove of treasure magnitudes more than they had before. We have made them richer, in a way."

"What about the traps, the suit of armor, the undead kobolds?" Penny asked.

"Well, that's easy, it's all ways to protect our assets," Cornelius explained further. "We're sitting on a literal goldmine, and we needed to make sure we could keep it that way. We've been living inside the mountain for years. The traps are just a way to keep nosy trespassers like you away. And the kobolds that work here have the joy of serving a master for the rest of time. You'd be surprised at how few questions your local necromancer will ask if you pay the right price."

"But why? Why go through all this trouble in the first place?" Oleander asked, trying desperately to find the logic in their captor's plan.

"You're looking at the reason, my dear kobold," Cornelius said, gesturing to his outfit.

"While we had money before this, we didn't have nearly enough to afford the garments we so desperately craved. Now we've got enough to keep us looking spiffy and wonderfully fashionable."

"You can't be serious," Oleander said.

"Oh, but I am. This fabric is imported from four continents away. It is no small fee, I'm sure you can imagine," Brookshire said.

"You caused all of this pain and suffering, separated us from our dragons, and threw everything into chaos for *FANCY CLOTHES!?*" Ember wailed. "This *can't* be happening."

"Of course!" Cornelius chimed in. "Come now, I know at least one of you would kill for a wardrobe like this," he gestured with his wand over to Tarot.

Tarot wouldn't meet his eyes as he looked at the tattered ruins of his own clothes. At how dingy and scratched his jewelry had become on the journey. He lifted his snout and sneered at the cat. "No finery is worth all this," he hissed the last word with contempt.

"You'd better pray to god I don't get my claws on you," Penny said, her voice cold as ice.

Brookshire laughed, booming voice echoing off the cave walls. He smiled at her crookedly and said, "My dear, the only god I've ever known is money. And it has served me very well."

"While this chat has been riveting, I'm eager to get back to my ball of yarn. I'm sure you understand we can't leave any witnesses so..."

Cornelius didn't get the chance to finish his sentence. The sound of a string snapping reverberated off the walls, turning Brookshire and Cornelius' attention to Shade. She had tucked her tail under the string as it wrapped around her, giving her extra wiggle room which allowed her to tear through it. She bolted towards Cornelius, catching him by surprise with a hard punch to the chest, knocking the wind out of him.

"Great creeping darkness, you talk too much," she spat as Cornelius fell over, clutching his chest.

As he collapsed, the strings binding the kobolds became loose and fell to the floor, the spell interrupted. Shade drew her sword to swing at Cornelius, but when she went to step forward, her foot landed in a small pile of gold that wrapped around her ankle and lifted her in the air before throwing her away. Brookshire's hooves were glowing with an ominous golden light.

"I do love a good tussle," he spoke before sweeping his left hand towards himself. Streams of gold coins rushed toward him, pooling at his feet.

Penny was the next to try and attack, rushing in towards Cornelius while he was down. He flicked his wand, and from the other side of the room came an onslaught of parchment flying towards Penny.

She readied herself and began spinning her staff, deflecting most of them as they flew at her, but catching a few papercuts as the odd sheet slipped past. Cornelius stood back up and waved his wand in a flourish. The space around him was filled with parchment, string, and an ink bottle with a feather quill in it that floated in front of his right hand.

Woof and Shade both went to swing at Brookshire, Shade with her sword and Woof with his claws, but were both tripped by the shifting coins under their feet. Shade managed to catch herself before falling, but Woof wasn't so lucky. He fell on his behind before being lifted into the air by a mass of gold coins and thrown at Tarot, sending them both flying across the room.

Ember and Oleander tried to strike at Cornelius, but whenever they approached, he would point his wand toward them, forming the swirling mass of paper into an impenetrable shield. Penny tried to approach Cornelius from his blind spot and could see that he was writing something on the parchment using the pen. When she lunged at him, her staff swinging, she saw him snap his fingers and the parchment he'd been writing on rolled itself into a stick of dynamite, fuse and all.

As the fuse began burning down, he threw it over his shoulder, directly into Penny's approach, blasting her away. She fell back, catching herself on her staff before getting back up and charging in again.

Attack after attack, the kobolds found themselves unable to break the duo's defenses. While Cornelius and Brookshire remained untouched, the group had amassed a legion of cuts, bruises, and sprains. As the duo was occupied by Oleander, Shade, and Woof's onslaught, Ember grouped with Penny and Tarot. "I need you both to attack Cornelius head on as hard as you can," she said.

"Oh sure, run into the waiting arms of Mr. Parchment Emporium over there. Did you forget that those letters can explode?" Tarot asked.

"You've got to trust me on this, Tarot, I've got a plan."

"Well, count me in. I *really* wanna get a hit in on that cat. C'mon, Tarot, let's show him what you're made of!" Penny said.

She dashed towards Cornelius and lunged with her staff. He saw her coming and pulled a mass of parchment into a protective shield to block the attack. He was then caught by surprise when Tarot came up behind her and swung his mace. The force of the impact shattered the parchment shield and flung the papers up into the air away from Cornelius for just a moment. This window of opportunity was what Ember was counting on. She readied a fireball to blast the papers out of the air and burn them up, but as she went to spit out the fireball, she was hit by a mass of coins in the shape of a fist punching her in the gut.

"I've had enough of your nonsense. This fight is over." With a wave of his hands, Brookshire brought piles of gold together around Tarot, Penny, and Ember. Shade and Oleander saw and tried to rush over to save them, but Cornelius had a chance to regain control and surrounded them with a swirling vortex of razor-sharp paper. Brookshire walked slowly over to the pile of gold that held Ember, laughing menacingly as he did so.

Ember struggled against the weight of the gold pinning her to the ground, writhing and biting at the open air, panicking in her desperation to escape. The coins were cold against her scales. She could feel her strength being sapped out of her.

"No! Ember!"

Woof jumped toward Brookshire, teeth bared and ready to bite, but Brookshire was too quick for him. He hit him square in the chest with a small stream of gold coins and catapulted him back towards the cave wall. He struck with a sickening *crunch* and fell down the wall to land in a heap.

Slumped over and breathing heavily, Woof watched as the Baron lifted Ember from the pile of gold and started to squeeze her neck. Ember scrabbled her claws against his hooves but couldn't get any traction. Penny and Tarot tried in vain to escape their gold coin prison. Oleander covered their face to keep the paper from cutting their snout while Shade slashed wildly at the vortex surrounding her. There was nothing they could do.

Woof whined and leaned all the way over. He braced his arms against the ground and brought his right knee up to steady himself.

He pushed off with a grunt and stood on shaky legs. He watched Ember's arms dangling at her sides, her muzzle open and gasping desperately for air. He threw back his head and out of desperation as well as rage, howled with all his might.

"AWOOOOOOO!!!"

All the other sounds were sucked out of the room. Woof's voice held the attention of everyone as he droned out his song. A feeling permeated and filled the kobolds as they glowed with a golden amber light. A feeling of unity. Together, they could win.

Woof dropped to all fours and took off running towards Cornelius, barking and snarling like a dog possessed. The cat was struck with fear at the sight of Woof's charge, too panicked to cast a spell. He was tackled to the ground, the paper vortex imprisoning Shade and Oleander dissipating as he lost control of his magic. Woof scratched and bit Cornelius with all he had, tearing off large chunks of his fine garments and spitting them out as he went.

On the other side of the room, Ember's arms twitched with life. Her movements were slow, but gradually, she reached her arms up and placed her claws on either side of Brookshire's hands. Brookshire still squeezed her neck, her face turning purple. Except, Ember couldn't feel it. She could only feel the love and passion of their group empowering her, sustaining and stoking a fire within.

She would not die. She was going to live for her friends.

She closed her hands around Brookshire's and pressed inwards with her claws. Her body pulsed with energy and heat spread out from her chest to her arms, legs, and tail. As the warmth spread over her scales, the spaces between became lit by an orange-yellow light. By the time Brookshire had noticed what was happening, Ember's claw tips were glowing a blinding white. The spots where she had dug into his skin began to burn and bubble as Brookshire let out a piercing scream.

He dropped her onto the ground, and she landed on her knees. She gasped for breath and coughed as Brookshire rubbed the burns on his hands. He had let his spell drop in the flash of pain and Tarot and Penny rushed to her aid. Brookshire went to kick Ember, but his foot was pulled out from under him by Tarot, who had slipped between his legs when he wasn't looking. He fell but rolled to the side while tossing Tarot off his foot. As he got up, he could see Penny standing a few feet away.

"I'm not done with you yet!" She shouted to him, eyes glittering with a pale gold light. "And you're not the only one who can move metal." She held out her hand and a coppery metallic aura enveloped it. She pulled towards her chest, a smile creasing the side of her snout.

The next thing Brookshire felt was the sensation of a metal staff connecting with the back of his neck. The momentum pulled him forward towards Penny as his shoes scuffed tracks in the ground. He stumbled and face-planted as the staff shot past him and into Penny's outstretched hand. Tarot stood next to her, his mace brandished and ready to strike.

Brookshire laughed as he stood back up. He dusted off his jacket while saying, "Insolent little lizards. You can't win. If we were able to capture your dragons, what chance would you have? Your corpses will do well as servants, at least."

He brought his hands up, palms turned upwards, and pulled towards himself, balling his hands into fists. The piles of gold that previously trapped the kobolds sped across the room and wrapped themselves around Brookshire until he was encased in an armor of coin.

Tarot and Penny took turns swinging at Brookshire's armor, chipping it away coin by coin. Tarot took a swing at Brookshire's leg, hoping to trip him, but missed as the armored swine sidestepped the swing. The mace had hit the ground and was stuck. As he tried to dislodge it, Brookshire wound up with a punch. Penny parried the blow just in time, a few gold coins plinking harmlessly off Tarot's horns as she did so. His eyes were wide and breath ragged, but he hefted the mace back up onto his shoulder for another swing.

On the other side of the room, Cornelius had gotten his feet underneath the snarling Woof and pushed him off himself. He got up and scowled at Woof. His clothes were ripped and torn, huge sections of his sleeves and pants missing, frills out of place, and his fur matted and stuck at strange angles from all of Woof's slobber.

"You mangy cur! I look like an absolute fright! I'll show you what a true dandy of a wizard can do when pressed!"

He swirled his wand around his body in a spiral and a great gust of wind whipped the parchment into a protective vortex around him. He fired off spell after spell, sending reams of paper to strike at the kobolds. Shade received several cuts as she deflected Cornelius's strikes, keeping Woof safe behind her sword. She rushed at Cornelius and swung her sword against the parchment barrier over and over, but the wall would not budge.

Oleander kept their distance and tried to come up with a way to get past Cornelius' defenses. Before they could formulate a plan however, Cornelius had managed to parry one of Shade's swings and sent her flying to the ground. As Cornelius readied a massive volley of parchment to cut Shade into ribbons, Oleander cast a spell. They fired off an enormous ball of light that shot past Shade and landed right at Cornelius's feet.

He jumped back to avoid it just in time and said, "Ha! You missed!"

Oleander wasn't aiming for Cornelius. The ball of light connected with the floor, casting Cornelius' shadow up and behind him - all the way to the ceiling. And from that shadow, Shade fell, sword drawn towards Cornelius. She pushed from the wall to give her some extra acceleration and aimed herself so that she would fall in the center of the vortex. Cornelius didn't see it coming as Shade's blade sliced through his neck.

SHHHNICKT!!!

The gust of wind softened Shade's landing. She tucked into a ball and rolled to a stop as Cornelius' head bounced against the floor before settling. His body crumpled in a heap soon after. The vortex spell dissipated, leaving the papers and string that were suspended midair to fall slowly and gracefully. The ink pot was not so lucky, smashing against the ground to splash up and give Cornelius's suit one last stain.

A few feet away, Ember had managed to get control of her breathing. She stood, inhaled deeply, and slowly exhaled a plume of black smoke. The light inside of her brightened until it illuminated her scales. Thin lines traced across her body and horns like trails of lava. She was burning and resplendent. The air around her moved in hazy waves.

What was cold, but a distant memory?

She crouched down and placed herself in a running position, and when she kicked off, she was rocketed forward by a small burst of fire. Brookshire panicked at the kobold's approach. He expelled his golden armor in a wave, sending Tarot and Penny to the floor. Clenching his hands together, he formed the gold into a massive ball before hurling it straight at Ember. She didn't flinch. She put her closed fist into her maw, and when she removed it, her fingers were drenched in a layer of red-hot molten lava. She wound up, and as the boulder of gold was about to hit her, punched it in the center of its mass.

The lava traveled out from her punch, melting the coins in a burst of heat and light until molten gold shot past her on either side. She leaped through the opening and twisted in the air, lurching forward with another burst of fire at her feet as she bared her claws. Ember dug deep gouges into the granite as she swiped them up and through Brookshire's torso, leaving a trail of white-hot fire in their wake.

Brookshire fell to the ground, clutching at the slashes in his chest. He tried to pull more gold to aid him but found that none would answer his call. Instead, he saw Penny racing towards him. Her staff glowed with that metallic copper light as it scraped along the ground, pulling the molten gold with it. She spun her staff above her head and as she did, the gold spiraled up and around Brookshire until he was completely encased in it.

Penny grabbed his face roughly and forced his mouth open with her claws. "Money is your God, huh?" Penny punctuated her question by stretching Brookshire's mouth open wider.

"Then choke on it."

She leaned her head forward and sent a flowing stream of copper coins down his throat. When she had filled his throat completely, she reached into the still hot pool of gold around his torso and used the molten metal to seal up his mouth and nose.

The last sound Brookshire ever made was the sizzle of cooking ham.

Penny shook off the rest of the gold and walked over to Ember, pulling her into a tight hug. Ember wrapped her arms around her back. She was still burning, but the light was starting to fade.

As Penny and Ember let go of each other, Tarot joined them, dragging his mace loudly against the floor. "If I never have to swing a weapon again, it will still be too soon!" He exclaimed in as triumphant of a voice as his tired body could muster. Ember and Penny laughed, and before long, Tarot was laughing right along with them.

When they met up with Shade, Oleander, and Woof, they saw that they were trying to open the jail cell and free the dragons. The lock on the cell was larger and more complicated than most, with a combination mechanism and one face covered in a cluster of glyphs and runes. With Brookshire and Cornelius dead, they were unable to force the combination out of them, leaving Shade to try to force a small lockpick under the runes.

As Woof and Oleander scanned the perimeter of the cell, Tarot cast a spell. He used the remaining magic he had, blue wisps of energy swirling around his right arm as he focused on casting one final spell. Threads wrapped around his arm, binding it in place as he reached out and grabbed at all the threads he could with his whole hand. He focused on the lock and the jail cell beyond and willed with all his mind for the outcome that would save their scales. Then, he pulled.

The surge of magic was enough to knock him to his knees, blue light flashing around him as the threads severed and wove back together, but his spell had gone off.

Shade shouted out triumphantly, "I got it!"

The door swung open and in the next instant, the first dragon stepped through the door and out into the room.

Auron, the gold scaled dragon of the forge, stood before the kobolds. He stretched his wings, wide enough almost to touch wall-to-wall, before stretching his massive chest and arms as well, and then his backside and his tail. He looked down at the kobolds, his curved horns and square face framing his gracious smile. "Thank you. You have no idea how cramped it was in there."

"Oh please," boomed a voice from inside of the cell, "at least you only had to worry about space for one neck." Carmichael, the beast dragon, had stuck his head out of the cell and was working on getting the rest of his frame through.

"Others don't have it so lucky." Another voice said as a second head in the shape of a lion poked its way through.

A third head in the shape of a goat was next to emerge and said, "Of course, I end up leaving last." The snake head on his tail hissed dissent as the last bit of his body cleared the cell. The goat head turned back to address the snake head and said, "You know you don't count; you're always going to be the last out of a room."

A streak of black dashed across the room and smashed the desk with all the papers and string into pieces. Dusk, the dragon of shadows and thieves, smiled at the destruction he had wrought on the cursed stationery. His body was sinewy and long, all curves and one long muscle that gave him the appearance of being a living shadow.

Shade didn't miss a beat and walked over in front of her dragon. She crossed her arms over her chest and tapped her foot angrily. "We need to have a talk."

Dusk looked around the room and went to put a foot forward, but Shade stopped him.

"Oh no, you're not leaving yet. Not until you know what kind of trouble you've put us through to get here."

A small ball of light came out of the cell next and floated over to where Oleander was standing. They began to tear up as they asked, "Is it really you?"

The ball of light danced around Oleander's head and then they were crying in earnest. The other kobolds were confused at first, but as the light grew in size they understood. Myfanwy stood only a foot or so taller than Shade, but their presence was somehow larger. They had antennae and round eyes just like Oleander and sported their own pair of moth-like wings. Their tail was an abdomen that jutted behind them, and their feet had notches in the back to help them hang onto the leaves of plants.

Oleander cried into their fur and Myfanwy brought up one of their legs to stroke at the back of Oleander's head to comfort them. "There, there, Olly. Everything is going to be okay now. You see? I am fine. Olly, Olly, Oxenfree! You can come out of hiding in my fur, my little savior."

Oleander laughed as they brought their snout up out of Myfanwy's chest. Myfanwy licked away their tears and Oleander hugged them tighter to themself.

"What a joyous reunion! I'm pleased to know that even after all of that time, I'm able to move around without much trouble."

Fortuna, the dragon of probabilities and prophecies, stepped out of the cell next. Her scales were sky blue with patches of white along her shoulders that made it look like clouds were moving across the midday sky. She had two horns on top of her head that were a bright pink and draped between them were various pieces of hanging jewelry.

Tarot knew right away that she had been kidnapped when she stepped into the room. She was hardly wearing half of her usual jewels! He rushed over to her and began to gush about the adventure he had been on.

Blast was the next to wake up and step out. He emerged from within a pile of coins, his red scales and horns contrasting their golden glow.

"Blast! You're safe after all!" Ember rushed over to her dragon and hugged his leg. Blast didn't budge and merely grumbled. A few seconds later, he wormed his finger in between Ember and his leg to pry her off. Ember let go of his finger and dropped to the ground, disappointed. Blast cleared his throat and said, "Thank you all for saving us, but the show's over. It's time we return to all our work. Ember, I expect you at the mountain by noon tomorrow."

It took Ember a moment to register what he had said. She was too shocked at his insistence that they just go back to normal. When it did hit her, she could feel herself getting mad. *This* was who she had been risking her life for?

"Are you kidding me? Do you have any idea what we've gone through to save you? Only to find you curled up in your pile of gold, raking in more money than ever before while us kobolds are working ourselves to death?"

"She's right, you know. None of this would have happened if you hadn't been so selfish, Blast. Brookshire and Cornelius told us everything—this was all your idea," Shade said.

"You have my word it will never happen again," Blast purred.

"That's not good enough!" Ember snarled. "I want to know that we're going to be protected from more than just this. You would still be in that cell if it weren't for your kobolds, and you're not even going to give us so much as a raise?"

"I will not tolerate this insolence any longer. I have never taken advantage of my kobolds."

"Of course you took advantage of us! What do you call making four kobolds lift a boulder up an incline when you could just cut it in half with your tail and be done?"

"I will not have you question how I delegate responsibilities."

"You won't let us question at all! And that's the problem!"

"This is entirely too much to take in right now, especially with everything else that happened today. We didn't even get to the undead kobolds," Penny said.

Carmichael's eyes went wide, "There are *undead* running around?!"

"So, I suggest we get all of the dragons together with all of the kobolds so that way we can explain what happened. But first, we should find a way out of here."

"For once, I agree. Then there is the matter of the gold, of course," Blast said.

"What about it?" Ember asked.

"I think it's only fair that we get our normal cut from your pay."

"Not a chance. We've been working our tails off for this gold. Kobolds died for a lie and you want their money?" Woof asked.

The dragons in the room shifted uncomfortably in place. There was quiet murmuring and they looked at each other uneasily.

"You haven't done anything in over a year. Kobolds earned it, kobolds can spend it," Oleander stated.

"Now let's not be too hasty, Olly," Myfanwy said.

"And what if we decide to just take it?" Blast asked.

"Well, if six kobolds could save you from this cell, how many do you think it will take to put you back in it?" Ember asked.

Blast didn't know how to react to that. It was the first time he had been directly threatened in what must have been a millennium. He turned to his fellow dragons and asked, "You're going to let her get away with saying that?"

Fortuna stepped up to him and leveled her snout at his. She snapped her fingers and a flash of blue appeared around them for a moment before dissipating.

"Yes, we are. And Blast, dearie, before you ask after this when everyone is out of earshot, I did look into the future. No, it doesn't go well for you. No, we don't help you. It's as simple as that."

Ember looked up at Blast and saw an emotion reflected in his eyes that she had never seen before. Fear.

Fortuna turned around and addressed the kobolds by lowering her snout to be closer to them. "I'm excited to see what your group does in the future. I've seen dozens of realities in which you do a lot of good. I'd be happy to be of assistance."

"Great! Now that we have that sorted, let's get out of here. I need a warm bath and a thorough scale scrubbing," Tarot said.

Dusk slid over to Shade and took her hands in his claws gently. He rasped in a quiet voice that was barely used, "Thank you, Shade. Your deeds will not soon be forgotten."

And then he was gone, sliding out of her sight and into a nearby shadow.

The other kobolds all escorted their dragons down the largest hallway they could find. Blast passed by Ember and told her, "This is not over. And do not return to the volcano. You will not be welcomed warmly."

He left without her, tail swishing angrily behind him as he padded down the long hallway. Ember heard a sleepy voice speak next to her ear. "Do not hold hate in your heart for him, little one. I've been giving him nightmares ever since he got us into this mess. Perhaps after a few nights of rest, he will relent." Somnir, the dragon of dreams and sleep, wiggled out of the cell and plopped down next to Ember. The fur on her wings brushed Ember's leg as she passed, softer than any other fur Ember had touched.

Penny grasped Ember's hand as she walked by with Auron. "Do you want to come along with us?" she asked. "We'll need the help, now that we're down a few kobolds. And the forge is nice and warm."

Ember thought about it for a moment and then laughed. "Sure, why not?"

The world did not change overnight when the kobolds returned with their dragons. When the rest of the kobolds learned what had happened in the mountain, more and more began to believe that something else needed to exist as a balance with the dragons. The belief came into its own once each of the kobolds were paid their share of the gold.

A portion was withheld to pay for medical care of the kobolds injured by the dragons' negligence and another portion was used for a mass funeral for those kobolds who died or were turned undead in the reckless pursuit of wealth. The remainder was divided equally among the kobolds, who—with it—devised their next big project.

They pooled their funds and bought a building in town where they would be able to meet regularly. They created a group which would communicate their needs and advocate for kobold rights. That way, no kobold would have to fear while serving their dragon. They would know that other kobolds would have their back and fight for them.

After a quick vote, the name was chosen to much fanfare and applause. And thus, the 'Association of Kobolds' was born. The very first kobold union. The name stuck due to its abbreviation. In this way, the union could make sure that everything was A-O.K.

Life settled back into its comfortable routines, with the added wrinkle of occasional A-OK meetings between kobolds and dragons. It was a difficult process to convince some of the dragons to recognize the A-OK. Blast in particular was a sticking point, but even he had to eventually admit that having happier kobolds was better for his bottom line.

Besides the occasional dragon, the only real dissidents of A-OK were the oldest kobolds, who were the most traditional in their ways. They were used to working for the dragons in a certain way and the union was a bigger shakeup to them than even the magical letters. The A-OK made sure to let those that were wary know that they'd be welcomed with open arms if they changed their minds.

Tarot took at least three baths when he returned from Accosto Mountain. He used some of the gold he received to replace the clothes and jewels that were damaged over the course of their adventure. He was careful not to spend too extravagantly; he hoped never to develop the same avarice or narcissism as Brookshire and Cornelius.

He continued to work out of the same room in The Draught of Dreams, but instead of pouring over letters, he looked through contracts and agreements for A-OK. It was a lot of paperwork to go through, but he'd gotten pretty good at organizing stacks of parchment over the previous year, so he wasn't worried. It was his expertise, after all.

Comfy let him stay in the inn free of charge in exchange for his services. And he could make those decisions without consequence. With the money he received, he was able to purchase The Draught of Dreams. He still worked for Somnir occasionally, but he could set his own prices and his own hours. He often used this newfound freedom to help the kobolds who needed a nice meal and a warm place to stay for the night. The lost revenue was worth it.

Oleander wouldn't let Myfanwy out of their sight for months after they made it back to their forest. Eventually, they grew more comfortable with Myfanwy going about their day without them nearby, but it was a difficult process. Old habits die hard, and Oleander had to find a way to be Myfanwy's bodyguard while also giving them space. For their part, Oleander did their best to let go of that obsessive need to protect them.

Shade made regular visits to Myfanwy's domain as well. After a while, she and Oleander had decided they would try dating and see where that might lead. It was a little difficult at first, what with their discordant sleep schedules, but they were making it work. After being a bodyguard for so long, Oleander enjoyed the feeling of being protected. Shade loved how Oleander's personality complimented her sarcasm while keeping her grounded. She showed up often in her full plate armor, sword strapped to her back. She had long since stopped pretending to be something she wasn't. Thievery just wasn't for her, but that was alright. She was doing a lot more for her friends and her community, which made her happy.

Ember and Woof fell quickly into a relationship after the initial shock of the dragons returning. No longer residing in Blast's volcano meant Ember could live in the town, allowing her more time to spend with Woof. She leaned on Woof to provide her with emotional support as she got used to living away from the volcano. Getting cut off from the rest of Blast's kobolds was hard for her to adjust to. As the A-OK branched out, she was able to rekindle those connections, but it took a while.

Woof was scared that his relationship with Ember would ruin their friendship, or that Ember might realize that he wasn't very special. This wasn't the case at all. She stayed by his side and made sure to remind him that he had plenty to offer. Even he needed reassurance every once in a while, and Ember was glad to provide it.

Woof's back had been fractured in the fight against Cornelius and Brookshire. He was recovering, albeit slowly. Running was still a bit of a challenge for him, what with the cane and all, but as long as he rested and gave it time he would recover. The pain would still be there, since magical healing had its limits, but Woof felt like the kind of kobold who would take that in stride. He ended up getting heavily involved with the A-OK and sat on more meetings than any of the other six. That was just like him, though—always making sure that others were taken care of.

Penny had kept her word and allowed Ember to work with her in the forge. It was good for both of them in the end. Ember was looking for a renewed sense of purpose after being rejected by Blast, and working in the forge helped. Penny needed someone to help her through her grief for Tinpin, and teaching Ember how to work the forge was incredibly healing. She could pass on what Tinpin had taught her to someone else and keep his memory alive in a small way.

Working so closely together, Penny and Ember had to admit that there were feelings between them as well.

Ember was scared to tell Woof about her feelings for Penny, knowing how attached he was to her, but was surprised to see him wagging his tail in response.

"Ember, I think that's great!" he said, smiling. "I like Penny a lot too. I'm okay with anything, so long as it doesn't affect what's between you and me." He gave her a slobbery lick on the cheek to reassure her.

True to her promise, Fortuna worked with the Association of Kobolds as they set themselves up. She acted as a bridge between the kobolds and the dragons at the beginning, but as the A-OK gained ground and legitimacy, she stepped back from having to initiate those conversations. Her presence around the other kobolds was something they had to get used to.

A lot of kobolds were rightfully nervous around dragons after everything that had happened. She would work out of the shared A-OK building, coordinating with Tarot on the bigger projects, and eventually the other members of the union warmed to her. She proved her willingness to help multiple times by using her probability magic to warn the A-OK of issues before they came up, and that certainly didn't hurt. Her predictions weren't foolproof, but they gave the kobolds an advantage in planning how they were going to negotiate with the dragons.

She seemed to understand the kobolds' needs easier than the other dragons. She knew from personal experience the frustration of communicating her gender to those who didn't understand, so she was willing to see things from their point of view. The Association of Kobolds had a long road ahead of it, but with Fortuna on their side, the future was looking bright, indeed.

On a sunny day in the middle of summer, Ember and Penny rolled down a grassy hill on the edge of Carmichael's territory. When they came to a stop, Penny kissed her neck and Ember took a moment to look up at the sky above her.

"I can't believe it, no whale," she said.

Penny stopped and looked up at her, "Did you hit your head on the way down?"

Woof hobbled over and said, "No, she's just like that." And then he licked the top of her head between her horns. Ember laughed and said, "Hey Woof. Where've you been lately?"

Woof rubbed the back of his head and sighed, "The Association has been having me run my tail off for what feels like months now. I had to pull Tarot aside and let him know I was taking a break so folks wouldn't go looking for me right away."

Penny laughed despite herself, "You get out of working long hours for the dragons and right into working long hours for kobolds."

Ember didn't find it as funny though. "You're not overwhelmed, are you?"

Woof looked down at her and replied, "No, not yet at least. I'd much rather spend all this energy if it's going to help out the other kobolds. We've been drafting up a proposal for the dragons to give kobolds some time off. We've earned a break after everything that's happened, and I want to make sure the other kobolds get the time they need to keep from burning out. We're also still trying to find out what's been giving so many kobolds problems sleeping lately." Ember didn't look any less worried, so Woof put a claw reassuringly on her shoulder and said, "I've been sleeping fine, Ember. Most days I hit the bed and I'm out like a light."

"Have Somnir or Comfy looked into what's causing it?" Ember asked.

"I don't know if Comfy has had time lately, but I think Somnir has been looking into it. It doesn't really help that even the dragons have their hands full with catching up with their kobolds."

"Oh! Does that mean they agreed to Tarot's idea, finally?" Penny asked.

Woof smiled. "Yep! The 'Proposal for Adequate Dragon Attention' was agreed on by all the dragons and kobolds present at the last A-OK meeting. Now the dragons must make time for visiting with their kobolds. They get to choose how to schedule those visits, but we've already told the kobolds to report to the A-OK if their dragon isn't following up on that."

Ember snorted, crossed her arms, and said, "I still think we could have focused on something more important first." Dragon relations were still a sensitive spot for her.

Woof gave her a sympathetic look. "It's making sure we're working for what a majority of A-OK members want. Besides, that just means they'll be too busy to make any new schemes for a little while."

"I sure hope so, Woof. I'm not sure I can handle another dragon-sized problem right now!" Penny said.

"I think we're going to have our hands full for a while yet. There are rumors of fights breaking out between the freshwater and saltwater kobolds, Carmichael is on the hunt for that necromancer and hasn't found them yet, last I checked the Kingdom of Anwillon's royal family was at each other's throats, and Dusk hasn't said anything about—"

"Alright, alright! That's enough shop talk for now. Come on down here and take a load off, Woof. You sound like you've certainly earned it." Penny said with a smile.

Ember grabbed him around his waist and gently pulled him down to the grass. Woof let her guide him until he lay on his side next to her. He scooched himself over slightly and reached his arm behind her shoulders. Penny, on Ember's other side, had cuddled back up to her and breathed a small sigh of contentment.

They laid there, letting the sun warm their scales, and Ember felt safe and happy. She wrapped her arms around the kobolds she loved and drifted off to a peaceful sleep.

A Gentle Rustling of Leaves

A wind, gentle and chilling, swept through the discarded leaves on the forest floor. Autumn arrived once again in the realms of mortal men, but there are realms beyond that of those that can be perceived with the naked eye.

It always started as a sense of form. Fuzzy, though not with fur. Unshaped and formless. The wind would blow through leaves all day and none would feel a thing. Until one clung to the breeze a little too tightly. Then another and another. And soon enough, a swirling pile of leaves would be carried by the wind. The form, though fluid and changing, was starting to take a shape amidst the greens and yellows of the leaves. A tail behind and a muzzle in front as it raced along the countryside through the early morning dew. If one was versed in the ways of forest spirits, it would have looked for all the world to be a fox in those swirling leaves and wind.

Her name, it came to her as if waking from a dream. And she knew at once, it was Selene. The grass was once again beneath her paws, the wind back in her leaves. It was a queer circumstance to have so much knowledge about herself so soon after waking. Though she paid no mind. It was the way of animals to know things innately, so why should she be any different? She knew as well that her time here was short. A season at most, if she was lucky. She resolved to leave no meadow un-frolicked, wheresoever the wind would carry her.

As she ran, her coat changed colors with the shifting of the leaves. Sometimes it would be more green and yellow, where the leaves were still freshly fallen. At other times it was a bright orange and red, streaking a sunset across the sky. She only slowed when the wind would die down, settling her leaves into the earth for a quick nap before she was whisked up and away again. Often, she would play games with the fae and faeries of the forests on her journey. They liked to fly around her and between her legs as she skipped and pranced through the flowers. The fae taught her secret games that only spirits could play, and she relished in the warmth of making new friends. Truly, a gayer celebration had not been seen since the return of springtime.

She did not want to leave her new friends, but the wind carried her off all the same. And so, she ran with it, instead of against it. For there is no greater fool's errand than to try and fight the wind.

She came across an odd shape near the edge of a lake and gratefully, the wind blew her in the direction of it. As she came closer, she noticed something quite peculiar. The shape was that of a dog, that much was clear, but of the particular breed, Selene could not determine. If she tilted her face one way it was clearly a bulldog, but in the next moment it could be a collie. Beagle seemed to be the most likely from what she could surmise. In all cases, the coat was brown and black, and the dog stood proudly at attention. Even stranger, the dog stood on the water of the lake. Selene tried her best to speak with her voice, though it often came out as thin and crackly.

"Good day, fine fellow! Might I have your acquaintance?"

The dog looked over to the outline of Selene and her leaves before giving a small nod. He walked across the lake until he was standing at its edge.

"Good day to you too, forest spirit. You've caught me at a good time, I'm enjoying my leisure."

"What do you call yourself? Are you of the River?"

The dog laughed. "You'll have to excuse me if I don't trust giving my true name to the faefolk. But yes, in a sense, I am of a river."

If offense was to be taken at his tone, Selene did not notice. "It's nice to meet you all the same. I'm Selene!" Selene let the wind blow through her and her leaves fell gently on the surface of the water. "Is this your river?"

"No, far from it."

"You said you were at leisure, but you look to be guarding something."

"Quite perceptive, but a coincidence I assure you. Occupational habits are hard to break."

"What, then, is your occupation?"

"Why do you care to know?"

"I've not had one myself, but to look at your posture they must be dreadfully stressful!" Selene barked a laugh.

Yet the dog was joyless. He looked down at her and said in a low growl, "You've no idea."

Without missing a beat, Selene cocked her head towards the dog. "Then tell me in the most detail you can muster! It sounds as though it weighs on you. Better to tell now than to let your worries sink you later."

The dog sighed but sat down on the water next to Selene.

"How familiar are you with the space beyond death?"

Selene had to think on it a moment, but replied, "I've a feeling I might have been there once but the memory fades even now."

The dog nodded his head, "Spirits come and go, but mortals stay. It's my job to help them cross the River Styx on their way over. I'm Charon's guide dog."

Selene could not contain her excitement. "I'm talking with the Cerberus! But where are your other heads?"

The dog shook his head. "You're thinking of Hades. Different fellow entirely, I assure you. Charon pilots the ferry for the mortals to the land beyond."

"Oh, I see. But then, what do you do?"

"The water there is colder than ice and runs deeper than a mountain. If a mortal falls in, I am their lifeboat back to the surface. They can grab onto me, and I will never sink."

"Are so many mortals prone to diving into the lake of the dead?"

"You would be surprised."

"That must get woefully tiresome."

"Absolutely. It is such a burden that I cannot even enjoy my leisure. Even now I am staring out across this lake anticipating some fool to fall in!"

His paws were up around his eyes and Selene could sense his frustration. She pondered for a moment before coming up with an ingenious plan. She turned to the distressed dog and said, "I know just what you need! It will surely help you relax."

She motioned for him to follow her to the edge of the lake that had many stones and pebbles stacked up along its bank. "I'm going to teach you a game that the fairies taught me."

She bent her neck down and made a motion as if to grab one of the rocks in her mouth, then flung her head to the side over the lake.

"You pick up the rock in your mouth and try to make it spin as you throw it. Small flat stones work the best, and you should try to flick your head slightly, so you throw it sideways. Now you try!"

The dog looked skeptical but did as Selene instructed and picked up a rock in his mouth. With a gentle toss, it went sailing out over the water and skipped a few times before sinking into the lake. The dog only seemed more confused until Selene explained, "You count the times the stone has skipped on the water. And the best part? You're allowed to let them sink!"

The dog smiled in surprise and bewilderment as he chucked rock after rock into the lake, skipping stones as fast as he could pick them up. Selene danced around the ripples that would form in the water and before long, he was chasing after her across the lake. They carried on with skipping stones and chasing each other until the moon was high above them in the sky. Exhausted and spent, the dog lay on his back in the middle of the lake.

"That was the most I've enjoyed my leisure in years. Thank you, Selene."

"I should be thanking you! I'm used to the feeling of my wind through the prairie grass, but running along the water was entirely new for me."

She turned to face the dog once more and found him fast asleep. She could feel the wind stirring her on someplace else. Before she let herself be carried away, she left enough of her leaves as a blanket to keep him warm.

Selene did not recognize the forest she had found herself in. It was unlike any she had seen before. The trees seemed to grow upside down, with the roots extending out into the sky and the treetops planted firmly in the ground. The sunlight shone brightly through the gaps in the odd canopy, lighting the forest floor. The ground she was walking on consisted of leaves and when she would shuffle through them, they would break off and float into the sky. She walked between the trees, until she came unto a clearing of sorts. The trees thinned out and a line of them on either side led her up to a strangely shaped tree in the center.

The first thing she noticed was its size. It was easily the biggest in the forest and must have been here for centuries. When she was close enough to walk around its base, she could make out the shape of a resting face on the trunk. Stranger still, the tree was the only one in the entire forest that was right-side up. Its canopy was filled not with leaves, but with beautiful pink and white blossoms. Selene could not help but stare at the wondrous flowers. So transfixed was she, that she did not notice the face on the trunk begin to stir.

There was grumbling and mumbling as water-blue eyes with mossy irises slowly blinked open. A gentle cracking could be heard as the face's mouth opened and showed the bright orange of freshly stripped bark underneath. Still feeling the effects of their long sleep, the tree shook their head back and forth to wake themselves up, whipping the vines that adorned their head.

Selene cried out and ran to hide in the nearest pile of leaves.

"Do not fear, little one. I mean no harm. You may come out."

Their voice was low, as if from the earth itself, flowing like sap dripping down bark. Selene crept slowly from her hiding place until the wind pushed her leaves more forcefully towards the base of the trunk. Fully looking at them, she could tell what the face reminded her of. It was a memory buried deep in her, but one she knew all the same. The face was more of a snout and the shape looked quite like a large lizard.

The word for 'dragon' popped into her head, but it felt off somehow.

"Ah, one of the Wind's children. You've nothing to fear, I welcome all into this grove," the tree said.

"Thank you, Old One. I did not mean to intrude. The wind carried me here and I'm ever so sorry for waking you."

"No trouble at all. It has been some time since I've had company."

"Then I am happy to give it!" Selene brightened considerably, her tail beginning to wag. "I am called Selene, and it is a pleasure to make your acquaintance."

"You've got the spirit of the Wind, that is for certain. But I am not familiar with your form. What body are your leaves an imprint of?"

"Surely you jest, I am certain you must have seen a fox before I?"

"On the contrary, you are the first. I must admit it is a lovely form. Suits you and her well."

"Begging your pardon, but your form is curious to me as well. You are a tree, but also a great lizard. I know of dragons, but I thought they cavorted openly with Fire."

"They are relatives, of a sort. Would do them well to remember when they were of the Earth, but it's not my place to say."

"Are you lonely here?" Selene looked around the forest as if to indicate a great truth she had just discovered. "None of the other trees I passed could talk."

"They can speak, I assure you. You cannot hear them, for the language has been lost to age."

"Do they speak fair of me?"

"They speak no ill."

"Just as well then!"

Selene looked down and could see that some of the blossoms from the Old One had fallen to the forest's floor from when it had woken up. She longed to hold one in her paws but was unsure if the wind would allow her. She turned to the Old One and smiled. "I must say that your foliage is exquisitely beautiful! If I could, I would carry it in my body and show the rest of the world your beauty."

"By all means, take as many as you can hold. I've no objection."

"I've not lifted blossoms before, only leaves. What if I'm unable?"

"Selene, you shall never truly know until you try. Impossibility is a word of those who do not dare to try."

As Selene swirled her form through the pink and white blossoms at her feet, they became a part of her, mixing and floating with the leaves of her body.

"Old One! I've done it! Oh, look how pretty it is when I swish my tail!"

The dragon in the tree smiled, orange bark cracking as the corners of their mouth pulled back in joy. "My blossoms are most becoming on you, Selene. You've given me a great gift today."

"I wish I could repay the kindness, Old One."

"Your presence is enough, Selene."

She wanted to stay, but she could feel the wind pushing through her again. With a bark and a laugh, she ran past the Old One and out into the unknown. She carried their gift of flower petals across the land and countless travelers marveled at their beauty.

One day, as she stopped on the side of the road to smell some flowers at the edge of a prairie, Selene saw a figure walking through the grass. The figure was an animal, most certainly, and it seemed to be staying close to the side of the trail. Domestics rarely found themselves far out in the country and so Selene resolved to meet the odd fellow. As she ran up and through him, his fur bristled out in all directions, catching some of her wayward leaves in the process. Once she had reformed in front of him, she could see him clearly. He was a tom with medium-length fur, and had a bright red collar tied around his neck. He was busy picking the leaves out of his fur as she introduced herself.

"Good morrow, humble tom. I am called Selene. What, pray tell, is your name?"

Instead of looking annoyed, the tom actually looked grateful. It was as if Selene was the first to treat him with common manners in a long time.

"Good day to you, Selene." He took a pause to bow slightly. "I am a mouser by trade and though I had another name at one time, I have recently taken on the moniker of Mouser."

"What unhappy circumstance caused you to forget your name?" Mouser threw his head back and mewled a desperate cry.

"Alas, I have been cursed!"

"Cursed?"

"Aye, cursed. I ate a strange looking mouse and now am naught but invisible and unheard in the nighttime. I should have known from the aftertaste it was to be my ruin."

Selene looked confused and tilted her head to one side. "But you are quite present to mine eyes?"

"True, but the afternoon Sun is still high in the sky. At night my fur becomes like a shade and the moonlight keeps me from being seen. My family hasn't been able to find me since. They only search at night, and they cannot see me no matter how loud I meow. If only they would search in the light of the sun, they would see me plain."

"Where do they live, Mouser? Perhaps the faeries could show us the way."

"I do not remember! I've been lost for so long I cannot recall my way back."

"Is there nothing you can remember of your family at all?"

Mouser put a paw to his chin and thought a while before his eyes lit up.

"They lived near a stone building and would always smell of burnt wheat. I've not been able to find the scent since."

"Then I shall find the scent and bring you back to them!"

"Alas, I doubt you'll have any luck. I have been lost from them for three years thence. Surely, they will have moved away?"

Selene laughed, "You should not give up hope so easily, dear Mouser. Let me at least try. Hold hope in your heart for a week more?"

Reluctantly, Mouser agreed, and Selene was off on the wind to search out the smell.

Selene was familiar with the scent of wheat, having played in the fields near the towns before, yet burnt wheat was a different thing entirely. She thought she had come close a few times but saw no buildings near her. Then, by chance, she was carried aloft by a strong gust of wind and found herself in a town she had not seen before. As soon as she picked up her nose to sniff at the air, she could smell the burnt wheat.

Following it, she arrived before a great stone building with a sign out front. The sign read 'Bakery' and next to it was a small cottage with a lively human family inside. Selene was glad to have found a family, but she was uncertain if they were Mouser's. He hadn't given her a description of what they looked like for fear that they had changed too great in appearance while he was away.

Then, an idea sprang to mind. She could lead him there and have him look for himself. After all, she knew the country much better than any town.

She left the town and let herself be carried on a wind back towards Mouser. As she travelled, she left a breadcrumb trail of bright red leaves for them to follow back. If her guess was correct, then the family would be reunited as a whole.

When she came at last upon Mouser, he was slumped against the side of the trail in a fit of despair. Seeing her roused him from his reverie as he bolted up and ran over.

"Selene! I'd given you up for good. Who have you brought with you?"

"What do you mean, 'brought with you?'. I was coming back to find you." Selene then looked behind herself and found that the youngest member of the family, a tot of no more than three or four, had followed her trail of leaves.

Mouser looked closer at the child and gasped in shock.

"Why, this is little Tabitha! I had last seen her as a babe in swaddling cloth."

Tabitha, seeing finally the cat in front of her, began to pet Mouser in the way that children do when they are not aware of the correct methods of petting. Despite such treatment, Mouser purred all the same. And from the ridge, shapes came running towards the sound of his contented purr. The mother, father, and three other children scooped them both up in their arms and showered them with equal kisses and scolding. Mouser cried in elation as he was lost no more. Selene's heart was warmed at the sight of their reunion. She allowed herself one rudeness and left without goodbye, so as not to spoil their moment together.

The season had grown colder these past weeks. Though she did not wish to admit it to herself, Selene knew her time in the realm was ending. The leaves that made up her body were dry and brittle. No Autumn breeze could lift her for more than a second before the leaves would drop back to the ground again. She felt heavier and slower without the wind blowing through her, and that feeling of shapelessness was growing again. She laid herself down at the foot of a large shady tree and curled up tight into a pile. Muzzle and tail wrapped round what was left of her perception of a body. As she faded out and her spirit was carried off to that place beyond our perception, she smiled at the time she was given that year. It was a very good Autumn, indeed.

Do not cry, gentle reader, for you must know.
That Selene was a spirit with purpose to show.
The importance of time we are given to wander.
Life is easy to squander, hold no regrets.
For these are the lessons, please don't forget.
And if you are cunning, and spritely, and gay.
And you look very closely on a cool Autumn day.
You may be surprised at what you can see.
In the simple serenity of the rustling of leaves.

Acknowledgements

This book would not exist without the collective effort of all my friends and family. It's my name on the front cover, but there are always more people behind the dragon that writes these stories. So, I'd like to take a moment to thank:

Joseph and Sandy Miele, Sharon and John Johnson

For supporting me in my creative passions and reminding me family has my back.

Kyle Mason

For being a part of my life and showing me how to be passionate about my stories and characters. I wish with all my heart you could see this book finished.

All my friends who have done beta-reads of stories, helped with questions I had, or just listened to me gush about my characters. I am incredibly lucky to have you as a part of my life.

The Voice of Dog Podcast and the Friends of the Fireplace chat

For bringing so many of my stories to life through narration and being incredibly supportive of my writing. I hope I can repay the help this community has given me.

Sandy Golden, for her amazing work as editor on this book. These stories shine brighter because of her dedication.

Everyone else at Fenris Publishing for taking a chance on my anthology.

And you, dear reader. Thank you for buying this book. It means more than I can properly express in words.

It may be cliche to say, but you all really are the wind beneath my wings.